8MEN

A NOVEL

MARCUS SMITH

This is a work of fiction. This book is pure conjecture, although there are historical figures and events the dialogue and plots are fictional. The author asks the reader to continue to study the historical facts laid out in this work.

ISBN: 979-8-9892885-1-9

Valeir Publishing, Inc.
Landover Hills, Maryland

"If we are on the outside, we assume a conspiracy is the perfect working of a scheme. Silent nameless men with unadorned hearts. Conspiracy is everything that ordinary life is not. It's the inside game, cold, sure, undistracted, forever closed off to us. We are the flawed ones, the innocents, trying to make some rough sense of the daily jostle. Conspirators have a logic and a daring beyond our reach. All conspiracies are the same taut story of men who find coherence in some criminal act."

DON DELILLO

FIRESIDE CHAT

The year is 1941. The world is in the grips of war; every quadrant of Earth is in battle with the exception of the United States of America. The American people are happy being isolationists—they remember what a toll World War I was to the country's resources and the massive death count sustained by U.S. soldiers. Many Americans believed then, as they do now, that the current war, dubbed World War II, is a conflict between European countries and should be solved by them. Unlike the previous war, this war is being fueled by the ambitions of the crazed maniac, Adolf Hitler. Hitler is bent on world domination, but he knows that he must conquer his rivals in Europe before tangling with the American giant. There have been very loud grumblings within the United States Congress that President Franklin Delano Roosevelt is trying to find a back doorway to get into the war in Europe. It is widely believed that America is the eventual grand prize to Hitler's march across the world. Hitler believes America is a cesspool of mongrel races, financed by some of the very Zionists that he ran out of Germany a few short years ago. The president is very aware of Hitler's book *Mein Kampf* in which he detailed the things that were wrong with his country as well as the world. He thinks the world should be under the rule of the Aryan people—he thinks that the lesser races would benefit by being ruled by people of Aryan descent. In *Mein*

Kampf, Hitler describes how the races must be pure and the mixing of the races could lead to a hybrid race of savage beasts. The president's understanding of Hitler's core beliefs has made him uneasy and nervous about allowing him to march across the world.

In the president's mind, America is everything that Hitler hates—It is a melting pot of different ethnic groups from all over the world.

But the overwhelming force sure to attract Hitler's ire is the number of prominent Jews in America. He would eventually attack America for that fact alone.

President Roosevelt knows that he must get into the war in hopes of fighting Hitler in Europe instead on the streets of Los Angeles, New York and Washington, D.C. The president knows that with a win in Great Britain, the Axis Powers, made up of Germany, Italy, and Japan would quickly be surrounding the American territory, making it almost impossible to defeat them. President Roosevelt doesn't know what he is going to do, but he knows that he must force Germany's hand.

"The American public has spoken, they do not want to get involved with the conflicts occurring on the European continent," says President Roosevelt from behind his oak wood desk in the Oval Office during his interview with Wesley Gilliam, a columnist from *The Washington Post.*

The president is trying to squash rumors that the U.S. military is preparing for war in the Pacific and sending ammunition to assist the Brits and the Russians in the European theater.

"Mr. President, it has been rumored that these plans have been in place since late 1939, well before last year's election. Anonymous sources say that the United States has been trying to bait both the Japanese and the Germans into attacking the U.S. so that the U.S. will have no choice but to enter the war—how do you respond?" inquires Gilliam.

The president takes a long pull on his handmade cigarette filled with North Carolina's sweetest tobacco, picked in Mebane outside of Rocky

Mount. He holds the cigarette in his ivory cigarette holder, which was a present from an African king. The president blinks several times and gives a Chester cat grin before answering the question.

"We have no problem with these countries; we are not going to bait anyone into a fight—if we did that, we would be nothing more than common thugs. Of course, we are keeping a very close eye on the developments happening in Europe—a destabilized Europe is not good for anyone. The American people don't want to get involved with European fights, and as steward of the American government, I must abide by the people's wishes. With regards to the Empire of Japan, we are trying to resolve our issues diplomatically; in fact, our governments are trying to come up with a treaty to avoid any such aggression," responds the president.

The room begins to fill with cigar smoke, bellowing from the cheeks of the stout and slightly balding gentleman standing in the corner. The president gives the man a slight grin and waves him over.

"Wesley Gilliam from *The Washington Post*, it is my esteemed pleasure to introduce you to the prime minister of Great Britain, Mr. Winston Churchill," announces the president.

Both gentlemen shake hands.

"I will excuse myself, gentlemen," replies Gilliam.

Both the president and the prime minister acknowledge Gilliam as he leaves. Churchill walks over to one of the large bay windows that overlooks Pennsylvania Avenue with a very determined look on his face. He takes a long pull on his cigar, emitting the smoke looking like a cloud formation before a major storm. Churchill looks down upon Pennsylvania Avenue. He notices the Americans walking, clueless to the carnage occurring in Western Europe.

"This time next year, the very people that walk up and down these streets unwittingly today may be running from the constant rhythm of

German air raids… When, Franklin? When will America join the fight? My people are dying; our military is becoming more depleted by the day. The Germans, they will overtake us in the next six months. The god damn Russians will surrender in weeks—that son of a bitch Stalin will cut a side deal that will allow the Nazis to focus all their resources back on Great Britain—I don't know who's worse, Stalin or Hitler, they are both crazy as shit. Stalin thinks that if he gives Hitler a piece of Russia he will be satisfied. He will not stop until he has achieved complete world domination," Churchill rants.

"I understand your frustration, Winston—" begins Roosevelt, but he is interrupted.

"With all due respect Franklin, you don't have any understanding of what is happening. Your cities aren't being shelled every day and night. You don't have to build mass graves for your citizens, including the corpses of dismembered infants whose mothers can't stop crying."

Churchill turns in a militaristic position.

"Mr. President, please. The people of Great Britain—no, scratch that…the people of the world need America's help. Hitler is spreading across Europe like the Black Plague—he is killing everything that stands in his way. He believes that his Nazi regime will rule for a thousand years. Do you think that Hitler will not come to America after he conquers us?" proclaims Churchill.

"He will use Great Britain as a staging post for his initial battles with America; you have to know this," suggests a convincing Churchill.

The president agrees with an affirming nod.

"You are probably right Winston, but the mood of the country as a whole is to stay out of European affairs. Last year's election was very difficult…many Americans became isolationists after The Great War. Nobody wants to lose a mass amount of American soldiers again when the war is not truly ours," declares the president, as he notices Churchill's mounting frustration.

"Of course, we will get in at some point, but we need the correct catalyst," the president devilishly remarks.

"Franklin, whatever do you mean?" demands a confused Churchill.

"The American people will have to be convinced that we must go to war…and that we must be complicit that we have an all-inclusive American war effort," the president exclaims.

"After Hitler went into Poland, I knew it was a matter of time before he would try to conquer the world," states the president.

Churchill looks surprisingly pleased that the president seems to understand the severity of the costs of America not getting involved.

"Show the American people that their safety and way of life are in jeopardy—they will get behind you," remarks Churchill.

The president comments back, "It is not that easy. They will believe I am warmongering. We will have to come up with another way…" The president takes a deep breath before saying, "Winston my friend…America will get involved in this war. I just need to find a way. Something that all Americans could get behind," asserts the president.

On December 6th, 1941, Aaron Nielsen, an American naval pilot, is patrolling the waters off the coast of Midway Island in the Pacific Ocean. Nielsen's patrols were normally filled with dodging the beautiful sun rays reflecting off the ocean's surface and the occasional bird that climbed to his altitude. Nielson had grown fond of singing Frank Sinatra's little ditty, "This Love of Mine," as he passed through the clouds—unfortunately, the clouds probably didn't enjoy his singing style, which was somewhere between a tenor and a baritone. When he came out of the clouds, Nielson saw a long line of objects in the distance.

"What the hell?" questions a bewildered Nielson to himself.

Nielson flew this path hundreds of times, and he had never seen an additional land formation; he is literally hundreds of miles from land in any direction. Nielson thinks he'd better radio back to base.

"Base, this is Nielson, over." The base answers back, "This is base, over." Nielson starts to feel real concern; he investigates, "Base, do we have any practice exercises slated for any of our battleships?" Nielson sees the Japanese flag flying from a long line of battlecruisers. The base answers back, "No, pilot, what do you see?" Nielson answers back, "WAR!"

The president is sitting at his desk signing documents when his secretary barges in.

"Mr. President, the Secretary of the Navy is here to see you sir; he says it is urgent that he speak with you," utters his secretary.

William Dewey Jacobs salutes the president as he rushes into his office.

"Mr. President, we have a situation in the Pacific," reveals Jacobs.

"Admiral Jacobs, to what do I owe to this pleasure?" replies a jovial President Roosevelt.

"Mr. President, our naval pilots have spotted a Japanese armada advancing on the Hawaiian Islands. We have intercepted several coded messages between the Japanese government and the Japanese diplomats here in Washington. The messages keep mentioning Pearl Harbor sir," admits a flustered Admiral Jacobs.

Pearl Harbor had served as a military outpost and allowed America to keep a close eye on their rivals in Asia, namely the Empire of Japan. America placed an embargo on the island nation in the fall of 1940, essentially strangling the nation from receiving exports. This action was in response to the Japanese occupation of French Indochina. Many in the international community felt Japan would have to respond with force.

"Has the Japanese government been in contact with the crews of any of the ships in the Armada?" questions the president.

"No sir, but I would think that if they are planning any kind of attack the ships would exercise radio silence," concedes an anxious Admiral Jacobs.

"Admiral, you know we are in very tense discussions with the Empire of Japan," discloses the president in a firm voice.

The frustration builds within Admiral Jacobs as it manifests on his face through the creases on his forehead.

"Mr. President, the Japanese armada is sailing toward Pearl Harbor. We must warn Admiral Kimmel and the rest of the Pacific fleet immediately," Jacobs barks at the president.

"Admiral Jacobs, would you like to tender your resignation, or would you like to sit down and talk about this situation?" the president proclaims in a scolding manner.

Admiral Jacobs understands the severity of the situation and decides to talk in a calming tone. "Mr. President, we have reason to believe that the Empire of Japan will be launching an attack on the Hawaiian Islands."

"Admiral Jacobs, I understand your concern, but we are in discussions with the Japanese. If we go on ready alert, we could touch off an international incident," suggests the president.

"Mr. President, we believe that an attack on the Hawaiian Islands is imminent," pleads Admiral Jacobs.

The president pulls out a bottle of Jack Daniels.

"Oh boy, there are times like these in which I need some smooth firewater, something with a punch without the nasty aftertaste," conveys the president as he chuckles.

"Dewey how long have I known you?" asks the president.

The president begins to pour Jack Daniels into two square glasses. Admiral Jacobs loosens his tie.

"I gather I've known you at least 25 years Franklin," Admiral Jacobs estimates in his deep Alabama drawl.

"I remember your skinny ass coming into the Department of the Navy wants to make changes… You always wanted to get things in order. You pissed a lot of good ol' boys off. They thought, 'How the hell is this wet-behind-the-ear Yankee going to tell us what to do?'" says Jacobs.

Both men share a laugh. The reality of the situation wipes the smile off the president's face.

"Dewey, I need you to answer a question for me, not as the Secretary of the Navy but as an American citizen," requests the president.

Admiral Jacobs nods to the affirmative.

"The United States has stayed neutral through all the conflicts in Europe and Asia, but I fear that our inaction will lead to war on our very shores. Do you think we need to get involved with the war in Europe?" challenges the president.

Admiral Jacobs takes a long gulp of the Jack Daniels.

"Jesus Franklin, this is not an easy answer," pleads Admiral Jacobs. Admiral Jacobs is searching for the words to articulate his point of view.

"Umm… The Great War cost us a lot, and many Americans are afraid of taking on such loses again without it benefitting us. I don't want to see any more young American boys die for these European conflicts—hell, let them fight it out. The more they fight the stronger our position becomes. The day they all unite is the day we become weaker," admits Admiral Jacobs.

"I agree with you Dewey, but Hitler," utters the president as he takes a drink.

"That son of a bitch definitely has some screws loose; he is set on world domination. There have been reports of him killing and burning his own people. I think he is the wild card," concedes Admiral Jacobs.

"We must take the fight to the Germans and Japanese before they bring the fight to us, but how?" questions the president.

"Mr. President, go to Congress. Tell them what you think and tell them that you believe we must mobilize our forces," pleads Admiral Jacobs.

"Dewey, that sounds good, but they are thinking about the next election, not the fate of the world. I am not trying to over-dramatize this, but if we allow the Brits and Russians to fall in Europe, this will allow the Axis Powers to fight us at full strength on American soil. You have to know that once Hitler conquers England, he will ramp up his efforts," states a visibly shaken President Roosevelt.

"We must act now then," declares Jacobs.

"I don't know how, but the regular congressional debate takes six months. They will be launching attacks from across both oceans," conveys the president.

Admiral Jacobs starts to pace back and forth, talking to himself.

"We can't…but it may be the only way…but the American boys, they wouldn't serve this," rambles Jacobs.

"Dewey, what are you rambling about," queries a puzzled President Roosevelt.

"Mr. President, what I am about to propose must be left in this office, and I must have your word that neither of us will ever talk about this again," demands a calculating Admiral Jacobs.

"Sure, Dewey," responds an apprehensive President Roosevelt.

"Mr. President, I frame this proposal with the possibility of our American people being completely galvanized; Congress will not dare to oppose a declaration of war, and we would be able to stop the Axis powers in Europe," announces an emotionally spent Admiral Jacobs.

The president pours two glasses of Jack Daniels for himself and Admiral Jacobs. Jacobs swallows his drink in haste. The Admiral had just given the president his way to get into the war. He proposed that they would not alert the Pacific command of the impending attack by the large

Japanese Armada. The president could count on the American people's need for revenge as the justification to get into the war. Admiral Jacobs takes a deep breath then swallows his drink.

"Lord my God, please forgive us. Please have mercy on our souls," says a repenting Admiral Jacobs.

DEATH OF A KING

In April of 1945, America and its allies have turned the tide against the Axis powers in World War II. After four years of the Axis powers marching across Europe and Asia, the Allies have had major victories against German and Italian troops. The Americans fighting in the west and the Russians fighting in the east have stifled Hitler's plan for world domination by stretching his forces to the limit. The ground forces believe it could be days before Italy surrenders and a couple of weeks before the Nazis lay down their guns. The American and British fighter-bombers have been peppering the German artillery factories and fuel-supply facilities with hourly bombings, strangling the Axis powers' war effort.

All the news has not been good—President Franklin Delano Roosevelt's health has taken a turn for the worst. The most passionate American cheerleader for the war effort has been battling complications of his weakening heart. It has been rumored since the fall of 1944 that the president has been in grave condition. The Vice President of the United States, Harry S. Truman, arrives at Warm Springs at the request of President Roosevelt. Truman has only been VP since the election of 1944 just six short months before. Truman is a very straight-laced politician; the ideal statesman. Truman is the type of political leader Americans say they want, but unfortunately, he couldn't communicate his ideas in an effective manner. He could identify with the common man's struggle—he had worked as a laborer and then toiled in local county politics. He should have been someone that Americans would trust, but they saw him as weak and dumb—soon he would learn the ways to be a great figure in American history.

Warm Springs is the president's vacation home; it is an exact replica of the White House. It was constructed with four columns and windows, emulating its Washington counterpart. Roosevelt often went to Warm Springs to help rejuvenate his polio-riddled body. He believed the resort's pools had therapeutic waters and mystical powers. Roosevelt visited the resort originally in 1924, hoping to find a cure for polio that left him paralyzed from the waist down. Roosevelt believed in the powers of Warm Springs so much that he decided to build a home close to the resort, which became known as the Little White House—an exact replica of its namesake. In early April, Roosevelt suffered a massive stroke.

Truman walks into the room to find a very ashen-faced Roosevelt. Truman tries to walk quietly across the cherry wood floor, but the constant creaking makes it all but impossible. Truman takes a deep breath as he finally realizes the severity of the president's condition. The president's eyes are sunken, and his skin looks like paper mache'—and looks just as brittle. The president awakes to Truman standing over top of him.

"God damn Harry, you trying to sneak up on me?" whispers President Roosevelt.

Roosevelt and Truman share a momentary smile. The vice president tries to break the tension.

"We've got the Nazis on the run. We have pushed them back into Germany, and the Russians are pushing from the east," discloses Truman.

"Yeah, our boys are fighting their hearts out," the president suggests as he starts to cough uncontrollably.

Truman hands Roosevelt a glass of water.

"Thank you, Harry…I guess I am not looking so presidential," concedes the president.

"Mr. President, you are fine," expresses Truman.

"We must start to make transitional arrangements, the president states in a stern voice.

"Mr. President, let's wait until you feel better," says a consoling Truman.

"I am not going to get better. I am dying, dammit," admits an angry Roosevelt.

The president takes a deep breath and a gulp of water.

"Harry I am sorry; you didn't deserve that. I have not informed the cabinet yet, but the doctors think I have less than two weeks. I wanted to tell you…no I wanted to warn you, to be ready. People will be coming at you from all directions: some friend and some foe. Most will have their own agenda. You will need to follow your heart so that you can live with your decisions," reveals Roosevelt.

Truman walks over to a nearby window and looks blankly into his undeniable future.

"Harry, I know this is sudden, but I owed it to you. I am going to tell the chief of staff that you are to be involved in every domestic and military issue. We must win this war, Harry," proclaims an exhausted Roosevelt.

Truman reflects on his time in Missouri. It was just a little over 25 years ago when Truman helped organize the 2nd Regiment of Missouri's Field Artillery's preparation for World War I. He fought in the fields of Europe in that war, and now he was to be the commander in chief at the culmination of World War II. Truman gazed into the early Georgian spring sun as he pondered his many successes and his equally painful defeats. How could he follow the overly popular and successful Roosevelt to finish the enormous American effort?

"Harry…Harry, I know this is probably a bit overwhelming, but you must prepare yourself. Once you leave here, you should tell Bess what's on the horizon, but she must not tell anyone what is happening until I am gone." Truman shakes his head in the affirmative.

"The war in the European theater is nearing a close, but the Pacific will be the challenge. The Empire of Japan will not go away quietly," declares Roosevelt.

"I thought we were contemplating invading the island?" asks Truman.

"We were, but McArthur and some other top generals believe the casualties would be too high," claims Roosevelt.

"So do we continue to fight them in the mountains?" asks Truman.

"No, we have convinced two former Nazi scientists to defect to America. They have plans to create a bomb that could destroy several cities with one blast. Ironically, Hitler wanted to use this bomb in New York City and Washington, D.C. The possibility of this bomb must be explored," concedes an uneasy Roosevelt.

"What's wrong?" inquires Truman.

"Harry, if we use this technology, we will kill many innocent men, women, and children. We could be seen as uncompassionate and as heartless as Hitler himself. But do we allow countless numbers of American soldiers to continue to be slaughtered in the Pacific? These are some of the decisions that you will have to make, Harry. We are on the fringe of America becoming the greatest empire ever, but the snakes lurk in the grass, not just the ones you know of but also the ones we think are our friends. They sit and wait for us to stumble," states a coughing Roosevelt as mucus streams from the corners of his mouth.

"Harry, I apologize for being so cold to you. I didn't think you were ready for the rumble and tumble of Washington politics. I kept you out because, in my own way, you are the purest person I've ever known. You know the powers that be in the Democratic National Party wanted you to be vice; I wanted Byrnes," admits a smiling Roosevelt.

Truman taps Roosevelt's hand affectionately.

"I know. It wasn't the best-kept secret." They both have a shared smile.

"I thought and think Byrnes has a great foreign affairs mind and thought he would have been great tangling with the Russians and many of the European nations. He was just brash enough to deal with our generals and smart enough to deal with the so-called intellectuals on Capitol Hill. He is just too much of a good ol' boy to put him out front. My boss doesn't like his politics on race relations. We are here now; when I go meet my maker, you make sure that you and Byrnes come to an agreement and work together. He has a lot of good things to say; don't hold his redneck persona against him. He is really a stand-up guy… I must admit sometimes he is a junkyard dog, but he is my junkyard dog. Now make him your junkyard dog," says Roosevelt as he shakes Truman's hand.

KING MAKER

Franklin Delano Roosevelt died on April 12, 1945, at Warm Springs. On April 15th, people line the streets of Washington, D.C., hoping to catch a glimpse of the casket carrying the deceased president's corpse. There must be one million people along Pennsylvania Avenue dressed in black and shedding a collective tear for their fallen commander in chief. Roosevelt was the closest thing America has had to a sitting king—not to mention a king that has saved his loyal subjects from the tyranny of world domination and the savagery of an unrelenting economic depression. Roosevelt was revered by many cross sections of Americans: the Jews love him because he took on Hitler and the Nazi regime, the Negroes loved him because they were gaining more rights and a prominent place in American life and Middle America loved him because he developed and enacted programs to help them get back on their feet. All in all, Roosevelt touched many American lives, and he made people feel like he was for the underdog, and Americans understand the story of the underdog. Quietly, many in Congress across political lines felt the passing of Roosevelt would present a vacuum of power within the federal government. It must be understood that Roosevelt ruled the federal government for 13 years—an eternity for American politics. Roosevelt helped many Americans, but he disabled many within the power circles in Washington. He started to allow groups like Negroes, Jews and the poor-at-large to believe that they too were entitled to the American dream. That was all well and good for the campaign trail, but many of the programs Roosevelt initiated brought more people than ever to the table of opportunity.

The transition of power needed to be seamless to make sure that the American and European efforts weren't hampered by Roosevelt's death. The new president set up headquarters within the White House, but he remained respectful to the family of Roosevelt. Truman and Eleanor Roosevelt were very cordial—it was rumored that Eleanor lobbied the president to pick Truman in light of growing concern about Roosevelt's physical condition. Eleanor is an advocate of rights for colored people, and she didn't like the views of Secretary of State James Byrnes—the president's pick for the Vice President. Leaning on the advice of the former president, Truman has summoned James Byrnes to the White House for a meeting.

The funeral of Franklin Delano Roosevelt was a regal event. On this day, the U.S. resembled a 15th-century monarchy—rather than the great democracy it strived to be. Roosevelt was the great American king, and his loyal subjects had come to adore him one last time. People of all ages, colors and political affiliations for miles lined Pennsylvania Avenue from the U.S. Capitol to the White House to get a glimpse of their fallen hero's casket. Roosevelt became America's great king, Americans looked to Roosevelt for guidance—he was the country's steady strength for more than 13 years. He was the one constant they all could rely on, but now he was gone.

The dark overcast clouds could not have posed more darkness on the city than what many Americans were already feeling. Many Americans felt like they lost their greatest drum major and the greatest advocate for the common man and woman. Even though Roosevelt was a wealthy man and never struggled for anything in his life, most identified him as understanding the plight of the common man who struggled every day to put food on the table for his family. Many also felt like Roosevelt was single-handedly the reason World War II changed in the Allies' favor. What will happen to the U.S. now that he is dead? The newly sworn-in President Truman does not have the luxury of contemplating his legacy, but he must make sure America continues to fend off its foreign adversaries. Shortly after the memorial service for Roosevelt, current Secretary of State James Byrnes is walking around the reflecting pool in front of the U.S. Capitol, pondering his future. Brynes knows Truman does not like him, and he knows that many within the establishment do not care for him as well. James Brynes has a very long record of public service. He has a reputation for getting things done. There is a famous story of his time as a senator from South Carolina.

He told some of his Northern counterparts during a civil rights debate, "Are you gonna tell me you are going to make a White man from Alabama, Texas, Mississippi or even my beloved South Carolina give up his seat to a Nigger and you think that is going to sit well?" said Bynes.

President Roosevelt loved Brynes; they had different ideologies, but Brynes tells it like is—he always says you may not always agree with him, but you have to respect that he told you. As Brynes smokes a rum-dipped Cuban cigar, he thinks about what he will say to Truman when he tries to fire him. Brynes has a resignation letter in an envelope in his left jacket pocket. He thinks if Truman fires him, he could run for governor of his beloved state of South Carolina. With his popularity, he could do great things for the state. Brynes' strength is foreign affairs; he likes the small intricacies of dealing with foreign leaders. It is an emotional high for him to discuss matters that would influence the lives of millions and eventually history. As Brynes weighs all his future options, a young man walks over to him, obviously, a military man with his rigid walk and short crew haircut.

"Good Afternoon sir. The President of the United States would like to speak with you," states the young man.

Brynes takes a hard pull on his cigar before sarcastically saying, "I guess I don't have much of a choice now do I?"

Brynes takes the short walk to a government car. The president is sitting in his makeshift office while President Roosevelt's belongings are carefully being packed up. Truman looks out onto the hustle and bustle of Washington, D.C. He looks in the direction of the Washington Monument and thinks how Commander-in-Chief George Washington would handle this situation.

"You know the view down the hall is much better," says Brynes.

The two men shake hands.

"You don't want to seem heartless to the memory of Franklin. I loved him too, but he would understand the importance of what you will be dealing with," asserts a stern Brynes.

"I will move in tomorrow. I just wanted Eleanor to have a day to reflect on him," hints Truman.

"Mr. President, I know we both come from different places philosophically. I know you disagreed with Roosevelt keeping me in the cabinet, so I will make things easier for us all. Mr. President, I present you with my resignation letter." Brynes hands the president his letter. The president says, "Thank you" with a smile on his face, then tears up the letter.

"I need all hands-on-deck. You still work for the President of the United States of America. We have our differences, but what two

people don't." Both men smile. "I need you. America needs you, Mr. Brynes," affirms President Truman.

"Mr. President, you are the great mid-western liberal, the conscious of the nation, and I am the backwoods redneck from the hick state of South Carolina," says Brynes sarcastically. Roosevelt answers, "Ok Jimmy, you have sold yourself short. I haven't always been a big fan of yours, but I never thought you were a backwoods redneck. I believe some of your constituents are backwoods rednecks but not you. As a politician, I understand you must feed the mob mentality. If your constituents' self-interests are jobs, you must advocate for jobs. If your constituents' self-interests are tax breaks, then you must advocate for tax breaks—I fully understand that about you. Unfortunately, many of your constituents believe that the advances of colored people mean that their quality of life will instantly suffer."

Brynes nods in affirmation to the president's comments.

"Why the change of heart? We have never sat down and had a conversation. I used to see you at public events, and you always seemed to give me a glaring look," asks a baffled Brynes.

"I probably did have a scowl on my face. I really didn't like you; I found you to be very brash and uncompromising, but in recent days I have found a new appreciation for you. At the end of it all, we can't allow petty differences to separate us anymore," declares Truman.

"Were you struck by lightning?" jokes Brynes.

"No, I was struck by Franklin. He told me you were misunderstood. He said to look at your track record," says Truman.

"I know you have heard about my many spirited discussions with my Senate colleagues and the times I have berated attorneys at the Supreme Court."

"So, what did you come up with?" asks Brynes.

Looking at a paper tablet, Truman says, "You were a one-term governor of South Carolina, a senator—your Senate election win was by

40 points—you became the chairman of both the department of war and treasury."

Brynes smiles, "Wow, it sounds quite impressive coming out of your mouth, Mr. President. I know that sometimes the citizens of our country don't know what is good for them. I have tried to be a barometer for the common man.

As I have gone up the ladder, I notice that there is no difference between the common man and the perceived well-to-do person.

We all want peace and prosperity for ourselves and our families. So, when I talk to foreign leaders, I speak with that background—but if they intend to infringe on our way of life then they must be obliterated," says Brynes.

Truman affirms Bryne's determination. The president thinks that Brynes' junkyard dog mentality along with his political fervor could aid him throughout his presidency.

"So, what will my role be?" asks Brynes.

The president looks out unto the grounds of the White House, contemplating where he should place Brynes.

"Honestly, I don't want to limit you to one area. I want you involved in public and foreign policy as a whole. Job number one is going be to find a way to end this war. The European Theatre is all but won, but the Japs are a problem," admits a rattled Truman.

Brynes approaches the president in a serious manner.

"Are you truly ready to end this war?" asks Brynes.

The president shakes his head in affirmation but is afraid of Brynes' impending proposal. The president wonders to himself what Brynes could be referring to.

"If Roosevelt had a chance to end the war, why wouldn't he?" asks a shaken Truman.

MANHATTAN PROJECT

A young 20-something Harry Truman is walking through a desolate town, formerly known as Argonne, which is nested gently in the snow-covered Alps in Switzerland. Harry is serving in the 2nd battery infantry unit of the United States Army as a 1st lieutenant in World War I. He and his platoon have walked for days across the picturesque countryside. Harry had always dreamed of skiing in the Alps, but his first trip went from a dream to a nightmare instantly. He had a nightmare of countless women and children being obliterated. It looked like the Germans leveled the town without any regard for life. The town was littered with an endless amount of rotting bodies. Some bodies were decapitated; some were severed in half with the intestines and bones close by, probably ravaged by wild animals. The freshwater river had been replaced by rivers of dark blood running through the city, turning much of the normally ivory snow into a pink glaze covering the landscape. Harry is overcome by the bodies of two children—they look like they were hugging each other before they were apparently shot. Overcome by the repugnant smell, he bends over to throw up.

President Harry Truman is broken out of his of a daydream by the shouts of James Brynes.

"Mr. President, Mr. President," barks an intense Brynes. The president has a glazed look on his face as beads of sweat roll down his forehead. The president walks over to a liquor cart sitting in the corner of the oval office and pours himself a scotch in a presidential crested glass. The room is full of advisors and fully decorated military types; all are silent as they watch the

president's unnerved reaction to Brynes' presentation of the Manhattan Project.

"Mr. President are you ok?" asks a concerned Brynes.

The president appears to snap himself out of the trance he was in.

"Gentleman, I apologize. I think I'm coming down with the flu. Bess told me that I looked a bit flush—let this be a lesson to you young men: always listen to your wives," jokes the president as he coughs.

The entire room erupts into laughter. Brynes tries to deflect attention from his obviously shaken boss.

"Mr. President, why don't we give you time to collect yourself. How about we reconvene tomorrow at 10 am?" inquires Brynes.

The president shakes his head in the affirmative and waits for much of the group to leave.

"Excuse me, Mr. Einstein, can you spare a moment?" asks the president.

"Of course, Mr. President," says Albert Einstein, the famous German-born theoretical physicist.

"Thank you for staying. I was very surprised to see you here in this setting," admits the president.

"Well, America is building an atomic bomb, which is heavily driven by physics. It would only be prudent to bring in a physicist. I just so happened to be available," says Einstein as both men share a light chuckle.

"No, I just wouldn't expect such a scholarly gentleman such as yourself would freely participate in such anticipated destruction," probes the president.

"I freely participate in the effort, plus I must help," says Einstein.

"This bomb will kill and maim tens of thousands of people…maybe more," asserts a concerned Truman.

"Actually, Mr. President, many of our estimates believe the loss of life will reach well into the hundreds of thousands," pushes back a combative Einstein.

Einstein's correction makes the president pour himself another scotch.

"Mr. President, exactly what are you having a problem with?" questions Einstein.

"Isn't there another way? I understand why Franklin didn't pull the trigger," says the president.

"I have to correct you Mr. President, but you are wrong. President Roosevelt was fully on board with this course of action. You remember Pearl Harbor?"

The president interrupts "So this is revenge. We are supposed to be the world's moral compass," proclaims a confused President Truman.

"So, you would allow a foreign power to continue to wage war against you. Taking a life cannot be easy, but I have seen some of the weapons that the Axis powers have. The longer Japan is able to delay their surrender the more likely we will see destruction right here on Pennsylvania Avenue," declares a determined Einstein.

"How do you stomach the possibility of so much death," challenges the president as he takes another gulp of Scotch.

"I was in Europe when the Nazis started their reign of terror. People said it's just a couple of nuts. The idea started with one person, and it grew to the ideology of millions—we must stop Japan now or you will have the blood of hundreds of thousands of American soldiers on your hands—the Japanese will not allow surrender without certain defeat," says Einstein with a tear streaming down his face.

The president, looking into Einstein's eyes, shakes his head in the affirmative, realizing what must be done to stop more American bloodshed.

VJ-DAY

The day begins like any other hazy, hot and humid day in Charleston, South Carolina. Richard Teed is awake at 5:30 am to beads of sweat rolling down his face, caused by the blazing August Charleston sun. Ricky, as his mother and father call him, doesn't mind the heat so much this morning, because today is the first day of football practice. The beginning of his senior year is finally here. This is the year Ricky plans on making a difference. He sat on the bench for the previous three years, but started the last three games last year after his team's starting quarterback, Jonathan Morancy, went down with a painful Achilles tendon injury.

Jonathan was one of the best football players the town had ever witnessed. He stood 5'10" and weighed approximately 160 pounds. Jonathan's physical prowess was secondary to his quiet intelligence. He was not the typical student-athlete; he carried a 3.8-grade point average and was well liked by all. As his understudy, Jonathan taught Ricky all the nuances of the quarterback position. He taught Ricky that he must know what everybody else on the field must do— backward and forward. To use a military analogy, the quarterback was the general and the rest of the team were his soldiers. The triumph or the defeat rested clearly on the quarterback shoulders.

Coach told Ricky after the end of last season that, barring an incredible mental breakdown, Ricky would be the starting quarterback for the upcoming season. What a confidence builder that was; Ricky wanted to make sure that he felt that he made the right choice.

Over the summer, Ricky stuck to a regimented workout schedule. He made sure that he did 500 sit-ups and 200 pushups every day. Ricky thought that Jonathan was one of the smartest football players that he had ever seen, but it did not matter if his body could not carry him through the pain. Ricky was going to make sure that never happened to him…He was always going to be prepared, always a step ahead of the next guy.

Ricky finally rolls out of bed at 5:45 am. He is awaked by the freshly brewed Columbian coffee that his mother loves so much. Mrs. Teed prepares breakfast, laying out a spread as she always does. She cooked corn beef hash, grits, and toast. Breakfast is a definite treat. Like most mornings, Ricky tries to eat as much as he can, but there is no way he can eat everything his mother cooks. Ms. Teed has always over-cooked breakfast; Ricky's father eats enough for four people, so she is used to cooking large feasts. Ms. Teed cooks as if Mr. Teed is going to come through the door at any moment.

Ricky's father, Captain Richard Teed Sr., is a part of an elite special operations force that went into Japan shortly before the U.S. attack on Tokyo. His team went into Japan to scope out possible targets for Army and Navy bombers. Obviously, the sensitivity of his missions didn't allow him to talk about his job. Shortly, before he left for his mission, several generals came to visit him here at the Teed family home—at least Ricky thought they were generals. Two of them had three stars on the top of their uniforms. Ricky remembers them having a very spirited conversation. They were standing out on the street in front of the house; Ricky peeked through the white sheer curtains that his grandmother gave his parents on their wedding day. His father was very upset with the three gentlemen and arguing with them. Captain—that's what Ricky called his dad—was a very reserved man. When Ricky turned 13, his father told him not to call him dad anymore; he said Ricky was becoming a man and dad sounded to kiddy for a man. He didn't believe in getting upset for no reason. Ricky noticed that he was smoking one of the cigars that he bought during his time in Cuba: a true indication that war was brewing. Ricky overheard their conversation.

"You sons of bitches knew and now you want me to clean up your god damn mess?" said an incensed Captain.

Ricky knew his father didn't curse without cause. So, he wondered what had happened and what needed to be cleaned up. Captain is a very God-fearing man. It seemed out of character for him to curse and argue with people.

Ricky has only known of the gentle and caring side of his father; could there be a sinister and secret side lurking? Ricky guessed the threat of killing or being killed could change anybody's personality for the worse. The next day, Ricky's father prepared to leave. He sat on his parents' bed, watching his mother pack his father's standard-issue green duffle bag. Captain had participated in many different missions before, but something seemed very cryptic about this mission. Ms. Teed's hands seem to be shaking as she folded up his socks. Captain walked over to his wife and wrapped her up in a large bear hug. The hug seemed to give her some momentary comfort. Ricky would never forget their last conversation. They sat on their porch in the old green and white two-seat swing. Ricky had fallen asleep many days on his dad's chest as the summer air passed through his brown locks.

Ricky and his mother had not heard from Captain in little over a year. Ms. Teed sits on the family porch morning, noon and night waiting for her husband to pull up. The absence of Captain seems to have aged Ms. Teed 10 years. Ricky hears her many nights crying herself to sleep. Captain didn't talk about many of his missions, but he sat his wife and son down before he went to Tokyo.

"Ricky, I want to tell both of you that this is going to be a difficult mission, but we should come out with flying colors. If the unit pulls off this mission, we should win the war," claims Captain.

Captain made war seem so glorious; he was a superhero so Ricky just knew he was coming back. Captain represented everything that was good about America. He was a good man; he took care of his family, and he loved his country. Ms. Teed continues to cook Captain's favorite breakfast every morning: corn beef hash, grits and lightly browned toast. Captain didn't believe in burning the bread on purpose. She cooked his favorite breakfast in the hopes that, when he came home, it would be like nothing had ever changed. But things did change. Ricky felt a double loss: not only did he lose his father, he lost his mother as well. Things were very tough for his mom. Captain is the only man his mother ever loved. They dated since their sophomore year in high school. Ms. Teed has not slept through the night since they got word that he disappeared nearly two years ago. Every morning, Ricky's mother gets up and cooks breakfast and then goes to sit on the porch. She hopes that he arrives with a hero's welcome, pulling up on a white horse with trumpets blowing.

"Mom, I've finished breakfast." Ricky's mom doesn't respond.

"Ma!" yells Ricky.

"Yes Ricky," she answers.

"I finished breakfast," says Ricky.

"Ok honey," she replies as she drifts into her thoughts.

"I have to get to football practice. Today is the first day," says a gleeful Ricky.

Ms. Teed takes a deep breath. "You know we are very proud of you." Ricky's mom says while fighting back tears.

"I know Mom; I will continue to make you proud. I will be home after practice," affirms Ricky.

Ricky thinks about what plays coach is going to run this year while riding his bike down Ashley Avenue. Inherently, St. Martin's Catholic High School always runs the triple wishbone formation, with two running backs and a wingback coming out the backfield. It is always an effective offense, but ultimately it is overly predictable. In recent years, St. Martin's has started getting better athletes who can execute an array of complicated schemes.

On his way to school, Ricky always takes a shortcut down Calhoun to King Street. The shortcut eliminates about 15 minutes of riding time. The route passes by the famous Charleston slave markets. The area still resonates with the stench of death. Ricky arrives at the field at about 6:30 am and hears a voice in the distance.

"Teed, you're late," comes from the raspy voice of coach Albert Nelson. Big Al, as the school so affectionately calls him, is sitting on a folding chair eating a box of donuts and drinking out of a bottle of Pepsi Cola: not exactly a nutritious breakfast. Ricky walks over to Big Al, dumbfounded.

"Coach, it isn't seven yet."

Coach replies, "I never said it was. If you are going to lead this team, you need to be the most prepared person on the field. So, you might as well get in your mind that you have more responsibility than your other teammates."

Coach is setting the tone for his relationship with Ricky from the jump. Most coaches look at quarterbacks as their coaches on the field; Big Al is no different. Ricky remembers Jonathan telling him that over and over after he got hurt last year. "Coach wants you to know what you need to know and what everyone else is supposed to do." It seems his words were proving prophetic.

The team begins practice at precisely 7 am with a short speech from Big Al.

"Gentlemen, today we begin another campaign to capture the ever-elusive Catholic League title. We finished in second place last year gentlemen. There are no excuses for us not to capture the title this year," states Big Al.

Big Al thinks this year Ricky Teed will be leading the offense. The team will continue to run the I formation with some minor modifications. Big Al stares at Ricky as if to let him know that the speech was expressly for him. Are there any questions?" asks Big Al.

No one dares to raise their hand, even if they do have a good question.

"If there are no questions gentlemen, please give me two laps," says a smiling Coach Al.

After completing the nearly one-mile run, the team walks over to the coach. Many of the players are panting and gasping for air; most did not run or do anything to keep themselves in shape over the summer.

"Is this what I'm working with? You guys are out of shape. How can we win anything if you are out of shape?" asks the portly Coach Al.

Ricky thinks to himself that it is really ironic for him to sit back and criticize the team for being out of shape while his stomach seems to hide the belt to his pants. But there were some elements of truth to what he said.

After a half hour of passing and catching drills, Big Al wants the team to start practicing the meat and potatoes of the offense: the I formation, with two split flankers. Coach calls Ricky over before the team starts running the offense.

"Okay Teed, it is up to you; you run the offense. You know the plays, right?" asks Coach.

Ricky nods his head in shock. The coach never lets anybody call their own plays. Ricky is going to be the guinea pig. He runs back to the huddle, more excited than the day coach told him he would be the starter for the year. Once he kneels to deliver the play to the offense, he realizes what coach is talking about…he is now responsible for the outcome of the Saints' season. Ricky quickly understands that it is only practice, but he now feels like the weight of the world is on his skinny shoulders. The coaches relay instructions and plays into the players as they huddle in the shade. In the distance, there is a car blowing its horn. A voice can be faintly heard.

"It's over, it's over!" says the voice.

The team seems a bit confused. They don't know what to make of the sudden interruption.

The coaches exclaim to them. "Get back to practice, don't worry about that noise."

The car pulls up to the practice field. A young scrawny White kid rips across the field.

"Who in the plum hell is that running across my practice field?" Big Al asks.

Coach Sheehan, looking through binoculars, says in his deep Carolina drawl, "That's that god damn Chris White."

Big Al exclaims to White in the distance, "You owe me three miles White!" White continues running across the field, saying, "It's over! It's over!"

White runs over to the coaches and tells them, "It's over, it's really over!"

"What the hell are you talking about White?" Big Al exclaims.

"The war coach… It is over today," he says.

The coaching staff begins jumping up and down. The players on the field are extremely confused at this point.

"Practice is canceled for the rest of the week!" says Big Al.

The team stands on the field, perplexed by the recent turn of events. They have not been able to get a cup of water in the last two hours and now practice is canceled. Chris White runs over to his team and exclaims to them, "We won...the war it's over! We won!" exclaims White.

The entire team erupts into jubilation. It appears they all have forgotten about the 100-plus degree day that made their coaches run for shade. There is no way the heat is going to impede the team's joy. They all huddle and hug each other, knowing that everyone on the field understands the magnitude of the victory.

"There is a press conference in about a minute," White tells the team. "I brought my transistor radio...we can all listen to the press conference."

The team and coaches all run to the shade to listen to the upcoming radio broadcast. The entire team and coaching staff are huddled around White's small transistor radio. The broadcast has not begun; the station is playing "Chattanooga Choo Choo" by Glenn Miller.

The radio station's announcer, Butch Gaston, interrupts the song. "Excuse me, ladies and gentlemen, for interrupting the pleasant sounds of 'Chattanooga Choo Choo'; we bring you this important message: We now take you to Tokyo, Japan." The Japanese emperor, Hirohito, is holding a press conference. It is the first time most Americans—and for that matter, most Japanese—will ever hear his voice.

"Today I come before the people of Japan to announce the terms of the Potsdam Declaration, in which we surrender our arms of battle.

After the totally inhumane destruction of Nagasaki and Hiroshima, I was left with no alternative but to accept unconditional surrender.

Indeed, we declared war on America and Britain out of our sincere desire to ensure Japan's self-preservation and the stabilization of East Asia, it being far from our thought either to infringe upon the sovereignty of other nations or to embark upon territorial aggrandizement. Despite the best that has been done by everyone—the gallant fighting of our military and naval forces, the diligence and assiduity of our servants of the state and the devoted service of our one hundred million people—the war situation has developed not necessarily to Japan's advantage, while the general trends of the world have all turned against her interest. Let the entire nation continue as one family from generation to generation, ever firm in its faith of the imperishableness of its divine land, and mindful of its heavy burden of responsibilities, and the long road before it. Unite your total strength to be devoted to the construction of the future. Cultivate the ways of rectitude, the nobility of spirit, and work with resolution so that you may enhance the innate glory of the Imperial State and keep pace with the progress of the world," says the dejected Emperor.

Butch Gaston's voice is heard once again. "Now we take you to comments made by President Truman this morning." President Truman says the following…

"Good morning. My fellow Americans, I am proud to announce that the Empire of Japan has agreed to an unconditional surrender in the Pacific. At approximately 7 am Eastern Standard time in the United States, Emperor Hirohito formally announced by radio that his empire would end aggression in the Pacific and their entire military would stand down immediately. On this day, which will be known as VJ day in honor of our victory over the Japanese, we must take time to honor the Americans who gave the ultimate sacrifice to ensure that the greatest country in the world was protected from oppression and tyranny. We should use this opportunity to reunite this country and repair many of the strains that this global conflict has inflicted on our way of life. But today let us celebrate this monumental victory."

Butch Gaston says, "The address from the president was given at the Rose Garden at the White House. We now take you back to our regular broadcasting." The radio resumes with the upbeat "Boogie Woogie Bugle Boy" by the Andrews Sisters, a song about a young bugler being drafted into the army. The entire team, including the coaching staff, is jumping up and down in joy.

It must be understood that the country thought three years prior that they could be invaded after the sneak attack by the Japanese after Pearl Harbor.

`Many of the kids on that very field have felt the cost of war. Many of them lost family and friends without any notification or closure to their whereabouts.

It was never talked about, but the country felt very vulnerable after the attack. It was certain vindication that made the country's attackers surrender in their country. Ricky thought in a strange way, it seemed like retribution for them attacking us.

The country did not celebrate the victories over the other Axis powers like it did against Japan. Germany was probably a bigger global threat, but the country did not enjoy the destruction of Hitler's Third Reich as much as the annihilation of the Empire of Japan. As the team celebrates the country's victory over Japan, Ricky notices the school cheerleaders practicing. The squad is led by Jennifer Holtzman. Holtzman is the prettiest girl in school. Everybody calls her Jen. She is tall and skinny, and she always smells like an ocean breeze on a spring morning. Sometimes Ricky daydreams about her—what would it be like to kiss her… Jen's school locker is in the same row in the senior locker bank. She is what every girl in school wants to be, and she is the girl every guy wants on their arm. She is in the running for just about all the senior superlative awards; best dressed, best personality, most likely to succeed and prettiest. Jen is one of the sweetest people you could ever meet. Ricky has had a crush on her since the first day he met her in freshman biology. He thought she thought he was a bit slow upon their first encounter. Ricky always seemed to trip over his words when speaking to her. Jen simply took his breath away. She was always an unassuming beauty. She wasn't your evil bitchy knockout; she was the type of girl that—sure, you wanted her to be your girlfriend—but if she wasn't, you were glad she was your friend. Jen waves Ricky over to their practice. He briskly jogs over. The entire squad is there with Jen.

"Good morning ladies," Ricky says.

Jen asks, "Why are you guys over there jumping up and down?"

Ricky replies, "Haven't you heard? The Japs surrendered today." The group of teenage beauties jump up and down in obvious joy. Ricky and some of his teammates watch as the young beauties jump and down in slow motion.

The girls reaction to the good news brings back memories of looking at some of Captain's old girly magazines. Jen looks like the stunning bathing beauty picture taken by Billy DeVross in 1942.

It is always a treat for the football team to watch the cheerleading practices. The splits and human pyramids are enough to get a young man out of bed, if not to just catch a glimpse of the somewhat tight sweaters and the high-cut, almost perverse skirts. Jen kisses and hugs Ricky.

"Ricky…Ricky are you ok?"

Unfortunately, Jen broke him out of his hormonal delusion of grandeur. But there is no better way of being awakened from a delusion than with the appearance of an angel.

"Sure, I'm ok," utters a delusional Ricky.

"This is great, isn't it?" Jen says.

She must have noticed the dumbfounded expression on his face.

"That we won the war," Jen says.

"Oh yeah, thank God it is over," Ricky answers.

"This calls for a celebration. Let's go to the soda shop!" Jen exclaims to the group.

The group agrees with Jen's assertion.

Jen asks Ricky, "Would you like to join us at the soda shop?"

Ricky hesitates, then says, "I would love to, but I probably should go home and check on my mom."

Jen walks over to Ricky and pinches his cheeks, then says, "Aren't you the sweetest? I told you, girls, he was the sweetest guy." Ricky doesn't think he could be embarrassed any further. He decides to walk back to the football practice with rosy, red cheeks and obviously sweaty palms. As Ricky starts walking back to the football field, he thinks that maybe now, if Captain is still alive, there could be a possibility that he will see him. If he were captured, hopefully, his captors would release him. Ricky never told his mom, but there were many nights that he had terrible nightmares about Captain being captured and tortured by the Japs. There were many rumors about the Japanese army's methods of torture. The most horrific thing that Ricky had ever heard was the Japanese use of vises. They would interrogate a captured American soldier, and if he didn't give them the information that they were looking for, they would place their body on a table and put a wooden vise around their head. They would then tighten the vise around the tortured soldier's head until the soldier's eyes would literally explode and spill out like cracked eggs, or the skull would crack, leaking out brain fluid.

Either method would result in cruel punishment. Ricky hoped Captain was killed on the battlefield; he thought that is how he would have wanted it. A superhero would die on the battlefield defending the American Way. He was built to be a soldier, not a confined prisoner.

FORT SUMTER

The city of Charleston, South Carolina is all abuzz with word of the Japanese surrender in the Pacific. The Empire of Japan is the last member of the Axis powers to surrender during World War II. Germany and Italy surrendered earlier this spring. The Empire of Japan was forced into submission after the destruction of Nagasaki and Hiroshima with America's new and deadly invention: the atomic bomb. The atomic bomb is a game changer. A country can destroy or severely damage a city without ever firing a gun. Most countries don't have the capacity or resources to compete with the U.S. on this front. This development propels the advent of the Atomic Age. Up until this point, the Brits, the Japanese, the Russians and the Germans were the big dogs on the world stage, but with the absolute destruction of Europe and Asia, it immediately thrusts America into the role of the big bully on the block.

Ricky rides down Ashley Avenue on his bicycle, feeling good to be an American. Ricky has never seen so much patriotic spirit in the city. Charleston always felt like a confederate city more than an American city. The south was always like its own country; everything below the Mason-Dixon always felt different than cities in the north. Cities like New York, Washington, D.C., and Chicago seem more like what people think of as American cities than Charleston.

The Yankees have always looked at towns like Charleston as backward redneck holdups, but now it feels like it has all changed. It seems like every house as far as the eye can see has an American flag flying in concert with the mainstay Confederate flag on their porches. Ricky feels proud to be an American on this day. Today's victory seems to balance out the despair the city felt after receiving word of the Pearl Harbor attack in 1941. It was four long years, but Charleston sure does seem like it was worth it.

The jubilation is so great because the sacrifices were also so great. Many residents of the town lost at least one loved one in the war. Many lost so much more. Mr. Abbott, who lives further up on Ashley, lost three sons. One son was killed at Pearl Harbor. Ricky heard stories that Mr. Abbott's son was aboard the Missouri, which rests at the bottom of Pearl Harbor. The other two sons enlisted the day after America declared war on Germany. Unfortunately, they died on the fields of Okinawa trying to avenge their brother's death in 1944. Ricky saw Mr. Abbott earlier in the day; Mr. Abbott seemed to be so proud his sons served the American military. His sons sacrificed their lives for the security of the free world.

Even Mr. Samuel Brown is flying his American flag on the porch of his home. Ricky is really surprised to see Mr. Brown flying his flag. Mr. Brown is a colored man who lives across the street. He has lived on Ricky's street for as long as he can remember. Mr. Brown has been the victim of harassment countless times from some of the local rednecks. Many of the rednecks that harass him are jealous because he's a colored man who owns a home in the upper middle-class Ashley Avenue neighborhood. Mr. Brown is a teacher at the local colored school. He teaches history, and it is fascinating to listen to his take on things. Mr. Brown is somewhat of a conspiracy theorist; he always thinks there is a sinister motive behind everything.

Mr. Brown lost his son Granville several months ago. His son was a member of the elite Tuskegee Airmen corps. Mr. Brown's son died in a very important air battle over the city of Berlin in Germany. He was shot down after defending an air bomber that he was tasked to protect. It was said that the bomber that he was protecting disabled the German military's headquarters, which turned the tide in the European Theater for the Allied powers.

Consequently, Mr. Brown was awarded the Purple Heart in his son's honor. Granville was given the greatest honor for his participation in the war, but when his body was sent back to America, the State of South Carolina refused to allow his family to bury him at the Jefferson Lee military cemetery with full military honors.

Charleston, like much of the nation, is still in the grips of Jim Crow rules, not allowing Whites and Negroes to cohabitate or rest in peace next to one another. Mr. Brown was forced to bury his son at an out-of-the-way cemetery in the Black section of Charleston.

Most of the country lost many of its residents to the war in Europe and Asia. The defeat of Japan should help the country get back to some kind of normalcy. The victory is not just a celebration of winning the war but also the relief that no foreign army will occupy the homeland. Americans were whipped into a frenzy after Pearl Harbor—it was really the first time any part of America was attacked since the Civil War. Americans thought that they could be attacked at any moment, and this conflict affected Americans way of life.

People are lined along the battery on East Battery Street; the Battery is the primary gathering place for large outdoor events in the city of Charleston. This area is significant because Fort Sumter, which sits about one mile offshore—was the site where the shots initiating the American Civil War began. Waves slap gently against the boardwalk while locals and visitors alike enjoy swinging in oversized porch swings and strolling along the shoreline.

The fort was one of the main military installations of the Confederate Army during the Civil War and a symbol of Charleston's Confederate past. The Battery is the social meeting place for Charleston's young people. It is truly a picturesque scene; sitting at the mouth of the Charleston peninsula, which is where massive ships with large masts and sails once docked and where Civil War cannons proudly stood, facing the battery and the Atlantic Ocean.

The victory celebration looks 10 times greater than the city's 4th of July celebration held a little over six weeks earlier. The fort looks like it is the 4th of July, but it surely doesn't feel like it. There seems to be a constant, steady breeze floating across The Battery. The palmetto trees are rustling in the wind, with boats sailing and racing across the harbor, stirring the smell of the salty sea air. The sun setting behind the fort tells the story of the evening. It appears fitting that the spot in which America once was at war with itself could also be the place where healing from such a horrific event would begin.

Ricky looks across the harbor; there are nothing but smiles on the faces of his fellow Charlestonians. He sees Jen and some of her cheerleading buddies standing on the dock.

It seems like the entire town and every enlisted man in the area are celebrating. Jen notices Ricky looking at her.

An enthusiastic Jen waves him over. As Ricky walks toward her, he can feel his heart beating faster and faster. Ricky thinks, *what am I going to say? Jen is an absolute angel.* As he approaches the dock, Ricky feels a shortness of breath. She has a hold on Ricky that he just can't seem to shake.

"Hey Ricky, we are all over here," Jen says as she walks toward him.

She grabs his hand and walks him over to her group of friends. When Jen grabs Ricky's hand, his heart starts to beat faster and faster. His pulse is beating so hard she asks him, "Did you run down here? You sound like you are out of breath."

Ricky says to himself, "*Shit, I hope my hands aren't sweaty.*"

Jen's friend, Hope Fitzgerald, welcomes Ricky over to the group, saying, "Hey Ricky," with a seductive grin.

Ricky always thought Hope had a little thing for him. She is actually a very attractive girl. The Fitzgeralds live about three blocks away from Ricky's house, over on Jefferson Street. He has known Hope since nursery school. They both attended St. Mary's preschool. She always seemed to be younger than Ricky, even now, even though they are the same age and will be graduating next June. Hope stands about 5'0", with bright red hair and the cutest freckles a girl could possibly have. If Ricky didn't have an insatiable crush on Jen that blinds him to every other girl, he would definitely be interested in her.

There are people with smiles as far as the eye could see. It is certainly a family event, and many brought their entire families. Charleston has always been a segmented city—normally the elite and commoners don't co-mingle—but on this joyous occasion, there are no elite or commoners—just Charlestonians. Ricky wishes that Captain could have seen this event, but he knows that Captain would be proud of his town today.

"Hello Ricky," Jen says as she is waving her hands in front of Ricky's face.

"I kind of slipped off into my own world. I guess I was daydreaming," claims a foggy Ricky.

Jen pulls a penny out her skirt pocket and asks, "A penny for your thoughts."

Ricky responds, "I am just impressed with the turnout for the celebration."

Jen answers, "It is quite impressive. I guess this is how the first 4th of July celebration felt. But then again, I guess those patriots who lived in Charleston weren't so happy with the result of the war." Ricky is infatuated with Jen because she is the total package: brains, beauty and a great personality.

But then again, I guess those

Ricky likes just talking to her. She isn't hard on the eyes either. She is one of—if not the smartest—kids in the school. She is a finalist for valedictorian, which means she would be the school's first female to achieve the honor.

There appears to be some commotion over by the pier pavilion. It is Charleston's mayor, William Rose, walking through the crowd, greeting the Charleston community. It is a perfect opportunity for Rose to stump for votes. As politicians do, he is trying to hitch his administration to the victory of the day. The mayoral election is just a little over a year away. Rose recently gave the U.S. government permission to create some experimental housing for poor people within metropolitan Charleston. Much of the housing is for low-income whites, but there are several developments slated for Negroes. This did not sit well with much of Rose's conservative base. They called him a traitor and even a "Nigger lover" in some circles. So, the prospect of the country's victory in World War II could not be overlooked for political gain. The mayor walks out to the screened gazebo at the end of the pier. It is set up with a podium for the mayor to speak from.

"Could I have your attention?" the mayor asks the crowd. Much of the crowd noise starts to subside, but there are still those who are not pleased with the mayor.

Ricky hears someone in the distance: "Go to Hell Rose, you Nigger lover."

As if on cue, the mayor grins at the dissatisfied crowd. "Ladies and gentlemen of the City of Charleston, I, Mayor William Rose, would like to welcome you all to our celebration here at The Battery. We are here to celebrate the Allies' victory in Japan," says Mayor Rose.

The crowd goes wild.

"Charleston, like most American cities, has paid a very hefty price as a result of this global conflict. We must, as a community, come together and help those that have had tremendous loss and tragedy. This is a wonderful opportunity to bring this city together."

The mayor's speech starts attracting some boos from the crowd. The crowd even begins with chants of, "Rose the Nigger Lover." Ricky thinks this is harsh. The mayor actually seems like a good guy, but he is trying to change some things too fast. The major point of contention for most people in Charleston with Rose is the possibility of housing developments for the city's Negroes.

The federal government has proposed funding and building housing for the low-income Blacks of the city of Charleston.

Of course, this doesn't sit well with most of the good ol' boys of Charleston. They want to know why the city, as well as the nation, would give their good tax money to Niggers. Even though the country had just had its greatest victory ever—only six hours later it is being used for political gain.

GRADUATION

Gazing in the mirror at the young man in the cap and gown staring back at him, Ricky barely recognizes the young man who used to whine about getting up to go to school. Ricky wonders, *Does the tassel belong on the right or left side of the cap? I wish Captain were here not just to help me with the tassel but also just to be here.* Ricky has not taken too many large steps without Captain, and this was definitely the biggest step. Ms. Teed is sitting on the porch daydreaming about days long since gone. Ricky knows she is proud of him, but he wishes she could show it a little more.

All the hard work and studying were for this day: graduation day—the day where you must leave the kid games of high school behind to become an adult in the real world. Ricky has imagined receiving his diploma many times before, but it seems like the lead-up today has been so anticlimactic. Maybe if Ricky were actually leaving home, it would feel differently. From St. Martin's, Ricky will go directly to The Citadel military academy. Ricky has wondered for months why he agreed to first apply there and then accepted to go there.

"Oh yeah, I am going there to become a military officer. That is what my parents would want. I guess that is what I want too," declares Teed while looking at himself in the mirror.

The graduation ceremony is set for 5 pm, so there was a whole day to frolic about.

Ricky is sitting on the porch with his mom when Hope Fitzgerald comes by. Ms. Teed was always very fond of Hope; she always thought Ricky and Hope would make a cute couple.

She always said, "I could have the cutest redhead grandbabies." His mother always thought that their families were so much alike. Hope's father was also in the military. He was a captain in the Marines and was in the second battalion that stormed the beaches of Normandy, France, on D-Day. He was among the many Allied causalities suffered that day; fortunately for him and his family, he survived to tell the story.

"Hi Ricky!" Hope yells from the street.

Ricky doesn't know if it is the sunshine or just his hormones, but Hope looks exceptionally good today. This fact is not lost on Ricky's mother.

"Hope looks very nice, doesn't she Ricky?" Ms. Teed says under her breath.

Ricky agrees with his mother silently. Hope does look very nice today. Hope always looked good, but there seemed to be a certain maturity to her look today. This is not the same Hope Ricky has always known; again, she was always cute, but she seemed to be rather curvy all of a sudden.

Ricky walked down to the street curb to meet her.

"Hey Hope, what's going on?" asks Ricky.

"Nothing much, I thought I would drop by to see how your graduation day preparation was coming," Hope said.

"It is kind of a blah day. I mean, we graduate today, but I will still be in Charleston in the fall," states Ricky.

"So, you have decided to go to The Citadel after all?" Hope asks. "Yeah, it is the best choice. I can look after my mom if I am here; plus, it is where my dad wanted me to go. How about you? Where are you going to next year?" asks Ricky.

"I am going to go to the University of South Carolina," Hope answers.

"I thought you were going to go to Harvard or Princeton? I thought you were Ivy League all the way. You may snatch yourself a Yankee to marry." Ricky starts to laugh.

"Really funny Ricky. I thought about it, just the school part," admits Hope.

Hope gives Ricky an adoring glance.

"I actually was accepted to both, but I couldn't stand going that far from parents. My dad is doing a lot better, but I'm not ready to be that far away from him and my mom," reveals Hope.

It is clearly an emotional issue for Hope. The thought of leaving her parents, her comfortable life and surroundings are coming to light.

Hope's piercingly beautiful mint julep-colored eyes swell with tears of sadness. Hope tries to hold back her tears.

"What now Ricky? Today is supposed to be the happiest day of our lives and here I am crying." Ricky reaches out to Hope and gives a caressing hug to comfort her. "Hope, everything is going to be alright; we are just graduating from high school. It is going to be alright," assures Ricky.

Ricky strokes Hope's flowing red hair as she lays her head on his shoulder. It appears to give her a reprieve from the impending heartache. But Ricky starts to think to himself. *Now what? I mean, sure, we are just graduating from high school, but our lives are about to change. Is it going to be for better or for worse? Maybe Hope's concerns aren't out of place at all. Could I just be naïve?"*

Later in the day, Ricky stands at the tattered screen door as his mom continues to get ready. Ricky notices Mr. Brown sitting on his porch drinking a glass of honey-brewed iced tea while fanning himself. Ricky decides to take a walk over to Mr. Brown's house. Ricky has not had a glass of honey-brewed tea for quite a while. "Hey there Mr. Brown!" shouts Ricky.

Mr. Brown responded quickly. "Hey there Ricky, come on over."

Ricky runs over to Mr. Brown's house as if the iced tea might be gone before he got there. Ricky runs up the large granite steps to the top of Mr. Brown's porch.

Mr. Brown is pouring a glass of the honey-brewed iced tea as Ricky climbs the last step.

"No reason for you to fret Ricky, there is enough," assures Mr. Brown as he hands the glass to Ricky.

Ricky takes the glass from Mr. Brown and drinks the iced tea in three large gulps. He then lets out a large burp.

"Thanks, Mr. Brown; that hit the spot."

Mr. Brown has a large smile on his face.

"I'm glad you enjoyed it," replies Mr. Brown.

He looks Ricky up and down.

"What you fitting to do? You looking clean," says Mr. Brown.

With all the excitement, Ricky neglected to tell Mr. Brown that he was graduating today.

"I am graduating from high school tonight," announces an excited Ricky.

Mr. Brown shakes Ricky's hand.

"That is good Ricky. I am so proud of you. You know I remember it like it was yesterday." Mr. Brown rubs his curly salt and pepper beard as he continues his thought.

"Your mother and father bringing you home from the hospital. You were bundled in a fluffy white blanket. Your mother smiled for weeks, and your dad sat on that porch every day right around sundown, holding you as he sat in the swing seat."

"Yeah, those days are now gone," Ricky says with a disappointed look on his face."

"You can't go pitying yourself son. It is unfortunate what happened to your father, but you have to carry on. You will be tested and disappointed many times in your life. It is the response to the challenges that will make you a man."

Mr. Brown takes out his dingy off-white handkerchief and wipes his tear-filled eyes and nose. The emotions started to get to him.

"You know, I wanted to crawl into a hole after Granville was killed. But that is not what he would have wanted. And your father would not want you to sit around pitying yourself," suggests Mr. Brown. Ricky agrees with Mr. Brown.

"You are right. I can't worry about what has already happened. I guess I am more worried about my mom. She is all I have left," asserts an inspired Ricky.

Mrs. Teed stands at the front door.

"Good morning, Mr. Brown. Lovely day, isn't it?"

Mr. Brown responds, "You make it even more lovely."

Mrs. Teed starts to blush.

"Ricky, time to get going," says Ms. Teed.

Ricky gets up and shakes Mr. Brown's hand.

"Thanks, Mr. Brown for the talk," says Ricky.

"Anytime Ricky. Anytime." Mr. Brown says with a large smile.

Ricky and his mom ride down Ashley Avenue in their green 1942 Ford Super Deluxe Convertible. Mrs. Teed looks like a schoolgirl; her 30-something skin glistens in the late afternoon sun as her long brown hair flows through the stale air. Captain bought the car so that he and his high school sweetheart could recapture and preserve their youth. Ricky is so glad his mother is able to clear her mind, if only for a brief second. This simple drive allows her a momentary peace.

They arrive at St. Martin's church at 4:45 pm. The church and school have never looked so beautiful. This could be the last time that Ricky sets eyes on this major mainstay in his life for some time. Mrs. Teed realizes that their invigorating ride through the city has come to an end she ties her beautiful brown locks up into her normal conservative hair bun.

St. Martin's Carroll Gardens are aligned with blue and white roses: the school colors that have meant so much to Ricky and even more after their much-heralded Catholic League football championship. The student orchestra entertains the audience by playing a breathtaking rendition of "Pomp and Circumstance." The Carroll Garden, as well as the day in general, couldn't be more beautiful. It is about 80 degrees with a light wind in the city of Charleston, which is truly a treat in the month of June; normally the city is sweltering with temperatures averaging in the mid-90s, with humidity out of this world.

After schmoozing and saying reluctant goodbyes, it is off to the city center to start the ceremony process. Ricky can't help but feel ridiculously happy and exhilarated. Ever since he was able to read and write, he and his parents had waited for this day…and now it was happening. When it is time to line up, the graduates take their numbers to be seated in order. When the organizer announces, it is time to start marching toward the cathedral, Ricky is hit by adrenaline. This is it. Ricky hopes he doesn't trip. He doesn't know it, but as they go to the cathedral, all eyes are on the graduating class as they walk and sit while the orchestra plays music, which makes Ricky feel particularly regal. The student orchestra plays a very melodic version of "As the Saints Go Marching In" that is very heavy on the stringed instruments. The happiest moment in that ceremony for Ricky is not shaking the hand of the vice chancellor but walking down the aisle, certificate in hand, and looking over and seeing his mother, through the thick of the audience, looking so proud and happy and waving at him.

Ricky wants to weep with happiness on the spot. The day is something that is very hard to describe. The day has made him feel that he has achieved something so worthy and so deserved. Father Kevin O'Blaney presides over the ceremony. He begins by leading the captive audience in reciting the Catholic hymnal standard "Hail Mary." As Ricky sits amongst the graduating class, he thinks, *what happens now?* Life begins today and he has no father to guide him. *Is going to The Citadel the right move?* Ricky believes he is as patriotic as the next guy, but he doesn't want to leave his family like Captain did. Maybe he is just worrying too much…but what becomes of his mother? She is not doing well. She is sad that Ricky is leaving her now but doesn't want to hold him back.

After the ceremony, Mrs. Teed and Ricky go back to the house, and Mrs. Teed goes directly into her room. She does not have the resounding joy one would expect a parent to have after their child graduates from high school.

Ricky walks into his mother's room, as she is looking out the bedroom window overlooking the patio deck. Many of the happy times the Teeds shared were spent out on the deck. Captain told Ricky that is where his mom told him that she was pregnant.

"Mom, is everything ok?" asks a concerned Ricky.

She smiles at him.

She replies, "Of course honey I'm ok. A day like today makes me think about the dreams your father and I had for you. He wanted you to grow up and become a strong military man just like him. I just wanted you to be healthy," claims Mrs. Teed.

She stands up and walks over to Ricky. She grabs his cheeks and looks deep into his eyes and declares, "You have fulfilled our dreams for you."

Mrs. Teed hugs Ricky.

THE BAY

The SS M. Smith is sailing up the Spa Creek out to the Chesapeake Bay, away from Annapolis, Maryland. The SS M. Smith is owned by media mogul Murray Smith; Mr. Smith owns several small newspapers and television stations throughout the United States and some in England. Mr. Smith grew up in the small town of Dattein, in the Northern Rhine section of Germany. He got his start by publishing the paper "Ygegenwehr" in the early 1930s; the paper addressed the growing wave of anti-Semitism in Western Europe and, more specifically, the amplifying message from the National Socialist Party. Mr. Smith and his family left Germany in the late 30s. He was warned by some friends within the German government—Smith and his family were to be tried and executed as instigators and traitors of the state. Many within the Nazi-led German government wanted to extort Smith out of millions before killing him. Since moving to Annapolis, Maryland, Mr. Smith normally took his 40-ft. yacht out during the mid-summer months of the year. Annapolis, Maryland sits about 30 miles to the east of Washington, D.C. Many of the government's movers and shakers move to Annapolis or become very familiar with it since it is home to the capital of Maryland as well as the United States Naval Academy.

Today is different; it is early May, and most of the recreational boaters in the region have not yet flocked to the area waters. The day is also abnormal because of Mr. Smith's sailing guests.

Senator Hampton Capers and Cecil Thomas are accompanying Mr. Smith on his mid-spring glide on Annapolis' Spa Creek.

Senator Capers is the senior senator from the state of South Carolina; he is also the finance chairman of the Senate Committee for the War Department. Mr. Thomas is the President of Steadman Industries. Steadman Industries was the primary producer of war aircraft for the United States Army and Navy during World War II. They produced well over 40,000 aircraft, including the B-92 bomber, which was used in the bombing barrages over Germany. They also built the famed "Star Striker," which was responsible for many of the mid-air dogfights that American pilots won. As a result of the war—Steadman Industries made over $85 billion dollars during the conflicts in Europe.

Senator Capers and Mr. Smith are dressed in polo shirts and khaki pants, the standard sailing uniform in the Annapolis sailing community. Mr. Thomas is dressed in a navy-blue three-piece suit, the standard uniform for the movers and shakers in Washington, D.C. Thomas feels very out-of-place.

"Capers, why the hell couldn't we just have met in Washington?" challenges an irritated Thomas.

Senator Capers smiles at Mr. Thomas mockingly.

"Don't you want to wave to one of your greatest customers, the U.S. Navy?" jokes Capers.

The yacht passes the Naval Academy's Hospital Point. "Capers, I have to agree with Thomas. What is this about?" queries a bewildered Murray Smith.

"Gentlemen, in the wake of World War II, there is a void in global order and, more importantly, there is an opportunity for us to influence it," announces Capers.

Both Thomas and Smith have a look of intrigue on their faces. "The world is getting smaller, and we need to control what comes in and out of this country," asserts Capers.

"How do you control information?" inquires Thomas.

Capers looks at Smith and says, "You control the media; you control the stories that the world sees, the good and the bad. When we go into countries, you and your media outlets will say we are liberating the people. Your newspapers and your radio stations will feature stories of the U.S. soldiers playing with the country's kids—all the while we will move our agenda along. And when necessary, you put out stories to keep things calm."

A puzzled Smith answers, "You want me to instruct my people to hide stories from the American public? That could be professional suicide."

Capers chimes in, "And you've never done that before. Do you remember when you sat on the Nazi spy story during the early forties?" Smith drops his head in humiliation.

"And do you remember when you gave those Nigger pilots those sub-par planes because some senators didn't want the possibility of those pilots claiming glory? Hey, I understand why you did it and why you were asked, but please don't get holier than thou with me," projects a smug Capers.

"How do we keep the world safe and make a lot of money in the process?" asks Thomas.

"I would like to form a group of eight men who could share information from their various expertise. I propose we incorporate some captains of industry and long-tenured senior officials within the government; all these men would share our worldview. We will need a constant flow of information," hints Capers as he looks at Kent Island in the distance.

"How do we fund this? Are you going to get your friends on Capitol Hill to fork over any money?" asks a concerned Thomas.

"No dumbass, you will ask for more money in your appropriations task orders for the next year, which I am the chairman of," Capers states in a sinister tone.

"Murray, next year I want you to apply for loans with the B&C Bank. They will loan you several million with the purpose of you buying 30 newspapers and radio stations throughout the country. Smith takes out a box of cigars. He gives both gentlemen cigars, which both promptly accept. Smith takes a long pull on the cigar. After blowing the smoke into the fresh saltwater air he utters, "Capers, you are one devious, sick, evil genius." Thomas laughs in agreement.

"So, are you gentlemen in?" asks Capers.

Thomas and Smith look at each other, then emphatically agree. They all shake hands as the sun sets over the tree line on Maryland's Eastern Shore.

RULERS

The city of Washington, D.C., has become the seat of power for the Western world since the end of World War II. The possibilities of wealth and power have become endless for the Americans, but the rising scourge of communism throughout Eastern Europe and Asia has many within and out of the U.S. government on edge. World War II spawned the global domination of the United States in the West and Russia's dominance in the East. Both countries began to wield their power unchecked throughout the world—officials on both sides knew that sooner or later the two sides would have to clash. The U.S. concentrated on being a facilitator for economic growth with American interests in countries like France, Denmark, and West Germany. The Russians concentrated on being a military presence and planning invasions of countries with which it shared a common border, like Poland, Yugoslavia, and Georgia. The countries' methods were different, but the objective of global influence was the same. Senator Capers felt the country needed his organization even more now; at the basis of his ideas he thought of himself as a patriot. He was a greedy and self-preserving patriot, but a patriot all the same. Capers knew that the Russians could make it hard for the U.S. to continue its dominance. Many politicians quietly worried that the

Russians would serve as a formidable military presence if a conflict were to happen.

The politicians were worried, but they knew they couldn't alarm the public about another global conflict in the wake of World War II.

Both sides learned very valuable lessons after World War II. The U.S. government realized that they must keep the public in the dark in order to further national security.

The Russian government realized its greatest asset was its military, and they knew they needed to invade neighboring countries to get their natural resources.

A long black stretch limousine rides down Florida Avenue in Washington D.C.'s northwest quadrant. The limousine contains five blindfolded gentlemen; all the gentlemen are immaculately dressed, looking like they are on their way to a board meeting of a Fortune 500 company. None of the gentlemen know of the others' presence, but they all know they are being summoned to a very important gathering of very influential men. The limousine comes to an abrupt halt, and a voice from the front instructs all the gentlemen to take their blindfolds off. The gentlemen take their blindfolds off and discover the presence of people they are all familiar with. A chauffeur dressed in a black suit and donning a top hat opens the door for the gentlemen. The gentlemen discover that the limousine has pulled into a dimly lit warehouse, Senator Capers greets them.

"Hello friends," says a jovial Capers.

A gravelly voice speaks from the shadows.

"Capers, I don't appreciate being blindfolded and not being told where I am going," states Valerius Torrantio.

"My apologies to you Mr. Torrantio, and the rest of you gentlemen, but we needed to keep this location secret until we found out if each one of you gentlemen decided to be in our brotherhood," says Capers.

Each one of the gentlemen looks puzzled about the purpose of their involvement. They are seated at a table with eight chairs resembling thrones, harkening back to the day of King Arthur and the Knights of the Round Table. The men take long looks at everyone around the table, wondering what their common links could possibly be. Senator Capers is seated at the head of the table; he is flanked by Murray Smith and Cecil Thomas.

"I know all of you gentlemen are trying to figure out your purpose here and what you have in common with the other gentlemen at the table. Let me put all of your minds at ease. We all wield unique power and influence. As patriots, we should do everything to extend our influence outside the country's borders. Understand, we are patriots, but we are still capitalists. So, we will be maximizing our investments and resources to make each one of us very wealthy men," discloses Capers.

The entire group shares a collective smile, with the exception of Valerius Torrantio.

"What do we have to give up, Mr. Senator. You are not cutting us in out of the goodness of your heart," says an apprehensive Torrantio.

Capers starts to laugh.

"I must laugh, my Sicilian friend. I know in the world you are used to you would think this proposal would deserve such caution, but we all will be tied together. You and your Sicilian friends could really benefit from this arrangement. Everyone at this table will benefit from each other, and we will all co-op each other's influence. Let's say that somebody from Mr. Torrantio's organization has any trouble with the law. Mr. Smith's newspaper and radio stations will make sure it is not reported to the public. I think Mr. Torrantio would appreciate it if his organization didn't receive any publicity. Let's say Mr. Carter's organization needs to move funds out of the country without too much congressional meddling; we would ask Mr. Torrantio and his friends to move it for us," suggests a self-assured Capers.

Valerius Torrantio's shakes his head in the affirmation.

"Can we get some introductions of our new brotherhood?" requests Torrantio.

"Of course, where are my manners?" declares Capers.

"This is Murray Smith; he is the President of MS media holdings. He presently has 20 newspapers and radio stations throughout the country. Seated next is Mr. Wesley Carter. Mr. Carter is the newly appointed chief of all foreign and domestic intelligence. Before any of you ask, he will not be Hoover's boss, but Hoover is supposed to run all domestic intelligence past Mr. Carter. We will see how that works. Next to Mr. Carter is Mr. Lance Bowen. Mr. Bowen is a third-generation oil driller. His family has had a mid-sized oil company since the turn of the century. They recently started drilling throughout the south, including Texas, Louisiana, and Mississippi. We are hoping to take Mr. Bowen's company to new heights. Speaking of taking things to new heights, my dear friend Valerius Torrantio is seated next to Mr. Bowen. Mr. Torrantio is the boss of bosses of the national syndicate. The syndicate has their hands in most illegal businesses throughout the nation. We are not as interested in Mr. Torrantio's illegal activity as many of his connections outside and inside of the country. Sometimes you need some arm twisting, and who better to do it—than my friend Valley. Last but not least is Cecil Thomas. Mr. Thomas is the President of Steadman Industries. His company was responsible for the many of the nation's warfare machines produced during World War II. This is our little club. Do you gentlemen want to be a part of our group? questions a confident Capers.

All the gentlemen raise their hands in unanimous agreement.

The 8Men have finished their lengthy meeting. The room is filled with a cloud of smoke from the cigars that the men smoked as they discussed their aspirations of world domination. Azalea Johnson, a middle-aged, slender Negro woman is sweeping the parquet floor as Valerius Torrantio looks out of a large window at the U.S. Capitol. Torrantio looks out onto the landscape of northwest Washington, D.C., along Florida Avenue. Torrantio looks down onto the street below; there is nothing but Negroes walking on Florida Avenue. Florida Avenue is the hub of Negro life in Washington, D.C., during the 1940s.

"I must say you have truly found an obscure location. Nobody will try to find us out here. Nobody around here but Niggers," utters a sarcastic olive skinned Torrantio.

Ms. Johnson stops sweeping for a split second as the scowl on her face expresses her displeasure with Torrantio's choice of words. Torrantio notices Ms. Johnson's reaction and immediately apologizes.

"I am sorry about that," Senator Capers also apologies to Ms. Johnson. "Azalea, I am sorry, my friend here doesn't always display his manners. You know those Yankees don't know how to act when they are in Dixie." Azalea Johnson excuses herself and leaves the room. Senator Capers walks over to the window overlooking Florida Avenue. He stands next to Torrantio as they both look out at the U.S. Capitol in the distance.

"How do you think your friends over there would feel about our little organization," asks Torrantio.

"Some would applaud a sitting U.S. Senator trying to circumvent the rules and laws of the land, and some would be furious that they didn't think of it themselves. Much of what we are about to embark upon would be done either way. I want to make money on it and create a consortium of people that can make things happen. Democracy is a beautiful thing in theory, but sometimes Joe Public does not know all the facts or can't understand them. Hell, sometimes we just can't trust them to make the right decision. Most people need to be told what to do," says Capers.

"It sounds like the syndicate," laughs Torrantio.

"In some ways, it is. That is why you are a part of this organization. Understand, there will be things that you will have to be the lead on," implies Capers.

"Oh, you mean the things you don't want to get your hands dirty with," responds Torrantio as he glares at Capers.

"You have found me out. The answer is yes. I will be pushing certain legislation that will help the group, so I can't appear to be involved. The first piece of legislation will be right up your alley. After World War II, the military realized that many of our cities would be isolated in the event we had a foreign invasion. Pearl Harbor really caught us with our pants down. Those god damn Japs could have gotten to Chicago before we could have properly responded. We knew that we needed to connect the entire country. This is where your organization could get involved," hints Capers.

"And that faggot Hoover is just going to let us do business with the Federal Government? He and his G-men are shaking my men down. His people are coming into our after-hours spots, and they are disrupting prostitution in the established red-light districts," alleges Torrantio.

"First of all, let me worry about Hoover. He will not be a problem. You must make it clear to your folks that any incidents with any police must stay peaceful. The minute your people shoot or cause a public dispute, I will not be able to protect you. We can't afford any attention on any of us. I need you to get your people from all over the country involved. We are going to build roadway systems connecting every city and state in this country," claims a convincing Capers.

Torrantio has a look of confusion on his face.

"'Why,' is your question? Imagine the commerce we can create if we are all easily connected. Think about the amount of liquor, or whatever you people sell, that could be moved if you cut down on travel time. Think about it. You could get on the road in New York and drive to LA," says an excited Capers.

"Why the hell would I want to do that?" sarcastically asks Torrantio.

Capers is getting visibly frustrated with Torrantio.

"Look, maybe you won't drive to LA, but Joe Public may want to drive there. But somebody has to build it…somebody has to get paid for it. Somebody will get the public works contracts, and somebody will be able to make inroads into the cities' public works and their connected contracts. This will also help our group out because the more cars on the road the more gas and oil they will need. We will make sure Bowen builds service stations along these highways before the land goes up in value," estimates Capers. Torrantio nods his head.

"I told you…you are one smart, devious son of a bitch. Sounds like one hell of a plan," responds Torrantio.

"Make sure none of your people know about the connection between us all. We don't want anybody connecting the dots," says Capers.

"Nuff said. That's how we operate anyway. Anyone talks, they die," affirms a stone-faced Torrantio.

"Keep your people on a need-to-know basis. You have already infiltrated the unions. Many of the union workers can do the work we are going to need to be done," says Torrantio.

"This can be a win-win situation for everybody—we will just win more. Understand we will be helping Americans," implies Capers. "Whatever you say, my friend. Just make sure we make boatloads of money. We are all Americans, but we are all capitalists as well," says Torrantio as he laughs.

"I notice that there were only seven men seated at the table during our meeting. Did someone get cold feet?" asks Torrantio.

Capers swallows the last swig of liquor left in his glass.

"No, nobody had cold feet. I am going to need someone to facilitate the activities of the group. I have my eye on someone, but I'm not sure just yet. I think I will have to create a mission to prove their worthiness," says Capers.

SCHOOL OF THE SOUTH

Ricky Teed is now entering his senior year at The Citadel service academy. It has been an up and down experience for him at the school. His mom became gravely ill at the end of his freshman year, which rendered him unable to play football at the academy. Ricky was not very upset about not playing; he seemed to have lost some of his love for the game: there was no Captain, no Jen and not the same type of camaraderie as he had at St. Martin's. Throughout his tenure at The Citadel, Ricky had maintained a 3.9 grade point average. He decided to major in foreign affairs and minor in warfare tactics. Warfare tactics were just a polite way of saying, "Ways we will teach you to kill." Ricky decided after Captain's death that he would go into the armed forces, but he wanted to be fully prepared. He wanted to know why we got involved in conflicts a half a world away and where those conflicts aligned with American interests. He knew the brewing battle would be between the U.S. and Russia. The end of World War II left much of Europe and Asia in ruins, but many of their natural resources were there for the taking. Both the Americans and the Russians understood that they needed to seize the opportunity.

Ricky was the model Citadel student; he studied four hours a day, he kept a clean area, and his uniforms were kept immaculate. Ricky followed The Citadel's honor codes to the letter. He promised himself that he would never shame the memory of Captain's exemplary reputation at his alma mater.

His wall was a multitude of commendations from the dean and various instructors. Unlike Ricky, his roommate Zachery Capers was a polar opposite. Zachery was a C-minus student at best; he had been on academic probation several times throughout his tenure at The Citadel. Zachery would have been promptly kicked out after his freshman year if his father, U.S. Senator Hampton Capers, had not interjected. Zachery had a cumulative grade point average of 1.6—maybe that was acceptable at some schools, but it was unacceptable for The Citadel.

Hampton Capers is the grandson of the Confederate president, and his namesake, Hampton Capers. The Capers clan were multimillionaires, making much of their wealth in real estate and cotton. The Capers family business was politics—Capers, like his father and his grandfather, was in politics. His father was the mayor of Charleston during the turn of the century but never ascended to national office. Hampton had plans for Zachery. Zachery was from a long line of Capers men who attended The Citadel before going on to receiving the opportunities and riches set before them. Zachery's days of privilege would soon be over as his father saw it— The Citadel was the first step in the process.

The tudentts from The school spent many nights at Ulysses' Bar, a short mile away from the school's front door. Ulysses' brought together the students and members of the community at large. Most nights are uneventful, but every now and then, there is a ruckus or two. Teed asks a reluctant Zachery to go to Ulysses' after a very tough week of hand-to-hand warfare. Many of the young men in the class with Teed and Zachery decide to come out to Ulysses.' The young men are happy they can complete the class in one piece. They all go to a back section of the bar and order several rounds of drinks; they are having a really good time. The group runs out of beer in one of their pitchers. Pee Wee, one of Teed and Zachery's classmates, decides to get a new pitcher. Pee Wee stands at a mere 5'4."

"Hey guys, I am going to get a pitcher," says Pee Wee as he stumbles to the bar.

A cute barmaid comes over to Pee Wee.

"What can I get you, honey?" asks the barmaid.

"A pitcher of Bud," responds Pee Wee.

There are some rumblings coming from the other end of the bar. Pee Wee is completely oblivious to what is going on. Moments later, a large shadow has overtaken the short-statured Pee Wee.

"What the hell are you doing here?" questions

the very deep-voiced giant standing over Pee Wee.

Pee Wee is stammering and stuttering, "Umm…Hum."

"You Citadel pussies always come up here and try to sweet talk our women," says the giant redneck.

"Sir, I am just trying to get a drink. I don't want any trouble," pleads Pee Wee as he noticeably trembles.

The commotion at the bar gets the attention of Teed and Zachery.

"Looks like Pee Wee could use our help," hints a smiling Zachery.

Teed and Zachery walk over to Pee Wee.

"Hey Pee Wee, everything alright?" requests Teed.

"Hell no! Everything is not alright," interjects the giant redneck.

"Can we buy you a drink to take care of this misunderstanding," asks Zachery.

"You think I can't buy my own drink? You fucking Citadel pussies ain't shit," says the Giant redneck as he throws a haymaker at Zachery.

The punch completely misses Zachery, and the giant redneck nearly falls to the floor from the force of his own punch. Some other patrons come to the defense of the big redneck.

"Come on guys, let's not do this," implores Zachery.

"I don't need no help," says the giant redneck as he motions the crowd back.

"I am going to kick his ass by myself," announces the giant redneck. The giant redneck gets a running start toward Zachery. Zachery sees the big redneck coming toward him in slow motion. Again, the big redneck throws a haymaker at Zachery. The punch completely misses Zachery again. Zachery steps back after the punch and he steps with lightning speed toward the big redneck. Zachery throws a short but accurate punch to his opponents' windpipe. The punch instantly makes the big redneck start choking and stumble backward. He falls to the ground gasping for air by grabbing his throat. The collective breath of the bar is sucked out as the blaring sound of police sirens fills the air. Moments later the police rush in to take out The Citadel rebel rousers.

WORTHY

The fight at Ulysses' Bar and Grill was over pretty quickly, but it may have caused some long-ranging problems for Zachery Capers. He was charged with public drunkenness and assault. The assault charge was dropped by the big redneck. The shame of the ass-whipping was already too much for his ego; he didn't want the humiliation of being viewed as a rat. Even though Teed was not in the ruckus, he was given a minor disturbing the peace charge. The police wanted to send a message. After a night in the lockup, Zachery and Teed exit the front of the police station. They are trying to get back to The Citadel in order to catch their 10 am Ancient Warfare class.

"It's eight fifteen. If we hurry, we can still make Ancient Warfare," says Teed as he and Zachery walk out of the station.

As Zachery and Teed make their way out of the station, Zachery stops in his tracks. He notices a large limousine parked at the end of the walkway. Zachery looks like he has seen a ghost.

"What's wrong?" asks Teed.

The rear door of the limousine opens. Out steps Senator Hampton Capers.

"Shit!" exclaims Zachery.

"Shit is right," responds Hampton Capers.

Hampton Capers motions for Zachery to come to him. Teed sees the seriousness of the situation.

"Hey, I am going to go ahead and get back to campus," suggests Teed.

As he starts to walk in the opposite direction he hears, "Mr. Teed, your 10 am instructor is aware that you are going to be missing your class. Please join us," Senator Capers asks politely, but Teed feels the request is more of demand, so he decides to comply. Moments later, Teed and Zachery are sitting in the limousine with Senator Capers. Zachery is looking at Senator Capers like a scared five-year-old, he remembers the days of being unable to please the elder Capers.

"Goddammit Zachery, you are pissing away your future. You haven't done anything worthwhile in the last four years. Your grades have been horrible. What would you do if you didn't have the last name Capers?" questions Senator Capers.

Teed had always thought Zachery was an asshole, but this brief encounter with his father made him realize that the apple did not fall far from the tree.

"Dad, I—" appeals Zachery as he is interrupted by his father.

"I don't want to hear another word from you. How can you almost shit away everything because of kicking some low-life redneck's ass?" asks an upset Senator Capers.

Teed thinks to himself, *why doesn't Zachery just tell his father that he was defending one of his Citadel brothers?*

Senator Capers continues to berate Zachery.

"Your mother has coddled you for years; it has made you soft," claims Senator Capers as he is interrupted.

"Senator Capers, Sir, I have to completely disagree with you. Zachery didn't pick a fight or try to piss away anything. Zachery was defending one of our Citadel classmates that was being picked on by the redneck. I don't know about all the other stuff that you have been talking about, but Zachery acted very honorably last night," asserts Teed.

Both Zachery and Senator Capers are surprised by Teed's words.

"Zachery, you did that?" asks Senator Capers.

"Yes," responds Zachary.

"Why didn't you say that before?" utters a contrite Senator Capers.

"Would it really matter? You have always thought I wouldn't live up to your expectations of me. Maybe, I won't be a great member of the Capers' legacy, but I will be a good person. And don't you dare say mom coddled me, she protected me from you and your henchmen. I screwed up in school just so I could get some kind of attention from you.

"And just maybe I wanted to embarrass you a little. No matter, you will soon have my Citadel diploma and then you can direct the rest of my life." Declares Zachery as he jumps out of the limousine.

"Son, I am sorry. I should have asked you your side of things," says Senator Capers as Zachery slams the limousine door.

Richard, thank you for coming to my son's defense. You both have shown you are the honorable men The Citadel trains. How would you like to do something honorable for your country?" asks Senator Capers.

WAR HORIZON

Most college students look at their commencement ceremony as transitioning to the real world. Graduation is the day when you become an adult: you stop depending on your parents and start to do for yourself. But if the student is a graduate of a military academy, it is just the beginning. The Citadel cadets will graduate as officers and then will be deployed into the army. In the past, the officers left the friendly confines of The Citadel for war-torn areas like Normandy, Berlin, Tokyo, and North Africa. Fortunately for these cadets, America is in a time of peace—they won't leave for wartime battle.

The Citadel graduation is far more formal and symbolic than Ricky's graduation from St. Martin's. The academy has an early morning prayer service in remembrance of several former cadets who lost their lives in a village outside of Seoul, Korea. The circumstances of their deaths have been withheld; the cadets are told they were on a peace-keeping mission with the United Nations.

After the prayer service, the cadets are aligned in perfect formation to begin their march into The Citadel's stadium. As the cadets march in unison, they receive thunderous applause from the onlooking crowd. The cadets are saluted by President Harry S. Truman. The entire city of

Charleston is in a frenzy with the president in town. Presidents don't normally come to Charleston, but the city is glad to have him.

Knowing the entire country is watching, the citizens of Charleston all fly their American flags to show their patriotism. Many residents of the city don't necessarily agree with the president's politics, but he is the commander in chief, and that demands respect.

After all the pageantry, the cadets sit in their seats to begin the ceremony. Superintendent Phillip Broughton asks the crowd, "Ladies and gentlemen, please bow your heads in honor of our fallen comrades that gave their lives in the pursuit of peace. Lord our God, please have mercy on the souls of those brave young men, and please do not let their sacrifice go in vain." The superintendent finishes his rather lengthy speech about all the hard work and the sacrifices the prospective graduates and their families have made to get to this point. Many in the graduating class and the audience at large were waiting to hear from the president.

Superintendent Broughton introduces the president, and he receives a 30-second standing ovation. Charlestonians did not have a chance to show their appreciation to the president after the victories in the Pacific and Europe. Some Charlestonians do not agree with the president's domestic politics; he wanted to integrate the armed forces and provide housing to poor Americans, but his victory in World War II has given him clout with the folks in the area for now.

The president steps to the podium, thanking the crowd for the applause. The president begins to speak in his Missourian drawl, "I am proud to stand before the future leaders of the Army, Navy and Marine Corps, and to celebrate the occasion, I thought I would bring along a small graduation gift. I, the President of the United States, hereby absolve all cadets who are on restriction for minor conduct offenses." The graduates and the crowd start to laugh. "The citizens of the United States appreciate your efforts thus far; you have survived the Dog Summer of Charleston and swam to Fort Sumter. You have made it to graduation day, and in a few moments, you will receive your diplomas. Your parents are proud of you, your teachers are proud of you, and so is your commander in chief. Congrats to you all," says President Truman. There is a thunderous applause.

"Ladies and gentlemen, our country is pursuing a clear strategy to stop the growing tide of communism; we want to stem the potential scourge of communism and its advocates. We want to preserve democracy and protect our homeland from the communists. We want to peacefully deny the spread of communism. America plans to make it abundantly clear that we will not tolerate the spread of the oppression of communism.

We will use every resource at our disposal to deny the communist states the foothold in Asia and Eastern Europe they so desire.

We will stop the communists from achieving the ideological victories they seek by working to spread the hope of freedom and reform across the globe. We understand that free nations do not support communism. We understand that to make the world more peaceful and our country more secure, we will need to advance the cause of liberty," remarks President Truman. The crowd gives the president another round of applause.

The crowd and the graduates listen to the president basically give them a pre-war speech. Presidents normally like to give pre-war speeches to a sympathetic audience such as a crowd of military men and their families. It normally makes them feel good to receive the adoration before the public-at-large tears the policy apart piece by piece. The president is gently taking the country to war against the communists. The Americans and the Russians have been having issues with the 38th parallel on the Korean Peninsula, but a full-fledged war would be insane. The communists have grown stronger; since Hitler's removal from power, they really have had no force in the region to combat their power. All the European nations were decimated by World War II. Most of Europe is still in the process of rebuilding; they are definitely in no position to challenge the Russians or the Chinese.

TIME TO GROW UP

Today is June 9, 1950. The day reminds Ricky of the many mornings he awakened at his parent's home to the merciless Charleston sun. The palmetto trees that line the entrance to the campus as well as many of the city streets of Charleston appear to be wilting from the lack of rain. Most college graduates spend the day after graduation getting drunk and having an all-around good time. But when you are a graduate of a military institution in the United States of America, your next four years have already been mapped out for you, including the day after graduation. Ricky walks over to the mess hall to get a bite to eat. It is hard to imagine that less than 36 hours ago, the mess hall was filled with enlisted men, families and a large military presence protecting President Harry S. Truman. Now it is a ghost town. Ricky doesn't blame everybody for leaving. He would be leaving also if it weren't for the top-secret mission that he was asked to be a part of. The mess hall is completely silent; it is not the social mecca it was just a week ago. A week ago, the seniors partied and ribbed the underclassmen about the impending graduation from The Citadel. The top-secret mission has Ricky rethinking his formal entrance into the armed forces. He parades over to the lunch line, which on this day does not have much of a line at all. Ricky assesses the day's culinary delights.

The cooks surpass some of their earlier week's triumphs with Salisbury steak, mashed potatoes, spinach, and rolls. What a joke. One thing the graduates will not miss about The Citadel is the food.

The Salisbury steak is a sliver of meat and some gravy that has a bit of a greenish hue to it. The mashed potatoes aren't really mashed; they are more like lumpy potatoes with absolutely no taste, not even with a hint of salt or pepper. The biggest health hazard appears to be the spinach; ordinary spinach is a robust Kelly green. This spinach is more mahogany than green. Ricky doesn't know what to pick from this bountiful smorgasbord, so he goes the safe route and gets two dinner rolls. He thinks that will hold him over.

Ricky notices Zachery Capers sitting at a table by himself. Zachery is pretty brave; he actually eats the food. Ricky goes over and sits at the table with him.

"Hey Capers, how are things?" Zachery looks up with a look of disgust on his face.

"Hey, Teed, this has got to be the shittest food I have ever tasted." Ricky nods his head in agreement as Zachery continues to devour his rolls.

Capers continues, "We put our god damn lives on the line for our country and we can't even get a decent meal?" Ricky jokingly says to him, "Why don't you get your dad to do something about it?" Disappointingly, Zachery says, "I already tried, but he told me I had to pay my dues like everyone else. You know he wants me to run for Congress when I get out of the marines."

Zachery makes another disgusting face. Ricky wasn't sure if it is the bad food or the bad taste of what his future will entail. Ricky doesn't know what to say at this point, so he asks, "What time is the unit meeting?"

Zachery answers, "I think 0530 hours."

He looked down at his watch; it is 0515 hours.

"We should get going," hints Ricky.

Capers shrugs his shoulders and gets up. They both walk out of the mess hall. At approximately 0528 hours, Capers and Ricky arrive at the briefing hall. They are apparently the last members of the group to arrive. The meeting is being led by Lt. William Rudder, one of the meanest sons of a bitch this side of the bible belt. He stands at an intimidating 6'4" and weighs about 280 pounds. He missed his calling. He shouldn't be in the armed forces; he should have been a professional wrestler.

"Gentlemen, you are late," came from Rudder's boisterous voice.

Teed thought back to the conversation that he had with Big Al about being a leader. Big Al always said, "You must be early so that you know the background which will allow you to be prepared."

Unfortunately, Zachery didn't receive that same lesson. He looks down at his watch, then says, "Excuse me, sir, it is 0529 hours, and this briefing was scheduled for 0530 hours so we are actually early," Zachery says with a Chesire cat grin as if to show Lt. Rudder up.

Zachery's outburst does not sit too well with Lt. Rudder. The Lieutenant starts to address the group.

"There is always one comedian in every group. Mr. Capers, I presume?" Lt. Rudder returns a slight grin to Zachery.

"Your reputation proceeds you." Lt. Rudder walks over to Zachery and towers over him.

"Understand one thing, young man." The Lieutenant picks Zachery up by his neck with one hand.

"You will not be the reason why my platoon doesn't succeed. If you want to be a clown, I will kill you right here right now. You can die with all military honors. You will not have to wait for the slant eyes to do it. Just so we understand each other, I don't give a fuck who your father is. Do we understand each other?"

Zachery shakes his head as his legs dangle in midair. Then he asks the entire group,

"Do we understand each other?" The entire group nod their heads in the affirmative. Nobody else wants that ass whipping. Lt. Rudder releases the crimson-faced and extremely embarrassed Zachery unto the cold marble floor.

"Now, if there are no further interruptions, we will be discussing your impending mission."

Lt. Rudder pulls down a map of the Korean Peninsula.

"This, gentlemen, is the Korean Peninsula. This is where the initial battle between communism and democracy will be waged. After World War II, the United States and the Soviet Union divided much of the land and the spoils of the losing countries. The Empire of Japan occupied Korea from 1910 until its defeat in World War II. The United States and the Soviet Union split the country along the 38th parallel line into South and North Korea. The original thought was that the two countries would eventually form one stable government after the Americans and the Soviets left the region. Unfortunately, the two sides took on the political ideology of their benefactors. It has become evident that military hostilities are more frequent than we would hope for.

The secretary of war and other military advisors believe that both the Soviet Union and the People's Republic of China are providing the North Koreans with ample munitions to crush any military campaign the South Koreans could muster.

This would allow communism to have a foothold in the region. In the interest of our national security, we cannot allow communism to spread like fascism did just five short years ago. Many of the Allies have not rebuilt their armed forces from the devastation of World War II. So, it is up to us to stop this threat now," proclaims a passionate Lt. Rudder.

Teed couldn't believe what he was hearing. The U.S. was going to attack its allies. America, the Soviet Union and China were allies just five years ago. They all fought to save the world, and the partnership helped extinguish Hitler's tyrannical pursuit of world domination. Teed raises his hand with a certain reservation. Lt. Rudder looks in his direction as he tries to define the significance of the 38th parallel. He does not appear to be pleased that Teed wants to ask a question. "Identify yourself soldier," barks Lt. Rudder.

"My name is Richard Teed, sir," replies Teed.

"What is your question son?" Lt. Rudder says to Teed with a glaring look.

"Lt. Rudder sir, you said that we going to war against our allies from World War II. What has happened to make us go to war against them?" questions Teed with his voice trembling.

Lt. Rudder takes a long breath before speaking.

"Son, the United States partnered with the Soviets and Chinese for one common goal: to crush the Axis powers, which consisted of Germany, Japan and Italy, not out of any overriding love for each other. As a point of reference, the Soviets and the Germans had an alliance with each other; it was only after Hitler reneged on their alliance that the Soviets declared war on Germany. China was in the same boat but with another axis-powered country: Japan. The Chinese and the Japanese have been at odds for well over 50 years. The first Sino–Japanese War was the name of their conflict; oddly enough it too was over Korea. These warring factions have always worried that the country that controlled Korea could control the Far East region. Our countries were never friends during the war; we just had common interests. Now our common interests sit totally opposite of each other. In short, the United States will not allow the scourge of communism to rule the world. Get on board," says Lt. Rudder.

HANGUK JEONJAENG

Hanguk Jeonjaeng is the South Korean term for the brewing conflict between the communist-backed North Korean government and the Allied-backed South Korean regime. This confrontation became commonly known as the Korean Conflict. The United States and its Western Allies have been doing a delicate dance for power in Europe and Asia with the Russians, the Chinese and their communist allies since the end of World War II. Many believe that the covert actions of both sides will soon spill over into actual warfare.

On June 7th, 1950, Lt. Rudder and his band of merry men are in transit to the Seoul, Korea airport. It is a beautiful day; the Seoul countryside looks wonderful from 30,000 feet, with its picturesque landscape of hilly terrain covered by endless green foliage. But Lt. Rudder knows that it is just a façade. He is a veteran of World War II, where he fought the Mussolini-led Italian army outside the romantic city of Tuscany. Lt. Rudder knows that there must be a good reason for keeping their mission secret. If it were no big deal, they wouldn't be sworn to secrecy. Secrecy is always code for extremely dangerous. The Lieutenant comes over to talk to Teed before the plane lands on the ground; he plops down in the seat next to Teed.

"I want you to keep an eye on Capers. I can't believe that son of a bitch is a part of this mission. If I had my way, he would be partying this weekend away for his bullshit graduation from The Citadel. His father and his grandfather are great men; they are both a credit to their country and public service, but the boy…maybe he will be worth something one day, but today he is not worth shit. From my understanding, his grades were terrible…he is disrespectful as hell, no honor. Where could he serve? He is too dumb for the Navy; the Army would simply kill him. He is not Marine material; hell, he is not ROTC material," Lt. Rudder says as they both share a laugh.

"Lt. Rudder, I must say I think Zachery is a good guy… Sure, he is a little rough around the edges, but an all-around good guy. There is no one I would rather be in a foxhole with. He has pulled me out of some serious scrapes. I remember we were in a bar outside of Charleston; there were some rednecks that had too much to drink and were talking about how the military screwed up the war. Unfortunately for us, we had on our fatigues…some big burly jackass reeking of moonshine came over and pushed me. I was not looking for a fight, but that is exactly what the redneck was looking for. After he pushed me, he caught me with an uppercut to the chin…I was dazed for sure, but all I saw was Zachery flying into action…he kicked their asses on that night. We both minored in war tactics—I think he got C grades at best—but he certainly retained everything we were taught. I remember he took down this one big redneck with one swift punch to the throat. The guy had to stand at 6'4" and weighed about 280 lbs. Zachery knocked him out cold. I was of no help." Lt. Rudder and Ricky laugh.

"Maybe he is not a bad kid, but he acts like an asshole," says Lt. Rudder.

Lt. Rudder looks over at Zachery, who has his eyes closed. He wonders if he could be wrong about him. The Lieutenant wonders if

Zachery is one of those kids who are assholes as people but may be the greatest soldiers because they know their objective.

The plane lands at approximately 9:30 am local time with no problem. The turbulence that is felt comes from inside the plane itself. The polarization of those on the plane is obvious; most of the cadets are visibly frightened. The cadets have only practiced hostile engagement, listening to the stories of their instructors and guest speakers, but now they could possibly be thrust into military action. The Marines take this deployment in stride. Many of the Marines have been on missions where they show heavy artillery with a modest number of soldiers.

"Gentlemen, check all your gear and make sure that you have reserve magazines. We don't foresee any problems, but we are in a foreign land, and we will be going into disputed territory. The locals will not be happy to see us…so please be alert. We all go home or none of us go home," says Lt. Rudder.

The team loads up a caravan of trucks with artillery and other supplies for their approximately 25-mile jaunt through the South Korean countryside. The team plans a course to Kijong-Dong. The city of Kijong-Dong is on the other side of the disputed 38th parallel line in the Republic of communist-controlled North Korea. The village of Kijong-Dong is believed to have been a prison camp for the Empire of Japan's prisoners of war. It is widely believed that the Empire of Japan, with the cooperation of the Nazis, performed many diabolical experiments on some of these prisoners of war. Because of the remote location of the village, many within the global community believe that some of the prisoners of war could still be in those prisons. The higher ups think the spring would have been the best time for a mission to free the prisoners, but they know that they must go in now or risk never finding the prisoners alive.

The cadets are longing for the 100 percent humidity days of Charleston. It has just rained, and the moisture-filled air makes it hard for the group to breathe. The stifling air is made even more difficult to breathe through the scent of rotting corpses. The very roads the soldiers are traveling on played host to some of the most intense hand-to-hand battles of World War II. Unlike the battles fought for Normandy and Berlin, the jungles of East Asia had to be conquered by soldiers on foot. The Americans had superior firepower, but their lack of jungle training was no match for the knowledge of the people who lived there. Ricky recalls Captain telling him, he never liked to fight in obscure places like a jungle.

Captain told Ricky, "Never fight someone where they can set the traps. Don't fight someone in their house because you will never win; they know all the good hiding spots. If the enemy is that much of a problem, then just blow them up."

Ricky has a slight giggle to himself in remembrance of Captain but a large bump jars him back to the present. The lead truck has blown a tire, so the entire caravan pulls over to access the situation. Lt. Rudder looks at the truck and then takes a look at his surroundings. He looks at his compass to see where they are. "We are almost there. We should be at the Yalu River; we probably have a 10-mile walk," says Lt. Rudder.

The team starts to gather their backpacks. Lt. Rudder sends The Squirrel ahead to scout the area. The Squirrel is a short Negro in his mid-twenties. He served with Lt. Rudder in World War II. Lt. Rudder swears by The Squirrel, as he is so affectionately known. There are stories that The Squirrel helped save the lives of over 100 American soldiers from being blown up in a minefield, finding a very well disguised trap in North Africa outside of Egypt. The Nazis had devised plans of luring Allied troops into grass-covered minefields. Up until that time, no one had perfected these types of minefields. The Squirrel's discovery aided the Allied forces in the liberation of North Africa.

The soldiers start off on foot toward Kijong-Dong with The Squirrel serving as a scout. The road, if that is what you want to call it, is an endless trail of thick mud. The mud is so deep and thick that it makes a suction sound as each soldier marches forward. Lt. Rudder realizes that he should have never got out on foot. The mass amount of foliage is so thick that you can't see more than 50 yards in any direction. The soldiers swat the leaves and the bird-sized mosquitoes that swoop down as they proceed on their marathon walk.

After the nearly three-hour walk, the small village is in sight. The village sits atop a slight incline in the endless horizon of mountain ranges. Lt. Rudder's group gets their second wind. There seems to be an extra pep in their step as they get to a gravel surface. The gravel road is a blessing for the group's footing, but the constant marching serves as an early warning system.

The Squirrel gets to the village first; he signals to the group to proceed slowly and with caution. There are signs that the village has been recently vacated. There are several smoldering fires burning and recently discarded bowls with traces of rice. The villages of the Korean Peninsula have been constantly under attack, going back to the time of the Ming dynasty up until the fall of the Empire of Japan after World War II. The Korean villages have been pillaged, their natural resources taken, and their women raped and ravaged. These types of villages have always known that they could not fight their aggressors, so very often they would flee to underground caves or tunnels. Normally, they would wait until the invading force left before resurfacing. Lt. Rudder and his platoon start to go through many of the individual huts, turning over everything that lays upright. He walks out of a hut without finding anything, and he lights up a cigar. He looks around the village. The village is eerily quiet.

"Something is not right here. Keep your eyes open."

Lt. Rudder's extensive experience starts to kick in, and he looks intensely at his surroundings. Lt. Rudder's sixth sense has served him well. Moments later, two Marines drag an older gentleman out of a hut. The gentleman looks like a witch doctor. The witch doctor has some type of war paint on his face, unruly hair and is dressed in a canvas robe. It is apparent the witch doctor is frightened. He starts to speak in his native language. Immediately, all the Korean soldiers and guides take a defensive position. Lt. Rudder sees the reaction of the Korean soldiers, and he grabs the witch doctor and lifts him off the ground.

"What the hell are you saying?" asks Lt. Rudder.

He grabs one of the Korean soldiers.

"What the hell is he saying?" demands Lt. Rudder.

The soldier is visibly scared while looking around.

"Soldier, what is he saying?" yells the Lieutenant.

"He is telling someone to come out and fight to the death," reveals the soldier.

Instantly, several of Lt. Rudder's soldiers are hit by arrows. One of the soldiers is hit in the head, killing him instantly. The other soldier initially hit in the chest is Citadel Cadet Pee Wee. Lt. Rudder looks out over the landscape and sees about 20 archers moving through the village. To his amazement, he sees a number of women and children running toward the soldiers, screaming and hurling large stones. Knowing that people of the village have been sent on a suicide mission, Lt. Rudder gives the order.

"Soldiers, shoot and kill everything moving," states the Lieutenant.

Two more soldiers are hit by arrows piercing their chests. As the soldiers begin to shoot, the villagers are mowed down by the soldiers' bullets. The sharp-shooting Squirrel hits two archers from his sniper's perch in the forehead. One of the villagers comes to Teed with a large knife. Teed is conflicted as he pulls out his gun. As he aims his gun, the villager takes a swing at him. Teed pulls the trigger but the gun jams. He knows he'd better kill this man, or he will never leave Korea. Teed loses his apprehension of hurting the villager. The villager swings the large knife unsuccessfully at him before Teed disarms the man and uses his own knife to stab him. After many of the men are killed, the even more enraged children and women continue to advance toward the Americans. The only American soldiers still standing are Lt. Rudder, The Squirrel, Teed and Zachery. The men come together, and Lt. Rudder gives the order.

"Kill everything!"

All the Americans take a deep breath and begin to unload on all the remaining villagers. Teed and The Squirrel are uneasy about shooting the villagers, but Zachery appears to relish killing them. The smoke-filled village begins to clear. The remaining soldiers access the body-filled village to make sure they are all dead. Teed and Zachery walk over to a near-death Pee Wee. The blood-drenched Pee Wee is fading in and out of consciousness. Teed kneels down next to Pee Wee to console him.

"Pee-Wee can you hear me," asks Teed.

"I fought in a war, didn't I Teed?" says a gasping for air Pee Wee.

"You did. Your mom and dad will be proud," says Teed.

Zachery is looking at Pee Wee. He knows Pee Wee's end is near. A lone tear rolls down Zachery's cheek. Pee Wee takes several short breaths and then he passes. Teed closes Pee Wee's eyes, then walks away. Lt. Rudder and The Squirrel are looking at several of the dead bodies; everyone appears to be dead, but one of the male villagers rises from the ground. Lt. Rudder and The Squirrel don't see the villager coming up behind them. The villager picks up a knife and starts to charge Lt. Rudder. Zachery sees the villager charging Lt. Rudder and runs to intercept him.

Zachery throws his body in front of Lt. Rudder. The villager misses Lt. Rudder as Zachery pushes him out of the way, but Zachery catches the blade in his chest. Zachery immediately falls to the ground. Lt. Rudder reaches for his gun; without hesitation, he turns and blows the villager's brains out.

THE G-MAN

President's Park sits south of the White House. The park was the brainchild of Washington D.C.'s architect, Pierre Charles L'Enfant. L'Enfant was believed to think that the new American empire would need structures to exemplify its budding power and prestige. He designed the city with many shapes, including circles, triangles, squares and even an ellipse. President's Park became known as the Ellipse, a public park that many of Washington's elite would come to enjoy the picturesque landscape. During the Civil War, the park was used as a Union camp to house a battalion to protect the president—on this day the park could be the site of a new conflict.

The Ivory Coast Orioles and the L'Enfant Senators are playing their annual summer baseball classic. The game had become more of a networking function for the parents than a childhood baseball game. The Ivory Coast team is made up of mostly children of ambassadors and congressman that reside in the very affluent area known as the Ivory Coast in the Upper Northwest Quadrant of Washington, D.C. The L'Enfant Senators are made up of the children of high-level government workers and certain Pentagon personnel that live on the outskirts of Washington, mainly in Arlington, VA.

Not known for his love of children, J. Edgar Hoover, the director of the Federal Bureau of Investigations, better known as the FBI, has decided to take in this year's game.

Hoover sits on a park bench within a rock's throw of the field but maintains his distance from all the action. Hoover decides to be a part of the action, asking one of his three well-positioned bodyguards to get him a hot dog, a bag of peanuts and a Coca-Cola from one of the vendors. In years past, the president would come to the game to throw out the first pitch or just to observe, but this year, with the country on the brink of its second war in five years, it was thought he should stay in the White House. Hoover wasn't at the game to enjoy the uncharacteristically cool summer day in Washington; he was there to have an informal meeting with Hampton Capers. Capers walks over to Hoover, sitting on the bench.

"Director," says a stern-voiced Capers.

"Senator," replies Hoover as he eats a peanut. Hoover hands Capers the bag of peanuts.

"I love this game; you don't seem to be having fun, director," implies a giddy Capers.

"We couldn't have met in an office or a damn restaurant?" questions a pissed Hoover.

"Where is your American spirit? This is the all-American game," asserts a smiling Capers.

"What the hell is so important that we had to meet out here," asks Hoover.

"Edgar, I really need a big favor," asks Capers.

"What the hell is it now? Is it another one of your redneck buddies?" demands Hoover.

"No Edgar. I need you to back off the Italians," concedes Capers. "Look, I know you are a powerful senator and all, but I can't allow their criminal enterprises to continue to grow," proclaims a pissed Hoover.

"What are they really doing? Girls, booze and gambling—all things that people want. All those things are harmless crimes," pleads Capers.

"Have you been drinking the Italian's wine? There is no such thing as a harmless crime. They are bribing every government official they can, and whatever citizen doesn't go along with the way they do business they kill. How the hell is that harmless?" challenges Hoover.

Capers rises to his feet in frustration. He knows that Hoover is not going to rationally agree to drop his pursuit of the syndicate.

"Edgar, they have pictures," claims Capers.

Capers hands Hoover a large interoffice envelope.

"What the hell is this?" asks a puzzled Hoover.

Hoover opens the envelope and has a surprised look on his face. He jumps to his feet. "Those sons of bitches!" exclaims an infuriated Hoover.

His outburst gains the attention of some of the people in the crowd.

"Edgar, sit down," whispers Capers.

"Why did you bring this to me?" asks a frustrated Hoover.

"They want you to give them some space to allow them to do their business," admits Capers.

"How did they get this?" requests Hoover.

"Does it matter? And before you ask, I had nothing to do with this. You and your G-men have been destroying their business; they wanted to get an advantage," states Capers.

"So, if I allow them to go about their business then these pictures will go away?" Hoover queries.

Capers nods his head in affirmation while eating more peanuts. "Does this have anything to do with your new little group?" asks Hoover.

Capers looks at Hoover in shock; he almost chokes on a peanut. Capers starts to cough and reaches for Hoover's Coca-Cola.

"I guess I have my answer," remarks Hoover.

Capers drinks Hoover's soda to kill his cough.

"No, Edgar I had nothing to do with this. I did meet with the Italians, but that is not why we were meeting. Look, is it going to kill you to leave them alone? Leave the victimless crimes alone. Leave the whores and the gambling alone," says Capers.

"And when they kill someone—because you know they will kill someone—what do I do?" asks Hoover.

"You charge that asshole with murder and only that asshole. You don't take this up the chain of command," states Capers. "They understand that if there is a murder that somebody has to fall," he adds.

Hoover sits back down next to Capers.

"So how do I know that these pictures won't see the light of day? They will blackmail me for the rest of my life," concedes a concerned Hoover.

"I promise you, if this gets out, I will bring the full weight of the United States Congress to bare on the syndicate," exclaims Capers.

"I hear you Hampton. I guess we both have secrets that we must now keep," says Hoover as both men rise to shake hands.

"I guess we do," says Capers.

"Hampton, be careful of the company you keep. The Nazis were seen as Patriots also," says Hoover as he walks away.

THE PRODIGAL SON

With a very heavy heart, Senator Hampton Capers descends from an Army 747 Boeing bomber. The senator has traveled to Seoul, South Korea to retrieve the body of his son, Zachery. The senator believed the Korean conflict would make Zachery a serious man; the senator believed that the conflict would help put his young son on the right track. The senator received verbal accounts that his son fought heroically; those accounts brought him momentary pride of his son's heroism, but the reality that his son would never be able to tell the story himself hurt more. The senator's wife did not accompany him on the trip. Obviously, she is still grief-stricken, but many say she was furious with the senator when she found out young Zachery was sent on a covert mission. Knowing her husband, Mrs. Capers knew this covert mission was in some way a father trying to make his son into the man he thought he should be. Zachery was close to his mother, but his father ruled their home with an iron fist—like most southern gentlemen of the day. Zachery had won his mother's affections because of his love for music. He wanted to attend Clemson University to study music; more specifically he wanted to play his beloved saxophone. If young Zachery had not been a Capers, he may have been an accomplished musician, but his destiny was not his decision. The senator knows that the vultures will be circling. The official purpose of the mission was supposed to be a peace-keeping detail to head off any potential problems on the Korean peninsula.

The group was not supposed to travel to North Korea, and there was no official need for Lt. Rudder's tactical team. The senator knew that at some point he would have to invent some kind of answer to beat back his adversaries in the Senate. As the senator walks down the steps to the tarmac, he is flanked by two of his 8Men partners: Cecil Thomas and Director Wesley Carter. The casket of Zachery lays about 20 feet away from the tarmac, draped by an American flag. The site of Zachery's casket takes the senator back to Zachery's first little league game. The senator had to convince his son to play baseball. Zachery had a fear of pitchers throwing the ball; he always told his dad that he was scared the ball would hurt him. The senator would say to his son, "Be a man, boy. If the ball does hit you, it won't kill you—it will only make you stronger." Those words ring in the senator's ears because that is exactly what he told his son before he left for this mission. The senator remembers his son had a very disconnected look the last time he saw him. He remembers his son's eyes were glazed over, looking like a man who witnessed a ghost or maybe a man that realized his own mortality.

As the senator looks out at the view of 20 or so other caskets, he wonders if it was worth it. The senator thought that his son needed this conflict. He thought that one day young Zachery would follow in his footsteps. His son would become a military officer, fight in an obscure occurrence in a far-off land, then come back to the states. The senator figured that once Zachery's military record was solidified, he could come back to the states and begin his political career. The senator had a similar trek. His father, the late Isaac Capers, U.S. Congressman from Charleston, believed that military service was the opening act to public service. He believed any self-respecting government official should serve in the military, he thought, *how could you act in the country's best interest if you weren't prepared to make the ultimate sacrifice?* The elder Capers instructed a young Hampton that upon his graduation from The Citadel he would be enlisting in the Army.

Hampton fought in World War I's pivotal Battle of Saint-Mihiel. The battle was touted as a turning point for the Allied victory. When Hampton returned from Europe, the elder Capers sent his contacts into full campaign mode. They made sure Hampton was in every victory parade within a 50-mile radius of Charleston following the war. Hampton won his campaign by a landslide. He thought that he could repeat history again for his son, but Zachery's untimely demise dashed those dreams.

The bereaved Capers kneels at the head of his son's casket, wondering what he could have done differently. He momentarily thinks he should have let him pursue his passion as a musician. Capers thinks back to the joy the saxophone brought to his son. When he was a boy, Zach played with the family maid's son and several other colored boys in an impromptu band. Capers recalls the joy on Zach's face whenever he played.

In the distance, a limping Ricky and a crutch-using Lt. Rudder approach the casket-filled tarmac. Both Lt. Rudder and Ricky salute Senator Capers.

"Sir, I am sincerely sorry for your loss; your son fought gallantly. He would have made you proud, not because you were his father but because you too are a patriot," expresses an emotionally moved Lt. Rudder.

Lt. Rudder again salutes the senator, then limps off.

"I want to express my sincere condolences, Senator," says Teed.

"Thank you, son. Tell me about the battle. Tell me how Zachery performed," requests Capers.

Hampton Capers is desperate to hear any details about his son's heroism so that he can make peace with this death.

"Sir, you would have been proud. He was a superhero. I saw him take down three of the villagers with his bare hands. One of the villagers he killed by snapping their neck and the other two he killed by using his 9-inch knife, severing their necks," states Teed as Senator Capers is enthralled in his story.

"He did great," proudly says Capers.

"He couldn't have better, sir," suggests Teed.

"Then how did he die?" demands Capers.

"He threw himself in front of a knife-wielding villager. The villager was intent on going after Lt. Rudder. Zachery saw the man and jumped in the way to save him. He just couldn't save himself," admits Teed.

"You know, I always thought Zachery was too stubborn to die; that's why I figured he would be safe here. He had a defiant spirit; I figured he could also defy death," mentions Senator Capers as a tear rolls down his face.

The senator walks away from the group, leaving Director Carter and Teed still standing at the casket.

"Thank you, for your service Mr. Teed," whispers Director Carter. Director Carter lights a cigarette as Ricky tries to get his thoughts together.

"Director Carter, did we get in trouble? Did we do something wrong?" asks a shaken Teed.

"No son, the unfortunate deaths withstanding, you and your team did exactly what we wanted you to do. War and death are unfortunate occurrences, but hopefully this small setback will provide for a brighter future," says Director Carter.

He shakes Ricky's hand.

"Thank you again son," declares Director Carter.

Ricky begins to walk away from the distinguished gentlemen when Senator Capers says, "Would you like to ride back with us Mr. Teed?"

LONG RIDE HOME

The Boeing 747 Army bomber that carried Senator Capers and Director Carter to Korea is a flying palace. The plane is an exact replica of the plane that brought Lt. Rudder and his team to the Korean Peninsula, but that is where the resemblance ends. The plane includes three separate sleeping quarters, a small kitchen, a communication center and a fully functional bathroom. Of course, the bathroom takes Ricky by surprise. Very few people in Charleston have indoor plumbing, but he would have never thought a plane would have an indoor bathroom.

Ricky feels scared and anxious; he doesn't know why the director and the senator want him to fly back with them. Lt. Rudder and The Squirrel get on another plane. Ricky thinks to himself that maybe they blame him for the failed mission. He has had a whirlwind couple of days: first he graduated from The Citadel a little over a week ago, then he was tasked with going to Korea on a perceived peacekeeping mission, finally he found himself in the middle of a gunfight that might be seen as the opening act of World War III. It may seem like an understatement, but Ricky's poor heart pounds uncontrollably. He was asked by the director to accompany the group of dignitaries to an American base in West Germany. Director Carter is talking with some military types in the distance while Senator Capers sits in his seat, looking out of a window, staring into the clouds.

The senator appears to be carrying a truly heavy burden with the passing of his son. Ricky walks over to the Senator to make small talk.

"It seems to be a beautiful day," says Ricky.

The Senator shrugs his shoulders; Ricky feels like the senator is brushing him off, so he turns to walk away.

"Sit son. I'm sorry—I know I have been an asshole," pleads an apologetic Senator Capers.

"It is understandable, sir," replies Ricky.

"You know we are entering into very dangerous times," says a very introspective Senator Capers.

"Sir, wasn't World War II the most dangerous occurrence of our time?" says a bewildered Ricky.

Senator Capers takes a long gulp of water before answering Ricky's question. "Son, World War II was nothing but the prelude to the new era. World War II for us was about stopping a madman and obliterating the Japs for Pearl Harbor. But the bomb changed the world forever—making us the most feared nation on earth," reflexes Senator Capers.

"But why would any country be afraid of us? We used the bomb as a last result, right?" asks Ricky.

"Sure, we did, but there is an anxiety that now frightens other countries. Historically, most countries weren't afraid of America; they always felt we were over-privileged playboys backed by the Zionist's bankroll. Now we are playboys with a weapon that could destroy our enemies from a distance. There has always been the apprehension of world leaders to send their country's impressionable young men into senseless battles. But now, if any of us want to attack from afar, what will stop us? The loss of life in World War II was devastating, but when we destroyed Nagasaki and Hiroshima in a matter tof seconds, we put a large target on America. Every world power is in a race to get an atomic bomb now," claims Senator Capers. "Why?" inquires a dumbfounded Ricky. Senator

Capers looks out of the window, trying to find a politically correct way to convey his thoughts to the impressionable Ricky. He chuckles before he answers. "Please excuse the way I say this son. Like every man, every country wants to have the biggest penis in the room. When we detonated the atomic bomb twice and the rest of Europe was left in ruins by the devastation of World War II, we officially had the biggest penis. You must understand that Russia, China and the other nations spared by the ultimate destruction of World War II are nations of immense pride. Since they did not create this weapon and we don't share the same outlook on life—they are now scared," remarks a rather coy Senator Capers.

Director Carter walks in the direction of Senator Capers and Ricky.

"Sorry gentlemen, I was in communication with the South Korean government. It would seem, Ricky, that your unit barely made it out in time. The North Koreans sent in three battalions supported by two other battalions from China and Russia. They were alerted that some western meddlers were searching through local camps," says Director Carter. After the end of World War II, the communist-influenced countries of Russia, China and North Korea formed an ideological pact to fend off the pursuits of western countries. The only viable western power at this time are the Americans. Josef Stalin's quest for European domination was only rivaled by that of Adolf Hitler. The one-time ally of Harry Truman did not want any signs of the Americans on the continent. Stalin felt he could build the Russian empire throughout Eastern Europe, but the perceived thought of American imperialism could thwart his efforts. Stalin looked at America like a cancer that seemed to take advantage of all situations. With all the previous powers in Western Europe, including France, England, Germany and Italy, crippled by the war, the Americans could come in and offer economic aid to enslave those countries to the Americans' will. Stalin always felt that America got into the war after the attack on Pearl Harbor; he felt like they knew what Hitler was up to, but they did not respond until the Japanese attacked them. Stalin felt the Russians and many of the Eastern European countries had endured the Nazis and the fascist movements only to give way to the Americans. It was too much for him to bear.

Senator Capers fixes himself a scotch with seven cubes of ice—he liked to watch alcohol melt the cubes. Normally, Senator Capers drank his scotch straight; he thought the mixing of the alcohol lessened the soothing nature of the drink. As Senator Capers and Director Carter have very strong drinks, Ricky drinks an ice-cold Coca-Cola.

"Ricky, we are very pleased that you survived the attack by the villagers in the Korean hills. We can see you are a very dedicated and resourceful young man. Judging by your academic record from The Citadel, you are an equally intelligent young man. Solider, let me cut to the chase; we are looking to form a covert organization outside of the normal bureaucracy of our military. We want you to be a very significant part of this," says Director Carter.

"Why me, Sir? You know I have never attended army basic training," asks Ricky.

Both the senator and the director start to laugh. Ricky looks at both of the gentlemen laughing and figures if he doesn't know why they are laughing they must be laughing at him.

"Ricky, you are going to be sent to basic training—a somewhat accelerated training. You survived a military ambush; most of your battalion were killed. You were one of three people who escaped; if it weren't the training then it was luck—hell we will take either one," says Senator Capers.

"It is time you get your rest Ricky. We have a long ride; you need to be well rested," affirms Director Carter.

Both gentlemen shake Ricky's hand before he goes off to one of the bedrooms.

After Ricky leaves, Director Carter asks, "Are you sure he is ready?"

"He is ready. This was the path I wanted for my son. He is now my son," declares Senator Capers.

"Well, we will see. We know he will get the best training available," admits Director Carter.

KATSA

Ricky is sound asleep. He is resting comfortably in one of the large rooms aboard the plane carrying him and a few American dignitaries to West Germany. Five large men shrouded in black enter the room. They grab Ricky and place tape over his mouth and hands, then place black dungarees and a black sweatshirt on him. Ricky is trying his best to fight back, but one of the large men dressed in black punches a defenseless Ricky on his left temple, momentarily knocking him out. The men continue to dress Ricky in all black; they stand his limp body up and place a large parachute on his back. The men walk Ricky over to one of the plane's large exit doors. The brisk winds of the door being opened awaken Ricky to a state of instant panic. The largest of the men shrouded in black picks Ricky up off the ground and says to him, "You will be alright. When you are picked up, make sure you say Shalom. They are your friends," says the large man.

The large man throws Ricky out of the plane. Ricky had limited parachute training while at The Citadel, but he knows that he has to pull the ripcord before he hits the ground. He thinks, *"Where the hell am I?"* He has no idea where he could be. He had been sleeping for several hours, so he could be anywhere in the Middle East, but he thinks, *why would they push me out of a plane in the Middle East?* He wonders if he has done something wrong; maybe he knows too much, but Ricky thinks to himself that he doesn't know anything. He has been kept completely in the dark; he went to the Korean Peninsula, almost got killed but still doesn't know what his mission was.

Judging by the sun, Ricky figures it must be around 6 am. Fortunately, he is not going to have to navigate through a foreign land in the dark, but the light will allow any interested party to track him. As Ricky pulls the ripcord of his parachute, he notices a lone truck in the distance. The truck appears to be riding on a dusty road in a hilly countryside. Aside from the headlights of the truck, there aren't any lights for miles. Ricky drifts down to the earth by angling the ripcord. His landing is a bit rough; the crosswinds carry the parachute, forcing Ricky to roll on the ground. Once Ricky is able to unravel the parachute, he has five semi-automatic guns pointing at him. The group of men don't look so happy to see Ricky's early-morning arrival. Ricky thinks about what the large man that threw him out of the plane said.

Ricky raises his hand and says, "Shalom."

The group of gunmen lower their guns and say "Shalom" back to him. One of the men asks Ricky in a heavy Israeli accent, "You are Teed?"

Ricky answers back "Yes."

Ricky thinks back to his accents and dialects class with Corporal Shanley at The Citadel. Corporal Shanley used to impress upon his students that they should know how the enemy speaks; he always wanted his students to be on the lookout for enemies trying to pass themselves off. But Ricky knows that these are a group of Israeli soldiers; they are friends of America. It begs the question, why was he thrown out of a plane to be picked up by the Israelis? After a lengthy trip, back to an unknown military installation, Ricky takes a well-deserved and overdue shower to relieve himself of the stench of war. He stands in the shower, wondering what will happen to him. He thinks to himself, *"why did a U.S. senator and the chief intelligence officer of the United States have me thrown out of a plane?"*

An armed guard comes into the shower area and says, "Mr. Teed, the director will see you now."

Ricky gets dressed, the guard escorts him down a bland hallway with no pictures on the walls. He winds up taking Ricky to the office at the end of the hall.

"Please wait here," states the guard as he leaves the office.

The office has four white walls with what appears to be a cherry wood table and two wooden chairs. For good measure, the office has a bowl of fruit on the desk. After sitting on the chair for a few minutes, Ricky decides to get an apple. He thinks to himself that this apple is the best meal he has had in weeks. A door opens and a well-groomed but stout fifty-something man walks through the door.

"Hello Mr., Teed, my name is Reuven Zaslanski; I am the director of the Israeli Central Institute for Coordination. I hope that my people have treated you well."

Ricky nods his head in affirmation.

"Good, my people have not always been known for their hospitality," the director laughs.

"Sir, why am I here?" asks a bewildered Ricky.

"You are here to be trained. You have obviously garnered the admiration of many in your government. You will be trained to be an intelligence officer and, for lack of a better word, an assassin," alleges the director.

"Why didn't they tell me? Why couldn't I have done that in America?" asks Teed.

"Mr. Teed, I can't give you all the answers you wish to have—but I can assure you we are the best at what we do. I will say, I believe you will be utilized by some very important people. Your country's intelligence community is very flawed, by your laws and procedures—your pursuit of life, liberty and justice for all," the director chuckles.

"Huh?" replies Teed.

"It allows your enemies to track your progress. While here you will be treated as one of us," says the director.

NAZI OASIS

After World War II, the state of Israel made it a priority to track down former Nazi officers and bring them back to Israel to stand trial for the mass murders of Jews throughout Europe. The Central Institute for Coordination was tasked with this mission. Because many of the former Nazis fled to distant lands under assumed aliases, it made it difficult to track and capture them. The country of Argentina became a haven for former Nazis. It is believed that many anti-Semitic sympathizers reside in Argentina and help to conceal the identity of former Nazis. During World War II, it was a rumor that much of the stolen jewelry and other family heirlooms of the Jewish people were fenced by Argentineans.

It has been three years since Richard Teed arrived in Israel to be trained by Israel's shadow organization. The newly named Mossad pursued all enemies of the state of Israel. Many so-called civilized countries shrieked at the Mossad's unconventional methods, but in secret they all understood their objectives and many aided them when possible. Teed, now a mature 25 year-old, is now looking the part of an international mover and shaker. Teed now sports a light brown beard with his trimmed quaff covered by a stylish fedora. Teed arrives at Ezeiza Airport in the Province of Buenos Aires in Argentina. Teed is accompanied by a strikingly beautiful woman that bares an amazing resemblance to Swedish actress Greta Garbo. Teed and his companion walk through the airport hugging each other while whispering into each other's ears.

The couple walks out of the airport and hails a cab to take them to the swanky Hotel Polmeria.

Three hours later, after an apparent intensive sexual session, Teed and his companion, Danya Franck, lay in bed smoking Parliament cigarettes. Parliament cigarettes gained prominence in the 1930s as a cigarette for the wealthy.

"These are rather rich cigarettes," comments Danya as Teed coughs from inexperience of smoking cigarettes.

"Why are we smoking?" questions Teed.

"We must immerse ourselves in this world. The scum we will be dealing with must think that we are of their world. So, we must smoke their disgusting cigarettes, eat their repulsive swine and drink their horrid liquor. Jehovah will forgive us for our sins," remarks Danya.

Teed watches as a shapely Danya gets out of the bed and walks to the bathroom. Teed can feel her impassionate resolve and her lifelong mission to defend Israel from its enemies through her stark words. The exotically beautiful Danya Franck is a pleasure to the eye, but she is as equally dangerous to those who catch her ire. She is an operative in Israel's Mossad secret military organization. Danya is a Hungarian Jew; both her parents were viral biologists forced to work on secret projects for the Nazis. Danya and her parents were placed into a little-known concentration camp outside of Budapest, shortly after the Nazis invaded Hungary. Her parents were working on a unique blood antigen that could help to improve the human immune system. The Nazis wanted to corrupt the Franck's' research; they wanted to create a pathogen to attack the human immune system. It was all a part of the Nazis' final solution to rid the world of Jews, the physically changed, gypsies, the mongrel races and homosexuals.

Even though she was a woman, Danya garnered the respect of her superiors as well as her colleagues; many within Mossad lost family and friends in the Holocaust, but she escaped while killing several Nazis. A feat not easily accomplished by many, especially a diminutive 15 year-old girl standing at 5'4."

It is unclear exactly what precipitated her killing rampage, but the rumor was that she decapitated three Nazis with a dull butter knife. Danya strolls back into the room.

"Tonight, we are going to find our mark. Tonight, we hunt the wolf," declares a determined Danya.

The Hotel Polmeria doubles as a high-roller casino on the weekends. It doesn't have the pomp and circumstance of Cuban casinos, but it does have its bigwigs. Unlike its Cuban counterparts, the Hotel Polmeria patrons come strictly for the intense gambling. The games of choice for this crowd are poker, roulette and craps. Each table carries a minimum buy-in of ten thousand dollars; they made the minimum buy-in high to keep the pretenders and riff raff out of the games.

Sitting at his usual perch at the roulette table, Albrecht Krause relishes being the center of attention. Krause has been on a tremendous winning streak on and off the roulette table. The early 50s playboy has been rumored to have bedded upwards of four dozen women since coming to the Argentinean capitol. He normally allows some beautiful senorita to blow on his dice for good luck. While they are blowing on his dice, Krause orders them drinks. Krause's newest conquest is a thirty-something Latina, with an hourglass shape and even prettier face. He always liked young women at least twenty years his junior; the new girl fit the bill.

Teed and Danya enter the heavily secured room dressed to the nines. Teed is dressed in a shiny black tuxedo and Danya looks elegant in a black one-shoulder-strap evening gown. Danya has captured the attention of all the men in the ballroom, as well as the ire of some of the less attractive women in the room.

"You have certainly gotten the attention of everyone in the room," whispers a nervous Teed.

"The only way to catch a sneaky wolf is to show him a beguiling prey that he can't pass up," states a seductive Danya.

"So, do we have a plan?" queries Teed.

"Why don't you buy a girl a drink?" suggests Danya.

Danya and Teed walk over to the bar.

"I'll have two scotches," says Teed.

The bartender pours scotch over the dice shaped ice. The hotel's management thought the specialty ice would be a signature piece. Teed reaches into his pocket and pulls out a wad of money.

"No thank you, sir." The gentleman at the roulette table has bought your drinks," says the bartender.

Krause raises his glass to Teed and Danya. He motions for them both to come over to his table.

"Game on," utters Danya.

Krause's lucky streak continues the roulette table through the night.

The presence of Danya has brought Krause luck that he has never experienced; he is up thirty thousand, and his previous high was fifteen thousand.

"You are my lucky charm. I have done well before but never this much," says Krause gleefully.

The shapely Latina that was Krause's previous lucky charm is steamed with her sugar daddy. The young Latina's womanly instincts are alerting her that her beau's loins have been aroused by another woman.

"Papi, are you finished yet? I am getting tired, I think it is time we leave," announces the young Latina in an overly seductive tone. Krause's interest has been shifted toward Danya.

"Sweetie, you can go. I think I will be here for some time. I think my luck can only get better," hints Krause as he looks Danya.

Danya winks seductively back at Krause. She turns to Teed and taps the table as if to give him a message.

"Honey, aren't you tired?" inquires Danya suggestively.

"Yes, I am going to turn in," replies a baffled Teed.

Both Teed and Krause's young Latina leave the roulette table area. Danya has gotten intimately close to Krause.

"So, who is the gentlemen you were calling Honey," asks an inquisitive Krause.

Danya laughs. "Do you really care?"

Krause laughs and shakes his head no.

"He is my husband; we have a business arrangement," reveals Danya.

"I like your arrangement," laughs Krause.

"So, tell me about you. You surely seem to command the attention of the room," probes Danya.

"My name is Albrecht Krause."

"Well Mr. Krause, my name is Heidi Schmidt," says Danya.

Danya knows that it is imperative to get Krause to trust her; she figures no easier way to get him to trust her than tell him she is from his fatherland. The name Schmidt is a very popular name in Germany. It is the equivalent of the surname Smith in America. Normally, Germans with the name Schmidt were pure Aryans. Danya is hoping that Krause will make that assumption. It has always been suggested that many with the surname descended from Aryans with origins near the Caucus Mountains. These people became known as Caucasians, or pure White people.

"So, what is a beautiful rich German woman like yourself doing here," questions a somewhat intoxicated Krause.

"I am here looking for fun. I wanted to go somewhere that I could let my hair down. Is this that place?" asks Danya as she strokes Krause's hair.

"Oh yeah, this is surely that place. You are an amazing woman," replies Krause.

"Let me show how amazing I am," says Danya.

ENEMIES LAIR

Danya and Krause stumble through the door of Krause's hotel room. They are embraced in a passionate kiss. The sexual tension is thick. Krause kisses Danya's neck as he palms her butt. Krause is pulling at her dress. He runs his hand up Danya's dress and discovers she is not wearing any panties. Krause's heart starts to beat faster with anticipation of penetrating Danya's five foot-something frame. Danya knows that Krause is now completely vulnerable; she always knew that her sexuality was the best way to disarm any potential male target. In short, once the blood rushed to the little head, the male target would abandon his normal common sense, which would make his extraction easier.

The stench of Krause brought back memories of Danya's rape at the hands of her Nazi offenders. As Danya remembers, the Nazis all shared a common stench of Biermann Ale. Biermann was the Nazis beer of choice; they drank it morning, noon and night while terrorizing their captives. The beer had a dark hue and was high in alcohol content. It resembled coffee and even had a faint smell like the beverage. A whiff of Krause's breath sends Danya into a rage; she knows that she must not tip her hand just yet, so she excuses herself.

"I am going to use your powder room. Why don't you pour us some drinks," suggests Danya.

A disappointed Krause agrees reluctantly. Krause takes off his tie and tuxedo jacket then throws them on the couch. Krause looks through his bar, he notices that he doesn't have any champagne or anything he would think a lady of Mary Schmidt's stature would drink.

"I'm sorry, all I have is water, cola and ale. What would you like to drink," requests Krause.

"What kind of ale?" responds Danya.

"Biermann," answers Krause.

"Sounds great," replies Danya.

Krause pulls out two 22-ounce glasses from the bar cabinet. He begins to pour the ale but is startled by the heavenly vision of Danya standing in the bathroom doorway completely naked.

"You are simply breathtaking," says a captivated Krause.

Danya walks over to a visibly awe-struck Krause.

"Do you like what you see?" asks Danya. Krause is tongue tied as he tries to say something. Danya stops Krause from further embarrassing himself. "Go get on the bed and take off your pants." In haste, Krause tears off his pants, wasting no time to get them off. Krause lies on the bed, waiting on Danya. "You look so good. Have you ever had a woman tell you to get on the bed?" asks an intrigued Danya. Krause looks at Danya, captivated by her beauty and her sexuality. He has never had a woman challenge his intelligence, let allow his sexuality. Krause in his mind believes that he has found the perfect woman. To Krause, his perfect woman is 20 years his junior, from his fatherland and very wealthy so that she can support his lifestyle of fine clothing, heavy gambling and heavy drinking. Mary Schmidt seems to fit the bill. Danya walks over to the bed where Krause is sitting waiting for her instructions. "Where do you keep your ties?" questions Danya with an enticing tone. Krause motions to the closet next to the bathroom. Danya walks over to the closet; she looks through the various ties. She picks out two ties—a blue and red paisley tie and a green tie with Krause's family crest. Danya walks back over to the bed; she starts to tie Krause's right hand when she notices that he appears to be getting aroused. She laughs to herself. She knows that Krause thinks he found the woman of his dreams, but he will soon find out that he has walked into his worst nightmare. After tying both of Krause's hands, Danya straddles Krause, sitting mere inches away from his fully erect penis. Feeling that now she is in full control, Danya devilishly laughs at Krause.

She smacks Krause across the face, immediately turning his right cheek rosy red. The smack turns Krause on; he asks Danya to smack him again. She hauls off and smacks Krause again—this time Danya draws blood from Krause's right cheek. Danya seems to be somewhat aroused by Krause's fetish of sadomasochism and the infliction of pain she has caused him. Danya decides to have a bit of fun. Danya grabs Krause's erect penis and places her vagina on top of it, only separated by Krause's underwear. The anticipation of sex seems to have gotten the best of Krause; he is a victim of premature ejaculation.

"Sorry," begs a disappointed and embarrassed Krause.

Danya starts to laugh uncontrollably, every bit of arousal she felt has ceased. She walks over to Krause's closet and grabs one of the numerous white shirts residing in his closet. A distressed Krause again pleads, "I'm sorry. I am just overly excited. Mary, I am sorry. This has never happened to me before."

Danya is visibly amused by Krause's misfortune.

"You are what I have been hunting for years. You are what I have symbolized as pure evil. You are nothing but a shell of a man," comments Danya sarcastically.

A perplexed Krause asks, "Mary, what—?"

Danya interrupts, "My name is not Mary Schmidt, my name is Danya Franck."

Krause starts to realize the severity of his situation.

"What do you want from me?" demands a terrified Krause.

Danya looks intently at Krause and says, "It is not up to me. But if it were up to me, you would be dead. Understand you will be made to answer for you past crimes."

PAST CRIMES

Albrecht Krause was one of Hitler's anointed youth, educated at Hitler's self-named school: Hitler's School for German Youth. Krause was one of the first graduates of the school. He and his classmates were looked at as the future of Germany. They typified Hitler's vision of the Nordic Knights that would bring the Aryan race back to its forgone prominence. Krause was amongst the SS troop that Hitler sent to eliminate his political adversaries in the famed Night of the Long Knives. He and his cohorts felt it was an honor to serve during the prelude of the historic rise of the Third Reich. Krause had a meteoric rise through the SS; he had a reputation as a merciless tyrant with his foot soldiers. He was also known to be an efficient administrator; he used death as a tool, not as an overall solution, unlike many of his SS colleagues. To Krause, if the Jews knew they were going to perish, they would sooner or later rise up and revolt. He thought it could be a win-win situation, if the Jews felt like they would live if they worked hard, it was a win for them, and if the Jews worked hard and if they produced, it was a win for the Nazis.

By the time the war ended in 1945, Krause was the senior Nazi official in charge of the southeastern province of the German-acquired countries. Unlike many of the other provinces within German rule, the southeastern province encompassed many Jewish scientists who worked on many groundbreaking scientific breakthroughs.

The Nazis endlessly explored an efficient method of killing what they described as undesirables. At the top of the list of undesirables were the Jews. Many Germans of Aryan decent, including Krause, blamed the Jews for every problem imaginable. Jews were blamed for mass poverty and the lack of Aryan-owned business in Germany. It was believed that the Jews controlled all the money and resources—purposely not allowing anyone but Jews to receive capital for businesses.

Krause sits in a darkened room partially lit by a dangling light bulb—that would swing back and forth for effect. Over the past few days, Krause has reminisced about his days within the Third Reich; it was obvious that his past finally caught up with him. Krause was wanted for war crimes connected to the Holocaust atrocities that occurred during World War II. He is still dressed in his finely tailored tuxedo he wore at the Hotel Polmeria. Obviously, Krause has been thoroughly worked over since he was taken from the hotel. Krause has been bleeding from every orifice. His left eye is slightly swollen, and his once ivory-colored shirt has been replaced by a pinkish tint.

In the distance, a door slams, it sounds like someone walks across the room with a heeled boot. A manila folder is thrown on the table that Krause is handcuffed to. The top of the folder has the name Albrecht Krause at the top. The overhead light comes on momentarily, blinding Krause. When his eyes adjust, he sees Danya standing at the other end of the table.

Krause chuckles to himself before speaking.

"You have to be the most attractive spy I have ever seen, and you are a Jew to boot. Absolutely brilliant; I have lost my touch," he concedes.

Danya stands at the other end of the table, dressed in a one-piece black cat suit, not intending to be fetching but fetching all the same. "I am pretty sure all the operatives you question relinquish any and everything you want to know. You can't help but be sexy," asserts a doting Krause.

"Mr. Krause, you seem very smug for a man that has been captured for war crimes. More specifically, you will be charged with countless counts of murder. I think that would qualify for a public hanging. If you make it to a trial," infers a stern Danya. Krause takes a long piercing look at her, then begins to laugh. An enraged Danya questions, "What is so funny? You killed countless amounts of Jews. You must know that you will have to pay for that."

"Mary, excuse me, Danya, I will not explain my actions. Quite frankly, I am pretty sure that no matter what I say there will be no redemption for me here today," concludes a somewhat amiable Krause. "Since it has been determined that I am such a deplorable human, what is the reason for my detainment in such a remote location? I take it since I am awake, I am needed," says Krause.

"We want to know where the rest of your cowardly comrades ran to," asks Danya.

"In the interest of half-truths, please don't insult me or your mission. Understand, I too was an operative, and no one puts this much effort into past murders. Yes, you and your people are upset about Auschwitz, Belzec, Treblinka and all the other camps, but my extraction was not about the camps. Your quest for me is about the future," asserts an insightful Krause.

An amused Danya pushes back, "If what you say is true, what information do you have?"

Again, Krause starts to laugh. "Come on darling, you must give me certain assurances that your position does not allow. I will talk; I will even give you the files of the special projects your superiors want—but after my demands are met."

The large door in the corner opens, and in walks Ezra Hirsch, the director of Mossad.

"Mr. Hirsch," says an amused Krause. Danya is caught off guard by Krause's recognition of the director of Mossad.

"How do you know him?" asks Danya.

"Again, darling I too was an operative. Mr. Hirsch has been around a long time," states Krause as he chuckles.

"Stop the damn games, Krause," demands the rigid Director Hirsch.

The director throws a small notepad on the table.

"Write your demands down," exclaims Hirsch.

The seemingly in control Krause throws both of his feet on the table.

"I don't need a notepad for these demands. They are quite short, and I will not negotiate any further. I want a pack of Polmeria cigarettes, a six-pack of Biermann Ale and a one-way ticket to America," demands a presumptuous Krause as he leans back in the chair.

HOME SWEET HOME

It has been seven long years since Richard Teed has set foot on American soil. He wondered how he would feel when he got back, but everything has changed. Teed has no nostalgic feeling about going back home. When he left America in 1950, the country was in the wake of World War II and in the early stages of the Korean Conflict—a skirmish that Teed and a group of unwitting patriots probably launched. He is flying home on an army plane that is taking some enlisted men back to Andrews Air Force Base in Maryland. Andrews is located about 15 miles southeast of Washington, D.C.

It is Teed's task to accompany Albrecht Krause to America. As a part of his deal with the Israelis, Krause wants to come to America. He wants to find out if America's streets are really paved with gold. During the flight, Krause talks about his sexual conquests in Argentina. He even eluded that he and Danya had a sexual interlude. Teed has grown tired of Krause's smugness. The only reason Krause is still alive is because he holds many of the Nazis' research secrets. He made sure that he didn't give them everything because he knew the moment they possessed the information he would be dead.

"I can't wait to get to America. I want to go to Yankee Stadium. I want to see your Babe Ruth," says a somewhat giddy Krause.

Unfortunately, Babe Ruth has been dead for a decade, but the way information traveled, he was still a folk hero to many around the world. Many foreigners came to the states to see the famed Bambino.

"Mr. Krause, Babe Ruth has been dead 10 years. I'm not sure if you have been told, but you probably will not be able to be in public often," comments Teed. Krause answers, "You expect me to come to the famed land of opportunity and sit in a room? I want to see this great experiment called America. I have always found it laughable that Americans say the Nazis are barbarians. We preach ethnic cleansing and yes, we did something about it. But your country also discriminates against your undesirables. Your poor Negroes helped to build your country and they are hanged and mutilated. You don't let them use public bathrooms…they can't eat in some of the very restaurants they are employed in. At least the Jews didn't help us build anything. Hell, we didn't get any free labor out of the Jews. Except during the war," he adds with a chuckle.

Teed is furious with Krause mocking America, but even in his jest Krause made a valid point. Teed thinks back to the death of Granville Brown. His neighbor died as a result of fighting for the American war effort, but he was given the same disrespect in death that he had been shown in life.

Several hours have passed and Teed has exhausted all the magazines provided by the flight crew. As he raises his head out of the Life magazine with the beautiful Sophia Loren on the cover, he notices a smirking Krause looking back at him.

"What the hell are you looking at," asks an infuriated Teed.

"You want to ask questions, don't you? Why would your country want me to be free? I will let you in on a bit of a secret. I am a treasure trove of information, and your country wants it," brags a contemptuous Krause.

Teed thinks to himself, *why do the U.S. government officials want to talk to Krause?* He wonders why the Jews would give him up. In Teed's view, the Nazis have been portrayed as the most diabolical regime ever in world history, so why would anybody want to talk to with them? Teed thinks that all world leaders would want to bury any and all things associated with the Nazis, but surprisingly most want to know what they were doing.

"What were you doing that makes everyone want to talk with you?" queries a curious Teed.

"Your curiosity has finally gotten the best of you," remarks a jovial Krause.

Teed's non-verbal expression concedes to Krause.

"Ok son, I have had too much fun at your expense. The truth is the world is becoming smaller, and what happens in one country will soon affect others.

We wanted to rule the world as Aryan people, but I don't think any of us wanted to ruin the world. World War II has forever changed the course of history. The weapons of mass destruction that were created as a result of the conflict are numerous. Some of the weapons were brought to fruition, but others even more deadly were still in production," reflects Krause with a hint of regret.

"What happened to the other weapons and where are they now?" asks a curious Teed.

"Son, I don't know. And I am scared out of my mind about it. Many of the weapons that we brought to production were defense related, but some of the others were doomsday type weapons," says a shaking Krause.

"What do you mean by a 'doomsday weapon?" questions Teed.

"In the event we gained world domination, there would be ways of getting rid of people or if we thought we were going to lose, we would try to destroy the entire world," hints Krause.

"What did you create?" asks Teed with fear.

"We made all kinds of weapons—really innovative stuff. We made a plane in which we could fold the wings. That was done so we could put that in a submarine; you know that was created especially for the planned invasion of America," divulges Krause as he chuckles.

Krause's revelation shocks Teed.

"The Nazis planned to invade America?" asks Teed.

"Oh yes. America was the grand prize. That is why we partnered with the Empire of Japan. They had a real disgust for America. If they hadn't jumped the gun, we would have won the war. Your country did not want to get into the war, but once you got in, it changed our fortunes forever," concedes Krause.

Teed looks at Krause with a loathsome look.

"You look at me with disgust or maybe it is what I represent to you. The power of domination is intoxicating. Sure, we were drunk with our power. What will America do now that it has the power? Make sure you judge your own countrymen as harshly as you have judged mine when your country's story is written," declares Krause.

FOGGY BOTTOM

After depositing Albrecht Krause with a trio of gentlemen wearing black suits, Teed jumps into a black four-door 1955 Ford Crown Victoria. The Crown Victoria was a vehicle primarily created as a two-door car, but the government ordered several specially made with the Crown Victoria's powerful V8 engine.

"Where are we going?" asks a somewhat inquisitive Teed.

Teed asked the question but he knew that his homecoming was going to start in the presence of one of two people. He would either be taken to see National Intelligence Director Wesley Carter or Senator Hampton Capers, Teed certainly wants to see both gentlemen.

Teed's return to the states brought back all the ill feelings he felt after his expulsion from the army plane flying over Israel. Since that day, he wondered to himself how they could throw him out of a plane not really knowing where he would land. He had just fought in a foreign land following orders from his higher ups.

Teed thinks to himself, *"is this how the American government treats its soldiers? The solider puts his life on the line only to be thrown to the wolves?"* He knows whichever gentlemen he encounters first he would make his opinion felt. The beautiful sunny day in Washington pales in comparison to the feelings that Teed is feeling inside. He doesn't know what his response will be to either of the two powerful men who abandoned him.

He constantly thinks, "*Why? What did I do wrong? Did I not complete my mission? Did I live when I was supposed to die? What was it?*" It doesn't really matter because he knows soon, he will get his answer.

The car Teed rides in pulls up to 2431 E Street in the northwest quadrant of Washington, D.C. The address has the appearance of a college campus at first glance, but upon further review the barbed wire rules out the thought of a collegiate environment. Off to the side, there is an inconspicuous sign reading the Office of Strategic Services (OSS). The OSS was the primary intelligence gathers during World War II. After the war, it was agreed that the U.S. government should be in the business of procuring information as it relates to American interests. The Central Intelligence Agency was born. The Central Intelligence Agency would ultimately be overseen by Wesley Carter—the same Wesley Carter who had Teed thrown from a plane over Israel.

In the short 6-year period since Teed left the states, Carter ascended from a simple advisory position in the Department of the Navy to a full cabinet position, holding the ear of the President of the United States. Teed is led through the halls of the OSS building by Director Carter's 25 year-old secretary, Lori Ann Mason. Teed is captivated by the resemblance to his high school sweetheart, Jennifer. Of course, the Lori Ann is a bit shapelier than Jen, but Teed still longs to see her again. He snaps himself back to reality; thinking about the task at hand. He doesn't know exactly why he is there, but he knows that it will require all his attention.

Teed has been sitting in Director Carter's office for little over an hour. He walks over to the large window that overlooks the Potomac River, with Arlington, Virginia, in the background. Teed thinks about what he will say to the director once he speaks to him. He thinks, "*how will I bring it up? Do I just ask what happened? Should I demand a joint meeting with Director Carter and Senator Capers? They are both responsible for what happened to me."*

Teed hears some voices outside of the director's office. He takes a deep breath, trying to anticipate what he will say to the Director. The door opens and in walks a newly bearded Director Carter. The beard seems to be out of place for the usually clean-cut Carter. The Director walks in, apparently in a jovial mood.

"Mr. Teed, glad to be back on American soil," says a pleasant Carter.

Teed looks at Carter with a look of disdain. He walks over to Carter, and he extends his hand to shake Teed's hand.

Teed extends his hand, giving a half smile to Carter. He pulls his hand back and punches Director Carter square on his already somewhat flat nose. The unexpected punch makes Carter's nose explode with a spray of blood. The punch throws him onto the cherry wood coffee table, which has pictures of Carter's family and some lesser awards for service to his country and community. The awards and pictures scatter as he lands on the table.

"I guess I had that coming," laughs Carter.

Carter's laughter seems to infuriate Teed that much more as he steps closer to follow up on his first punch.

The commotion of Carter falling onto the coffee table brings two rather large gentlemen brandishing two powerful Colt Python handguns. The Colt Python was created to inflict major damage to whatever the revolver pointed at. Even though the Python was a relatively new gun in the U.S., Teed knew the gun's reputation; some of his Mossad colleagues used the weapon, so he slowed his advances toward Carter. Director Carter laughs as he wipes his blood-drenched face.

"Gentlemen, this is my friend. We just have a strange way of saying hello to one another. Please…Please put the guns away; we will be alright," begs an apologetic Carter.

The gentlemen slowly put their guns down; they want a reason to fire at Teed. Director Carter motions to his security detail that everything is alright.

"Now, since you got your anger out of your system, are you ready to talk?" asks Carter.

"I'm not ready to talk. I want to know why I was thrown to the wolves. What did I do wrong?" demands Teed.

As Director Carter wipes his blooded nose, he reaches into his desk drawer. The director pulls out a check addressed to Richard Teed for $1 million dollars. Teed's eyes widen in surprise at the amount of the check presented to him. Teed's excitement is replaced by a sudden burst of anger.

"What is this, hush money?" yells Teed.

"No son, this is your money. You have earned every bit of that money. You can take the money today and walk away forever or you can take the training and the contacts you have acquired as a liaison with the Mossad and make history," suggests Carter.

Teed's facial expression shows his apprehensive curiosity.

"What would I have to do?" probes an apprehensive Teed.

"I want you to help us make history. But we must maneuver in stealth," comments a gleeful Carter.

Teed looks at Carter with doubt in his eyes, but the temptation of making history has piqued Teed's curiosity.

"While you contemplate your decision, I want you to take a ride with me," says Carter.

LANGLEY

The rise of communism has made many freedom-loving Americans fearful of the regimes in Russia and China. Many in the newly formed intelligence community are more afraid of the spread of communism than they were of the Nazi regime in Germany a short decade ago. Both the Russian and Chinese governments were quietly invading countries that shared common borders. These countries were systematically changed, with their central governments reporting back to Moscow and Beijing respectively. The countries changed from their various types of governments to those using communist's principals—instantly clashing with the common principles of capitalism. Most of these countries paid major taxes back to the mother countries; they also were forced in many instances to share their natural resources and human capital. Frightened by America's entry into the nuclear age, Russia and China wanted to exhibit they could match America's military might.

Director Carter persuades Teed to take a short ride to neighboring Virginia. As they ride, Teed marvels at the pictorial countryside of the Washington, D.C. suburb. Teed thought the Washington, D.C. area was a metropolis of skyscrapers and thought it had the bustle normally associated with New York City. To his surprise, Washington, D.C. is very similar to Charleston. Both cities have their urban centers, but in most instances, even at the most central part of the city, you are only 10 minutes from the countryside.

Teed looks at the somewhat bloodied Director Carter. The director pinches his nose with his pocket square. Teed looks at the director and regrets his prior actions.

"I am sorry…I'm sorry I punched you in the nose," admits a contrite Teed.

The director laughs as he feels his nose.

"Son, you are one of many who have taken a swing at me…usually they don't connect."

Both gentlemen laugh as Carter positions his head to stop the blood from rushing down his face.

"My emotions got the best of me…that will never happen again," affirms Teed.

The director's car stops out in the middle of a cleared patch of land.

"Teed, I want to show you something," says the director. Director Carter motions to him to get out of the car. For a brief second, Teed thinks that the director has brought him to an empty patch of land to kill him then bury his body. Teed has a gaze of doubt on his face.

"Relax son, if I wanted to kill you, I wouldn't need to drive all the way out here," laughs Director Carter.

Teed looks around and notices that the vast landscape is marked by survey stakes normally used when parceling land for subdivisions or to establish some kind of boundary.

"What are you building? Where are we?" asks Teed.

"Well, I will answer your second question first. We are in a little place called Langley, Virginia. This has always been a farm area…much of the area's produce goes to the city and even some parts of Maryland. To answer your first question, we will be building the future here. After World War II, some very connected gentlemen and I realized that the

West was caught with its proverbial pants down. We didn't know what was going on in our enemy's backyard. We had no idea what Hitler was planning, let alone the devastation the Japs were planning. Knowledge is power. We want this country to always be powerful, so we must know what others are doing," states Director Carter.

Teed has a look of confusion on his face.

"What does that have to do with this plot of land?" questions Teed. The director snickers at Teed's question.

"Son, I was trying to give you some background as to why we are moving in this direction. This will be the hub of intelligence gathered by the United States government. We are in the process of building a mega complex that will house thousands of intelligence agents. This organization will be called the Central Intelligence Agency. The sole objective of the agency is to make sure that we are safe from foreign powers," remarks an excited Director Carter.

"So why am I here?" asks Teed.

"I need a discrete agent who reports to a group that operates outside of the bureaucracy of the government. Some Americans can be a bit squeamish when it comes to making sure we stay safe. You now know the type of characters that won't hesitate to destroy the world and more importantly America," recites Director Carter.

"What can I do? I am no spy…except for my brief stint in Korea I have absolutely no military experience," concedes Teed.

"Please don't downplay your experience. You are a valuable asset. You have been trained by the best covert organization in the world. It shames me that America didn't have an organization like the Mossad. Are you ready to put your skills to work for your country?" challenges the director.

Teed looks out over the land, hoping to find an answer in the endless acreage of farmland.

"I will do it. What do you need from me?" inquires Teed.

Director Carter is beaming with the excitement that Teed will be joining their team.

"Great. I want you to meet a very important group of men. Let me set the meeting," says Director Carter.

MO MO

During the 1950s, the American La Cosa Nostra experienced its greatest period of prosperity. The Mafia had infiltrated most segments of American life. Prior to World War II, the mafia concentrated primarily on the victimless vices of prostitution, gambling and alcohol. The post-war era in America afforded the mafia the opportunity to become a part of the American fabric. The Mafia did not give up its vice operations but expanded to other mainstream businesses, primarily through the control of Midwest unions.

Unlike its East Coast counterparts, the Chicago mob, also known as the Syndicate, was not subdivided by family affiliation. The Syndicate was run by Al Capone's protégé, Sam Giancana. Giancana learned his ruthless tactics of murderous rule from infamous gangland enforcer Frank Nitti. Since the late 1940s, the Syndicate has enjoyed its lucrative gamble on the desert city of Las Vegas. Giancana basked in the money and notoriety of being one of the city's architects. Most of the East Coast families sent low-level enforcers to the desert to make sure the money count was correct. Giancana left nothing to chance; he thought the big wigs from New York were stupid. He thought, *what if their flunkies cut side deals with the pit bosses or table dealers? They could cheat us out of millions.* Giancana simply didn't trust anyone—well almost anyone.

The olive-skinned Giancana is sitting in his study smoking a cigar while talking to a famous entertainer.

"Frankie baby, you were great in Havana, they can't stop talking about you. I love when you and the boys are there together. The broads come from everywhere…great…great. Frankie, I want you to do me a favor…I want you and the boys to play at the hotel in Vegas. You som bitches will pack the place for weeks. Every broad from a 50-mile radius will come to look at you, and the jack offs they are with will have to come to make sure you don't knock them off," laughs Giancana.

As Giancana turns in his chair, he notices Valerius Torrantio standing in his doorway. Giancana starts to laugh with excitement. "

"Valley my friend, how are they hanging? Hey, Frankie let me call you back. What do I owe for this visit?" Giancana puts the phone down, sprouts out of his leather cognac colored chair and gives Valerius a kiss on both cheeks.

"How the hell you doing Valley?" asks Giancana.

"I'm doing well," replies Valerius.

"Tommy, come here, I want you to go upstairs and grab the briefcase off the floor in my office," demands Giancana.

The young twenty-something gangster scurries off, eager to fulfill Giancana's request.

"Why didn't you tell me you were coming? I would have had some of those calzones you love so much from Bellotte's," utters Giancana.

Bellotte's was known for having the best calzones in the Midwest and possibly the best the country. The calzones had a mixture of chewy mozzarella cheese, a sweet marinara sauce with assorted beef and pork wrapped in a tasty dough.

"Thank you, Sam, but I didn't come for that. I come out of concern for our Vegas operations. Our friends from New York are a bit concerned about your visibility on the strip in Vegas. They believe you are becoming a part of the nightlife in the city," suggests a concerned Valerius.

Again, Giancana starts to chuckle at Valerius' concerns.

"What does your father think about your concerns?" asks Giancana.

Valerius gives Giancana a disgusted scowl.

"I have not talked with my father, but like I said, I have talked to our friends in New York, and they weren't happy."

Giancana goes over to his record player and puts on Frank Sinatra's, "What's This Thing Called Love?"

"I love this song. He plays it every night in Vegas. You know that he has brought his friends to Vegas," reminisces says Giancana.

"I know Sam—" says Valerius as he is interrupted.

"I did that, getting Frank and his friends to the clubs—I did that. I haven't heard a thank you from any of *our friends* out of New York for that, but because I'm seen chasing a little tail they get mad," chuckles Giancana as he takes another drag from his cigar.

Valerius walks over to Giancana's bar. He pours himself a shot glass full of Giancana's previously unopened Remy Martin Cognac. The cognac starts down smooth but catches Valerius with a kick on the back end.

"Whoa, you never get used to that kick. Sam, I don't think anyone gives a damn about you chasing tail. I for one sure don't, but you are a suspected gangland boss, and you are being watched by the government. Don't bring any unnecessary heat down on the rest of us; I am pretty sure my father would agree with that," says a self-assured Valerius.

LEBENSBORN

During the rise of the Third Reich, it was Adolf Hitler's dream to create Aryan super soldiers. The dream was that these super soldiers would march blindly across the world into battle at the beck and call of their field commanders. Hitler believed that a soldier's will should be that of his commanders and not his own. But all good commanders know that a soldier's will may wane depending on the battle; they know not all soldiers have the fire in their bellies for war. The Nazis developed a program in which soldiers would be programmed to exclusively follow the command of their commanders; the program made some willing and others unwillingly into field zombies. The young men were trained in the latest hand-to-hand combat techniques. They were also trained to be world-class marksman and to withstand the fear of war. They were hypnotized into believing that they were the descendants of the mighty Norse Vikings; and were instructed through hypnosis that they must fight to the death. During his time with the Nazis, Albrecht Krause also oversaw the super-solider initiative as well as the Lebensborn program. The Lebensborn program was instituted to breed pure Aryan children with one goal of ultimate victory for the German Fatherland.

Even though Krause's loyalties have changed to the Americans, his personal goals of making the ultimate and obedient super solider continues.

The Romaine is the name of a sprawling property two miles north of the United States Naval Academy.

The property's namesake was the French-Jesuit Romaine LeBleouf. LeBleouf came to America to broaden the Jesuit message to the colonists in the 1700s. As a by-product of the Jesuit message, LeBleouf assisted in the underground railroad. The property's water access off of the Severn River and the short six-hour boat ride to the free state of Delaware made the property a major destination for escaping slaves. The Jesuits abandoned the property in the early 1920s to concentrate their message on the nearby metro centers of Baltimore and Washington, D.C. The United States Naval Academy decided to take over the property in 1925, originally as a retreat for its staff and visiting dignitaries. Upon inspection of the property, the Navy decided to scrap the idea. It decided to use the property to train elite regiments and experiment with new military tactics.

In 1948, the United States military created the Unconventional Warfare Capability Unit (UWCU). UWCU pulled enlisted men from the Army, Navy and the Marines. The purpose of the group is to form a covert group that could eliminate strategic targets without large military engagement. The UWCU group training at the Romaine became known as the Bay Boys because of the proximity to the Chesapeake Bay. Since the end of World War II, American generals knew that the American's one-time ally, Russia, would soon become an adversary. Because of the introduction of nuclear weapons, the United States and Russia knew that many of their new battles would be fought in the shadows of diplomacy. The days of conventional and strategic warfare were now over. Each side needed to make sure that no single event took the world to annihilation. The former Nazi scientist Albrecht Krause has continued his work on the super solider program with the assistance of the American military. Krause decided to incorporate the Americans' research on hypnosis into the program. The two-headed monster of the Nazis' super-solider program and the Americans' use of hypnosis is about to be brought to fruition. Krause has been secretly injecting twelve members of the elite Bay Boys with the super-solider serum over the past six months at the Romaine site. Krause watches as the Bay Boys perform amazing feats. The group performs overly accurate gun marksmanship from unbelievable distances and angles.

The Bay Boys are subjected to extreme physical tests; they are made to run a mile in two minutes, bench press 500 pounds 20 times and swim 10 miles.

After testing the groups' physical abilities, Krause tests the hypnosis aspect. The hypnosis was to take away the personal feelings of the solider.

During Krause's debriefing after his capture, he shared that the Nazis wanted to take away the humanity of their soldiers.

Krause said that the Nazis didn't want the conscience of its soldiers to affect any missions. Krause decides to put the program to the test by using two roommates: Henry Hulse and Raymond Stocklon. The men were inseparable during their time as Bay Boys. In a diabolical move, Krause tests the men's affections for each other by using hypnosis to see how far the men will go during a fight.

Hulse and Stocklon have unemotional scowls on their faces as they are led to a makeshift boxing ring in a basement tunnel in the Romaine. The damp and mold-filled air of the basement makes Krause feel at home; it brings back memories of his scientific conquests in Germany. The two burly young men are looking at each other with gazes of emptiness across the boxing ring. Both young men are dressed in Heather Gray T-shirts and shorts with the Army insignia on them. The two young men wait for a signal to begin battle, resembling the anticipation of a prize match. In the audience sits Senator Hampton Capers, Director Wesley Carter and Albrecht Krause. The young men are released to begin battle. Unlike a boxing match, the two men charge headfirst into each other. There is seemingly no strategy; the two men are blank slates bent on pure destruction. Minutes before the fight, the men were given instructions with hypnosis to fight until the other dies. Knowing that the American politicians could be a bit squeamish, Krause also placed a code word in the men's minds that would stop the men from killing each other. The men's savage instincts take over; they charge each other and are in a body clutch. Hulse has a hold of Stocklon's middle finger. Sensing a slight advantage, Hulse tugs on the finger until he dislocates it. Even though his finger is broken, Stocklon continues to fight on; his mangled finger does not stop Stocklon from biting a chunk of Hulse's ear. Blood trickles down from Hulse's ear, but he is completely unfazed as he battles on and gouges out the right eye of Stocklon. The blood spray shoots into the air, covering the two men and most of the makeshift ring.

"Enough!" shouts Senator Capers.

"Lebensborn," barks Albrecht Krause toward the two battling titans.

The code word releases the men from their hypnosis. Once the hypnosis wears off, the men fall to the floor in complete agony. Medical staff rush to the men to try to provide some type of relief.

Disgusted by the seeming fight to the death, Senator Capers walks briskly away from the gym. A concerned Director Carter follows after Capers.

"Senator, please wait," asks Carter.

"What the hell was that? We are training American soldiers to be barbarians—to literally tear the eyes out of their opponents. Just what are we doing?" questions a very concerned Senator Capers. "Your stomach a bit queasy, Senator?" laughs a mocking Krause. "How do you expect to have a powerful military if the people who lead them are afraid of the horror of war? Your military must be feared by the world. The Russians and the Chinese are building up their militaries. They wanted this program; I am pretty sure they are experimenting with others," affirms a cryptic Krause.

"He is a bit melodramatic, but he is correct. We must have the best soldiers, in the best shape, with the best state of mind for war. The other so-called superpowers are in an imperialistic mode. They want to destroy us. We must be the best; we must train the best," concedes Carter.

"So, we turn American boys into savage beasts? Those boys couldn't have been more than 21 years old. I'm pretty sure they joined the Army because they wanted to fight for their country against foreign aggressors, not to be test rats," states a frustrated Capers.

SIT DOWN

The citizens of Washington, D.C., have played host to many gatherings of world dignitaries, but today's meeting will be different than all held before. Unlike the meetings of the past, the Shaw section of the city will do the honors of hosting this event. The Shaw section of Washington, D.C., is a middle-class Negro area of the city made up of government workers and Negro business leaders. This area is home to the Negro landmarks of Howard University as well as the Lincoln and Howard theatres.

Teed is being driven through the streets of Washington, leaving the friendly and the somewhat comfortable confines of the area surrounding the U.S. Capitol. Teed had never seen this part of the capital city before; his few visits to the city never took him north of Constitution Avenue. Because of the confidentiality of the meeting, Teed is riding in a white milk truck in the event anybody is paying attention.

"You guys don't play when it comes to your anonymity," jokes Teed.

The driver looks at Teed in a condescending manner, prompting Teed to look out onto the streets of Shaw. As he rides, he notices young Negro children playing in the street on an early Indian summer day. Teed's driver pulls up to 1219 U Street in the northeast quadrant of

Washington, D.C., the same address where Senator Capers and Director Carter held their meeting with the 8Men.

A squeaky warehouse door raises, the milk truck proceeds through, and Teed begins to get an uneasy feeling in his stomach. He thinks to himself, *why would Senator Capers or Director Carter hold such an important meeting here?* The milk truck stops.

The driver says to Teed, "You wanna go up those steps. They will be waiting for you." Teed looks at the steps with a menacing stare.

"Up those stairs?" asks a concerned Teed.

The driver motions for him to walk up the stairs.

The 8Men are sitting around, awaiting Teed's arrival; the silence is deafening. Several are smoking cigars and drinking expensive scotch.

"What time did you tell him to be here?" demands a perturbed Senator Capers.

"I think he just arrived," comments Director Carter.

The click clack of Teed's shoes sounds through the long hall that leads to the 8Men's meeting room. He walks into the meeting room. He takes a deep breath as he scans the room of tight-faced men. Teed is overwhelmed by a feeling of hesitation. Each man sitting at the table is looking at him with contempt in their eyes, with the exception of Director Carter.

"He's a little young, Director," implies Murray Smith.

"We were all young at one time, Mr. Smith," rebuts Director Carter.

Director Carter walks over to shake Teed's hand.

"Gentlemen, this is Richard Teed," announces Director Carter as he motions him to a seat.

"Evening gentlemen," whispers Teed.

None of the 8Men greet Teed.

"Son, what are your credentials?" challenges Murray Smith.

"Well, I—" stammers Teed as he is interrupted.

"Gentlemen, we are not here to interrogate young Mr. Teed but to welcome him into our group. He will not have vast experience of the gentlemen sitting at this table. What he lacks in experience and influence, he more than makes up with his intelligence, his moxie and most importantly his loyalty," remarks Director Carter.

"I am supposed to trust my money to this neophyte?" arrogantly says Maximillian Love.

Senator Capers starts to laugh to himself.

"Senator," says a bewildered Director Carter.

"I am sorry, we are giving this young man a hard time about his lack of experience. As I look around the room, he is the only one that has truly put his ass on the line in battle for these United States. I know many of us have fought in war, but we signed up—we were trained…kind of knew what we were getting into. This young man went unwittingly into a battle halfway around the world and fought with amazing valor. He cannot even get the recognition for it," declares Senator Capers as he starts to think of his own son's death.

Director Carter notices that Senator Capers is getting emotional, and he decides to jump in.

"Gentlemen, Richard will be with us, so please, let's get to know him," says a stern Carter.

BELLOTTE'S

Italians come from all parts of Chicago to dine at the famous Bellotte's Italian Bistro. The restaurant sits in the Sicilian enclave known as Little Sicily on the city's north side. The sound of Italian music greets patrons at the front door with the restaurant's owner Christopher Bellotte. The restaurant has been in the Bellotte family for three generations. Christopher's grandfather, Grotto Bellotte, came to America in the late 1890s after the great mafia wars of southern Italy. The restaurant is best known for its pizza and calzones, with Bellotte's savory marinara sauce. Both the pizza and the calzones are baked to a crisp perfection: mozzarella cheese that could stretch for blocks baked in Bellotte's custom-made brick oven.

Valerius Torrantio has asked Sam Giancana to meet him at the beloved restaurant. Giancana beats Valerius to the restaurant; he is sitting in a booth with a bib on looking like a kid in a candy store. Giancana is eating a calzone stuffed with pepperoni, ham, bacon and sausage—a pig's nightmare. Sam is basking in the joy of Militiro, a sweet merlot from the Tuscan region of Italy. Valerius enters the restaurant dressed immaculately as always in a gray pinstriped suit. He is flanked by two large Italian men, also looking dapper. Giancana greets Valerius with a kiss on both cheeks.

"What brings you to Chicago? Let me guess, our friends are still mad about me chasing tail," mocks Sam as he sits.

Valerius chuckles as he unbuttons his suit coat, preparing to sit in the secluded booth.

"No Sam, I am not here about that. I am here about a very serious matter. Quite frankly, I need your help," pleads Valerius.

A twenty-something waitress obviously of Italian heritage comes to the table.

"May I get you something sir?" asks the waitress as she seductively winks at Valerius.

"I would like one of your calzones," answers Valerius.

"Is that all sir," replies the waitress.

"Yes, for now," answers Valerius as he scans the waitress from head to toe.

Giancana, Valerius and the waitress all share a quick laugh. After the waitress leaves the area, the playful Valerius turns deadly serious.

"I need your help as a go-between and some of your political power here in Chicago," requests Valerius.

"Whatever you need Valley. No one normally asks me to be a go-between. I normally am the one to be calmed down. This must be big," proclaims Giancana.

"In 1960, Jack Kennedy is going to run for president," comments Valerius.

Giancana has a look of bewilderment on his face.

"Who the hell is Jack Kennedy?" questions Giancana.

"Do you read the paper?" asks Valerius.

"Sure, the funny papers. Everything else is only good for wrapping fish," laughs Giancana.

"Well, he is the son of one of our friends," implies Valerius.

Giancana's face tells the tale; he has no clue who Valerius is talking about.

"The only Kennedy that I know is Joe Kennedy, and his oldest boy died in the war," responds Giancana as he looks into Valerius' face for answers.

"It is one in the same. His oldest boy did die in the war, but his second boy is Jack. He is a senator from Massachusetts," explains Valerius.

Giancana cuts a large slice of pizza and dips it into a cup of marinara sauce.

"Have you talked to Frank Costello? You know Frank has a contract out on that jerk off," remarks Giancana.

"I do; that's why I want you to broker a deal," states Valerius.

"Why don't you just tell Frank to do it?" inquires Giancana.

Valerius looks at Giancana with a look of distrust. He knows that the old timers are not kosher with him wielding so much power at such a young age. All the American bosses have the utmost respect for Valerius' father, Don Giuseppe Torrantio—the true boss of bosses. Don Giuseppe brokered the peace with upper-level American mafia, and he helped many establish their invaluable political connections.

"I was hoping that you could lean on your friendship with Frank. Remind him of the old days," Valerius somewhat begs. "Anything for you Valley. Consider it done," says Giancana.

Valerius smiles with delight but knows that this will cost him at some point.

THE GREAT DEBATE

The 1960 presidential campaign pit Vice President Richard Milhous Nixon against Massachusetts junior senator John Fitzgerald Kennedy. Both men are relatively young, considering their contemporaries. The candidates have participated in two groundbreaking debates with no apparent winner. The democrats have said that Kennedy seems to be the more collegiate of the two men and the republicans say that Nixon appears to be the more presidential of the two. The republicans also point to Nixon's current experience as vice president in these trying times, with the communists advancing daily as a major plus for their candidate.

Valerius Torrantio and Cecil Thomas are having drinks at the plush Waldorf Astoria in Midtown Manhattan. There is a small crowd watching the end of the third presidential debate between Kennedy and Nixon. The country is literally torn down the middle in support of both men.

"The election is looking pretty tight. Has anyone reached out to Nixon?" asks Thomas.

Valerius chuckles. "No faith Cecil, we are backing Kennedy. We are backing him all the way through to the end. Plus, I don't think there is anyone that is a friend that could get close to Nixon," says a convincing Valerius.

I just feel like we are betting all our money on one person," comments a doubtful Thomas.

"We are Cecil. We just have to ensure that he wins. Kennedy is going to win; we just have to get him the help he needs," remarks Valerius.

There is a commotion at the front of the bar. Valerius and Cecil are so enthralled in their own conversation that they never even notice. It is Joe Kennedy, father of Senator Kennedy. Joe Kennedy looks flustered as he approaches Valerius' table. Joe Kennedy has a newspaper in his hand. He tosses the paper onto the table.

"Polls are saying that the campaign is a virtual tie. I thought you people were going to help," pleads an incensed Joe Kennedy.

Valerius gives Joe Kennedy a murderous look, bringing Mr. Kennedy back to reality. Joe Kennedy has a volatile temper, but he knows in whose company he is in.

"Mr. Torrantio, I know you and your friends are working diligently to get my son elected, but it appears he is still coming up short," declares an apologetic Joe Kennedy.

Valerius looks around the room to see if anybody notices them talking. He relaxes his deathly stare in Joe Kennedy's direction. "Mr. Kennedy, we told you we would back your son out of the longstanding relationship our organization has with you. Your son must make things close," asserts Valerius.

"We are very close. If my numbers are correct, Illinois and Louisiana are the states that we need. I was hoping that you could get Sam and Marcello to do something," stammers Joe Kennedy as he looks through a pile of paper.

A demonically smiling Valerius comments back. "As you know, Sam is already on board, but Marcello will be a bit harder to enlist. He, more than the rest of us, lost a lot in the Cuban Revolution. And frankly, he doesn't trust your boys. I told him about your boys; these hearings are just a show…they must be playing possum or something. I know that your boys aren't stupid enough to fuck with our friends. Cause you have taught them what would happen if they fucked with our friends. Marcello wants some assurances that if your son becomes President, he will strike back at Cuba."

The Cuban revolution occurred a short ten months ago on New Year's Eve. Prior to the revolution, the mafia was king in Cuba. The mafia ran an assortment of businesses: gambling, prostitution, and other seedy ventures. All these ventures brought in millions of dollars every week. Most in La Cosa Nostra were feeling the financial loss. They all wanted payback, and John Kennedy would be the man to give it to them. Joe Kennedy was looking at Valerius hoping that he would notice a glimmer of sarcasm in his face.

Unfortunately, Joe Kennedy knew Valerius would ask for an impossible request. Joe knew his son had his own mind and any request made today, his son wouldn't feel beholden to, but what choice did he have?

"Mr. Torrantio, I will do whatever I can do to get these things done," says a somber Joe Kennedy.

Valerius chuckles as he listens intently to Joe Kennedy. "Understand Mr. Kennedy, whatever deal we make you and your son will be beholden to, so I would suggest that you speak with him and make it abundantly clear. We expect a return on our investment. Your *son* is our investment; we expect a return," proclaims Valerius.

Joe Kennedy nods his head, agreeing with Valerius. Joe Kennedy knows he needs the mob's help, but he knows this agreement will be nothing less than a deal with the devil.

WATERING HOLE

The country's political landscape was changing by the day during the presidential Campaign of 1960. The 8Men were backing Kennedy and they were going to pull out all the stops to ensure his victory. The polling data shows a virtual tie. The polls show 25 states leaning toward Kennedy and 25 states leaning toward Nixon. The 8Men do not want to take any chances; they turn to Valerius to see if his cronies can influence some voting precincts. The polling data shows very close races in the syndicate strongholds of Illinois and Louisiana. Valerius figures that if his mob ties can influence some votes in and around Chicago and New Orleans it could get Kennedy the win.

Unlike many cities in the Northeast, Washington, D.C., does not have a distinct area for Italians. The closest thing they have is Swampoodle. Swampoodle is the area surrounding the beautiful St. Aloysius Roman Catholic Church in Northwest Washington, D.C. The gathering area for Italians in the area is the Watering Hole. The Watering Hole is a restaurant with many Sicilian specialties, but because many patronized the restaurant purely for the drinks, it was thought of as only a bar. When he is in town Valerius, tries to make sure to get by to get his favorite stuffed pie. Valerius is sitting in a booth eating his large stuffed pie. Across the restaurant, Valerius sees Carlos Marcello entering the restaurant. Marcello notices Valerius and walks over to him. Valerius rises out the booth to hug Marcello.

"Don Torrantio, how did you find this place?" asks Marcello.

"I love to find food from Sicily. Not too many places in Washington. Can I get you something?" solicits Valerius.

"Glass of wine, I guess," replies Marcello.

Valerius motions to one of the waiters to bring a bottle of wine.

"So, you wanted to talk?" inquires Marcello.

"Yes, I wanted to ask you for your help," hints Valerius.

"Sure, whatever I can do, Don Torrantio," remarks Marcello.

"I am a part of a group that wants to influence the presidential election. And we want your help in Louisiana and Texas if you can help," states Valerius.

"I will do all I can do to help Nixon," asserts Marcello.

Carlos Marcello is a major point of interest in the government's investigation into mob activities in the United States. The investigation is being led by Bobby Kennedy. Marcello has privately threatened to kill Kennedy if the investigation continues to center around him. Valerius knows that he is going to have to do a good job of convincing him it is in all their interests to get Kennedy elected.

"Carlos, we need your help to get Kennedy elected," whispers Valerius.

Marcello is drinking a glass of wine. He chokes.

"Are you joking? You have to be joking," implies a pissed off Marcello.

"It is no joke. We want to get him elected," utters Valerius.

"What the hell? That son of a bitch, Bobby Kennedy, rakes me over the coals and you and your group want to make his big brother president?" says Marcello.

Valerius is looking for the words to confront Marcello about the 8Men's decision.

"If his brother becomes the president, he will have even more power. The son of a bitch already has a hard on for me; they will string me up if he is elected," says Marcello as he gulps a large amount of wine.

Valerius pours Marcello some wine into his empty glass.

"Look, I understand your apprehensions, but his father is a friend of ours. We want him to help us get a foothold in the legitimate world. He will help clean up our money and get respect our people deserve. Italians will be able to be captains of industry, not relegated to profiting off the rackets," states an impassionate Valerius.

"Don Torrantino with all due respect, I know the stories of what Joe Kennedy did, but his sons are legitimate. They both frequent the girls but bribes or anything illegal they just don't do. And the father has no control over the boys," begs Marcello.

"Joe Kennedy knows that if we do him this favor, he and his family are in debt to us. And he knows the consequences if our requests aren't made. So, don't worry about it," declares Valerius.

"I hope you know what you are doing," says Marcello.

"Can I count on your help, Don Marcello?" respectfully asks Valerius.

"Of course, you can count on me, Don Torrantio. What do you want me to do," asks Marcello.

"Well, I want you to help us with fixing elections in Louisiana. Kennedy is going to be weak there. He will need our help to win the election," admits Valerius.

"Done... One thing, are you sure you can trust them? I know their father is a friend, but they are not from our world," says an uneasy Marcello.

"Their father made certain assurances. He knows what will happen if they don't live up to this," concedes Valerius with an air of finality.

MAIN STREET

The tiny town of Vienna, Louisiana, is a typical small town in southeast Louisiana. Vienna is a short 40 miles away from the hustle and bustle of New Orleans. But liberalism and the inclusive nature of New Orleans does not travel the short 40 miles. The town is very conservative; it is not an area to be trifled in. The people are God fearing and believe that you stay to your own—White people stay to White people and Negroes stay with Negroes.

A dark model four-door Chevrolet rides down a somewhat dusty Main Street near the Vienna town square. The car pulls up to the town's City Hall. The town's mayors come and go, but the true power rests with Harvey "Bubba" Timmons. He is a third-generation powerbroker of the town and its surrounding area. His family have been grain farmers at the core, but the mass amount of land that his family has amassed makes them major players in local politics. They control the grain flow to farmers, and since they are the major landowners, they set policy. Bubba is the local son of a bitch. He doesn't care what anybody thinks of him, and he never gave two shits about anybody else. If you don't agree with him, that is your fault. He would rather that you don't agree with him so that he can roll over you, showing you that he is the boss. Bubba serves as Clay County commissioner. Clay County is named for Bubba's maternal great grandfather, Thomas Clay. Unlike the position of mayor, the county commissioner is an appointed position that insulates Bubba against electoral challenges.

The dark Chevrolet pulls up in front of the county hall, and out steps Richard Teed. He takes in the feel of small-town America. Teed proceeds up the gray marble steps of the county hall. He walks through to the office labelled the Office of the County Commissioner and is greeted by a 40-something, slightly chubby woman smoking a cigarette.

"Can I help you?" asks the woman in a raspy voice.

Figuring that the secretary is the gatekeeper to see Bubba, Teed knows it is imperative to charm the lady.

"Excuse me ma'am, my name is Richard Teed. I am here to speak with Mr. Harvey Timmons about the upcoming election," says an extremely polite Teed.

"Let me check," snaps the secretary.

The secretary waddles over to Bubba's office door. She opens the door and says, "There is a Mr. Teed here. He wants to talk to you about the upcoming election." The secretary turns her attention back toward Teed.

"He will see you now. Mr. Timmons is eating lunch but make your presentation and he will get back to you," says the secretary. Teed walks into Bubba's office and is disgusted by the amount of food on Bubba's desk. There is a full fried chicken, a basket of fried potatoes, a loaf of corn bread and a six pack of Pepsi Cola. Bubba does not have a piece of fruit or a vegetable on the table. He has a napkin tucked in his t-shirt, catching some of the residual food as it drops from his mouth.

"Son, where is your machine?" inquires Bubba as he spits a piece of chicken out of the side of his mouth.

Teed has a look of confusion. "Machine sir?" he asks.

"Yeah, aren't you here to sell your voting machines?" questions Bubba.

"No sir, I am a representative for Mr. Carlos Marcello," remarks Teed timidly.

"Marcello?" challenges Bubba.

"Yes Sir, he is a businessman out of New Orleans," replies Teed. Bubba rudely starts to laugh.

"Businessman; he is no damn businessman. He heads the mob in New Orleans. What business does he have here in Vienna?" suspiciously asks Bubba.

Teed looks for the words to describe the reason for his visit. He settles on the direct approach "Mr. Marcello would like to ensure that one of the presidential candidates wins here in your county."

Mr. Marcello would like to compensate you for your troubles," divulges Teed.

The fury builds up on Bubba's face as he rises from his seat.

"Let me tell you something, you little bastard. We don't throw elections around here. I take my constitutional obligation seriously. If I wasn't in the middle of lunch, I would have you arrested. You take a message back to your friend or boss or whatever the hell he is to you. Don't ever come back to Vienna again. We don't like his kind around these parts," proclaims Bubba.

Bubba looks deep into Teed's eyes.

"And let me tell you *boy*, if I ever see *you* in this town again, you won't make it out of the county. You understand me boy?" asks Bubba.

"You have made it clear sir," affirms a defeated Teed.

Teed descends the steps of the county hall with a defiant Bubba looking on, draped by his soiled lunch napkin. Teed takes one last look at the city of Vienna.

"Go on get boy," yells Bubba from atop the county hall steps.

Teed affirms Bubba's request with a nod. He opens the door to the black Chevrolet that is waiting for him, sits down and looks out of the window.

"I guess we will do it your way now," admits Teed to a shadowy figure.

"You tried your best. Timmons is a hard-ass redneck. We just need to soften him up a bit. Every man has his weakness; his just needs to be found," says Carlos Marcello as he leans into the light.

"He will fall into line. Let's get back to the quarter, I'm in the mood for some shrimp gumbo," states Marcello with a smile on his face as the Black Chevrolet speeds off.

CREOLE

The night of October 25, 1960, began like any other evening in southeastern Louisiana. The temperature was a balmy 80 degrees at 8 pm. The town of Vienna, if you want to call it a town, is very small; it was not even represented on most state maps. The official population of the town at the time was 316 people, but every night the population grew by an additional 50 to 75 patrons. The town was known for its main street full of brothels. The police in the area have always looked the other way with the appropriate bribes.

Distinguished gentlemen come from miles around to partake weekly, if not daily, in the town's bounty of voluptuous ladies. Bubba Timmons is a frequent visitor to the town of Vienna's lewd district. Bubba's obese stature does not make him a desired sexual object to most women, so the purchase of sexual relations is not farfetched. Bubba has a liking for Negro Creole women, not to be mistaken with the normal Negro woman. He liked his Creole women with a little bit of cafe au lait; not too much, but enough to get a tan.

Khandi LeBlanc is the object of Bubba's desires. Bubba has been a regular customer of Khandi's for five years. She treats him like he is a sexual god while talking about him behind his back. It is well known by all the girls in the district that Bubba's male prowess is more childlike than the big man persona he projects. In his mind, Bubba is hung like a racehorse, Khandi knows that he must believe this so he will keep coming back to spend more money.

The 1960 presidential election is a little under two weeks away. Bubba knows the next two weeks will be hellish to say the least. Bubba doesn't want Clay County to get any negative press for any botched election results. He knows he won't be able to see Khandi until he certifies the election results. He will need to be on his A-game just in case there is some hanky panky in the results. It is well known that his district can swing the entire national election.

The curvaceous Khandi enters the bedroom of Bubba's usual room at the aptly named Love Shack room 144. Khandi is wearing a white lacey bra and panties set with matching garter belts. Both panties and bra seem to be a bit too short on material, as her shapely body parts spill from the sides. As appetizing as Khandi looks, Bubba looks equally disgusting. He is dressed in a dis-colored A tee-shirt, a faded pair of khakis and some dusty work boots. Khandi always begins their sessions with a seductive dance, caressing then showing her butt and breasts to the undersexed Bubba. By the end of the dance, he has already begun to stroke himself. It always disgusts Khandi, but Bubba is the customer, he drops a small fortune on her, so she pretty much allows him to do anything. Khandi brings Bubba a drink; it is Bubba's usual moonshine in a 12-ounce mason jar—so he thinks. Bubba usually likes a taste of hooch before his trysts with Khandi; he feels like it intensifies the pleasure. On this evening, Bubba will have wished that his thirst for hooch went on unquenched.

Several hours later, Bubba awakens to a horrific scene. Khandi has been stabbed, with her neck cut so deeply she is nearly decapitated. The bed is saturated with her blood. Bubba looks around the room. He is terrified to see the spray of blood on the walls. Several men in dark suits are walking around the room; they all seem oblivious to the severity of the situation. Bubba lifts his hands; both have blood on them.

"Oh, my God," says a mortified Bubba.

"Mr. Timmons, you are in quite a predicament," hints Carlos Marcello. Bubba tries to focus his eyes on the blurry-figured Marcello.

"Who the hell are you?" demands Bubba.

"Who I am is entirely up to you. I can be a friend or a foe. I am hoping to be a friend," states Marcello.

"What happened? Who did this?" questions a confused Bubba.

Carlos looks at all the blood on the walls, bed and on Bubba.

"Mr. Timmons, you are the only person who has been here. Some acquaintances of mine were in the area. They heard about a murder in one of the rooms. I told them to extend you our help," claims Carlos.

"How the hell do I know you didn't set this up. I didn't do this. I don't remember anything…maybe you drugged me then killed Khandi," responds a combative Bubba.

Bubba looks at Khandi's carved up body and starts to tear up. He starts to talk to her disfigured corpse.

"Khandi, what happened? I couldn't have done this to you," weeps a remorseful Bubba.

"Mr. Timmons, I will show myself out." Carlos looks around the room. "I see you have everything under control. Hey fellas, let's go, Mr. Timmons will clean up. He will speak to the police and explain the blood everywhere and somehow stay out of jail for killing this beautiful Negro woman. I'm sure the New Orleans press will love a juicy story like this. You know Whites stay with Whites and Niggers stay with Niggers here. They will really love it so close to the election," announces a somewhat smiling Carlos.

"You fucking guineas!" exclaims a mad Bubba.

Carlos grins. "Mr. Timmons, is that any way to speak to your new partners?"

Bubba finally realizes that Carlos has the only possible solution for him.

"What the hell do you want?" asks a defeated Bubba.

Carlos grabs a chair and saddles up in front of Bubba. He pulls out a large cigar. He cuts it evenly with his platinum-plated cigar cutter and lights it, making sure the cigar burns consistently.

"Mr. Timmons, some friends and I understand that you are the certifying election official for Clay and Orleans parishes," says Carlos as a somber Bubba nods his head.

"We got an election to fix," declares a smiling Carlos.

INAUGURATION

The frigid air of the winter morning has brought the most powerful city in the world to a snarl. It is inauguration day 1961; the president-elect John Fitzgerald Kennedy will take office in twenty short minutes. The day's events are in doubt, a short twenty-four hours prior an unexpected snowstorm blanketed the Washington metropolitan area. Several army battalions from Ft. Belvoir and the D.C. National Guard were called in to shovel out the Capitol and several streets leading to the White House.

The 8Men convened a victory party of sorts at Jake's Bistro, three blocks away from the Capitol. Richard Teed enters the restaurant, stomping his feet, trying to get all the snow out off the bottom of his boots. Valerius Torrantio notices Teed as he walks into the restaurant and waves him over. Teed walks to the table where the other 8Men are sitting, except for Senator Hampton Capers and CIA director Wesley Carter. Both gentlemen are attending the inauguration. Currently, Vice President-elect Lyndon Baines Johnson is taking the oath of office. The entire restaurant is watching the festivities on a 20-inch television; the camera pans the crowd and finds a dignified Senator Capers dressed in a navy-blue camelhair topcoat bundled with several scarves.

"Look at that lucky son of bitch," proudly says an elated Valerius.

Teed looks at the television.

"I don't know about lucky; he looks cold," suggests a sarcastic Teed.

The crowd at the inauguration claps as Vice President Johnson kisses his wife as he completes the oath of office.

"This is a historic day. Kennedy is going to set so many things right," hopes Valerius.

Teed thinks to himself, *Wow, these people feel like they won the jackpot.* Valerius motions for the waiter to come to the table.

"I can't believe we won," admits Valerius.

"What did we win?" asks Teed.

Valerius affectionately hugs Teed.

"You really are from the sticks. Look, our man is president; we helped him get there. So, he owes us," alleges Valerius.

Teed shrugs his shoulders in agreement with Valerius.

"I'll be back. I think I've had too much wine," claims Valerius as he walks toward the bathroom.

Cecil Thomas is sitting at one of the tables close by smoking a cigarette. He is staring at Teed intently; Teed feels like he is looking through him. Thomas nods his head, motioning Teed to come over to the table. Cecil Thomas has a no-nonsense personality. Teed walks over to the table with the caution of a schoolboy walking to the principal's office after hitting someone with a spitball.

"I have noticed that everyone has been treating you with kid gloves. They all want to explain their world views and their philosophies; they want you to understand their perspectives. Son, you don't need to understand anything about me. You need to be up to speed on what we want to do and make sure that you make it happen," says a stern Thomas.

Cecil Thomas' reputation has certainly proceeded him; he is truly a no-bullshit person. He wants results; he never wants to hear excuses.

"Valerius was right to tell you that Kennedy owes us because he does. We have bribed too many people; we have moved heaven and earth to make sure Kennedy wins. If I had my way, I would have preferred Nixon. He would have given us all the wars we could have stood. As long as he thought the reds were involved; but he is a bit too wacky, he would have been hard to control. Since Kennedy's father has been a player in the underworld, we are hoping that he knows how to return a favor," says Thomas as he takes a deep pull of his cigarette.

"What favor do you want from him?" asks Teed.

Cecil Thomas scans the room to make sure no one was eavesdropping on their conversations.

"We simply want Kennedy to keep the status quo. We will soon be at war. We don't need him to get a conscience," says Cecil Thomas.

"You want to go to war, but why? asks Teed.

Cecil Thomas laughs at Teed's question.

"Son, war is a money maker. Industrialized countries make money from conflict. When this country went into war in World War II we were pretty much still in a depression. Once this country's war effort got ramped up, we became an unstoppable force. Look at us now, we are the richest and most prosperous country in human history. But we have been slipping, we have fallen into an era of peace," proclaims Cecil Thomas.

"Isn't that a good thing?" questions Teed.

"Someone is always plotting war. Is it you? Or are you being plotted on? And most importantly are you making any money? Can't forget that," concedes Thomas.

Teed is trying to process everything Cecil Thomas has told him. He is starting to understand the 8Men want to profit without worrying about the consequences.

"You ever been to Boston?" asks Thomas.

"No," responds Teed.

Thomas goes into his suit pocket, where he pulls out an airline ticket. He slides it across the table to Teed.

"I will see you tomorrow in Boston," Thomas tells Teed as he gets up to leave.

THE PATRIOT

Cecil Thomas typifies the American spirit. Born to a working-class family in Greenburgh, New York, Cecil has always been the short little runt with a chip on his shoulder. A debilitating childhood disease left a young Cecil without the full use of his left eye. Early on, the affliction rendered Cecil nearly blind. The limited blindness made a determined Cecil depend on his other senses. He was determined not to be anyone's cripple. Cecil regained the use of his left eye shortly before entering high school. After graduating from nearby Iona College, a 21 year-old Cecil enlisted in the Navy hoping to become an air pilot. Cecil was at the top of the Navy's inaugural airman training until it was discovered that he had suffered from blindness as a youth. Knowing that the Navy would need all its fighter pilots and, quite frankly, the best in the training program, Cecil's paperwork mysteriously rid itself of the blind distinction. He was a part of America's first air battle at the Axis powers' stronghold of St. Mihiel, France. It was important that the Allies disrupt the German grip of the coastline to gain entrance to the mainland of Europe. He was credited with 35 air kills, quickly making him one of America's best pilots. After World War II, Cecil turned down many offers from the Department of War to spearhead their air division of the Navy. He decided to become a vice president at Steadman Technologies. At Steadman, Cecil oversaw all plane technologies.

He even flew as the company's test pilot of its new planes, to the chagrin of the boss' daughter, his wife Denise.

It was always thought that Denise was the great influence on Cecil deciding to forgo extended military service for the lucrative opportunity of private industry. Cecil Thomas greets Teed outside Steadman's air hanger on the campus of Logan Airport in Boston, Massachusetts. Steadman's air hanger is a part of the cluster of hangers assigned to the Army Air Corps. Teed is awestruck; he notices miles of war weaponry. He sees tanks, guns large and small, and notices several fighter airplanes.

"Are we fighting a new war I don't know about?" inquires Teed.

Cecil Thomas, not known for his sense of humor, begins to laugh at Teed's assumption.

"No son, the country is not getting ready for war. America has to stay ready. War can happen overnight. We don't want to be caught off guard, like World War II," admits Thomas.

Teed looks confused about Thomas' answer. He wonders why the massive amount of war stockpiles with no war or potential conflict in sight.

"Why so much if we aren't going to war?" challenges Teed.

"I—or maybe I should say the group—wants you to sell these weapons to some Palestinian and Jewish fighting groups. They seem to be having problems with one another. And we imagine that at some point war will break out," Thomas mentions with a nonchalant attitude.

Teed looks at the long line of storage grates, trying to find an answer within the slats to respond to Thomas.

"Why would you want to cause war between them? They both are a depressed people; neither has anything," asks Teed.

Cecil Thomas takes a long intense stare at Teed. He shakes his head in disbelief. He can't believe what he is hearing.

"You know, the gentlemen in the group said you were a boy scout. I didn't believe them. Your experience in Korea, hell your time with the Mossad. I just knew that you were a hardened operative. But you really aren't," declares a somewhat confused Thomas.

"Sir, I believe that if war is necessary then we must fight the good fight, but to instigate a conflict…" baffles Teed.

"Son, don't overestimate your importance. Understand, these people have been fighting for over 5,000 years. Have you ever heard the story of Isaac and Ishmael? Long story short, these two brothers are the founders of the Jewish and the Muslim religions. Issac, the father of the Jews and Ishmael, the father of the Muslims. Both factions fight over the same homeland calling it their own. Both are actually right, they are cousins for God's sake, the land is theirs collectively," comments Cecil Thomas.

Teed has a look of confusion on his face. Cecil Thomas is not known as a religious scholar.

"So, you have relegated the Mideast crisis to a family feud?" asks Teed.

"Pretty much, but moreover to let you know these people are going to fight either way. Hell, I bet that most of the present-day fighters have no idea of the genesis of it all. The Good Lord Jesus Christ wouldn't be able to stop them from fighting. They don't like each other, so they are going to fight either way," remarks Thomas.

"What is our interest in that, sir," asks Teed.

"Money son. What other interest do you need? Muslim money, Jewish money—it all spends," replies Thomas as he laughs.

ALL

The Arab Liberation League (ALL) was born out of the frustration of the Palestinian people in and around the infant Israeli territory. The Palestinian people have felt the Israeli people have become occupiers in the land they have all shared for centuries. The league is the brainchild of Wafai Abdullah Rashad. Wafai is the eighth child of Khalid Rashad. The Rashad family are the first cousins to the royal family of Saudi Arabia. The family has made its fortune in the exploration of oil deposits in Saudi Arabia and neighboring Kuwait.

Wafai was educated at Yale University in the late 1940s and assimilated well into American college life. He was equally smart as he was mischievous. When Wafai was good, he was great; he earned a perfect 4.0 grade point average throughout his tenure at Yale. But his dark side craved the destructive vices of drugs and illicit sex. It was rumored that Wafai would study for upwards of eight hours, then use a little-known drug called heroin, then participate in day-long sex parties. After hearing about the rumors of his son's behavior, Khalid took Wafai on a pilgrimage to Mecca. The pilgrimage to Mecca was meant to bring focus to Wafai's life. It brought focus, but not the well-centered peace for his fellow man that his father intended. Wafai met with several clerics while in Mecca but was most influenced by the Islamic Brotherhood.

The Brotherhood is a militaristic and radical Muslim organization; their intent is to rid the Palestinian land of all traces of Christian and Jewish dogmas. No longer did Wafai believe that diplomacy was the only option to bring peace to the promised land. He now thought the Palestinian people must come to the table with the notion that there could be complete destruction if their demands are not met. After his time in America, Wafai knew that the West enjoyed its individualism and capitalism so much that the threat to it would rock the founding principles of those countries. He needed to introduce fear in the Jewish occupiers and their western cronies.

Teed walks down an unassuming street in Damascus, Syria. He enters the epic Umayyad Mosque. The mosque is a landmark for both the Christian and Islamic faiths. The vestibule of the mosque is filled with ancient relics. Teed looks at the relics in awe; many of the relics are artifacts that he remembered from his high school history and religion books. The first relic he sees is described as the original Torah. These seem to be a dime a dozen in the Middle East; Teed recalled seeing another original Torah in a Jewish museum in Jerusalem described the same way. The relic that really catches his eye is a large, tarnished silver plate.

"No fucking way," states an awestruck Teed.

"Yes way. Mr. Teed, I presume," says Wafai Rashad.

Rashad is immaculately dressed in a three-piece white linen suit with a crimson tie and pocket square. Teed nods in the affirmative. The card underneath the plate says, "The Silver Plate of Yahya," also known as John the Baptist.

"This is the silver plate on which Yahya's head was placed on after his decapitation," affirms Rashad.

Teed has an uneasy scowl on his face.

"I understand you have never heard the name Yahya before. Yahya was his Arabic name. You know him only as John the Baptist. He was also a prophet of Allah as well." The new information puzzles Teed. Teed wonders how John the Baptist, one of the preeminent figures in the Christian bible, could also be a prophet for the Islamic religion.

"Propaganda has highjacked our religions and our prophets. History has been changed to pit one religion against one another. Alas, the damage has been done," remarks a regretful Rashad.

Changing his focus, he pulls a pack of cigarettes from his suit jacket. It is the last of his bad habits brought back from America.

"So, your organization will deliver the weapons to our base of operations?" asks Rashad.

"Of course, we have an assortment of guns, explosives, pretty much whatever you need. If you need some tanks and fighter planes, we can get those for you as well," jokes Teed.

Wafai gives Teed a half-hearted smile.

"No Mr. Teed, we won't need the tanks and fighter planes, but we would surely take the guns and explosives. But please keep the tanks and planes on standby," utters Wafai.

Teed asks, "Why do you want war with the Jews? Can't you all work out your differences diplomatically?"

"Mr. Teed, my organization wants to level the playing field. The Palestinian people have inhabited the area now known as Israel for centuries. Right or wrong, the Jews left the area and spread throughout Europe and Asia. After World War II, your government and the British felt the Jewish people deserved a homeland. In theory, I agree with this notion, but why the land they left hundreds of years ago?" ponders Wafai. The information is bombarding Teed at light speed. The reinstatement of the Israeli territory in effect will probably resume the Holy Crusades. Teed has a terrible feeling that he may be providing the catalyst for the beginning of a new conflict between the Palestinian and Jewish people.

AFTERNOON STROLL

Walking on the streets of Damascus, Teed smells the sweet smell of a day long since passed. He feels the ice-cold barrel of a 474 Beretta in his back. A slender woman dressed in a tight black pants suit accented by Christian Dior sunglasses stands behind him.

"Hello Mr. Teed. Exactly why are you in Damascus?" asks the sultry voice.

Teed smiles; he recognizes the voice.

"I am here enjoying the pleasures of the Middle East. I am on a pilgrimage to rediscover my connection to my Christian roots. I am visiting biblical sites," claims a coy Teed.

"Bullshit," softly whispers the slender woman in his ear.

"May I turn around," asks a playfully cautious Teed.

As he turns around, Teed sees the angelic silhouette of Danya Franck. The four years since their last encounter had been very kind to her; the only hint of aging were several streaks of gray hair in Danya's stylish mane.

"Hello, Teed," says Danya in a seductive tone.

The feeling Teed once felt came rushing back. He remembers the passion of their love making in Argentina, but he knows that Danya's visit is not a social call. He knows if she pops up with a gun then there is surely something that she needs to talk about. Danya looks at Teed with a sexual twinkle in her eye.

"Teed, you are looking quite well," comments Danya.

He chuckles, lightly infuriating Danya.

"Danya, you know you look good; you know I think you look good. But this is not why you are here. You didn't follow me to this dirty alley to show me how well you look. You could've just called," says Teed. Danya looks around to make sure no one is watching.

"You are in danger. I couldn't sit by and allow you to be harmed," says a concerned Danya.

"What are you talking about? I am here on vacation," rebuts Teed. "*Don't lie to me.* I know you are here to sell weapons to Wafai Rashad. The plane carrying those weapons will be destroyed. We can't allow those weapons to hit the street," admits Danya.

She walks toward Teed and caresses his face.

"I couldn't allow them to kill you in the process," utters Danya.

She leans in and kisses Teed, but he pulls away.

"You're lying; you want information," says Teed.

Danya is fed up with trying to get through to Teed. She motions to a car down the street. The car swiftly backs down the alley to pick up Danya.

"Since you won't believe my words, maybe you will believe your eyes. Get in," demands Danya.

An apprehensive Teed gets in the car. Minutes later, he is riding in silence with Danya.

"Stop here," she demands of the driver. They stop on a dusty road overlooking the countryside.

"Why are you stopping?" questions Teed.

"Shhh." Danya puts her right index finger on Teed's lips.

"Please be quiet love. You might miss the show," whispers Danya to him.

In the distance, a large plane resembling the plane that brought Teed to the Middle East takes off from an obscure runway. The plane elevates to about 300 miles from the surface, barely able to be seen by the naked eye—when a large explosion occurs. The explosion splinters the plane into thousands of pieces. Instantly, Teed thinks of the explosions of fireworks at the Fourth of July celebration in Charleston, but he knows the ramifications of this explosion are far greater.

"*Did you do this?*" exclaims Teed.

Danya is momentarily stunned.

"We did do this. And we will do this again if we feel like the security of Israel is at stake," confirms Danya.

"Why didn't you just blow up the plane on the tarmac? Why kill innocent people?" says an exasperated Teed.

"There are no innocent people in this battle. There were more than six million innocent people that died in the concentration camps. We will not allow anyone to even think that we will be soft on terrorism," states Danya with a stone face.

OUR INVESTMENT

In 1963, the Kennedy administration was a little over two years in office, but many of its biggest champions had become dangerous detractors. Kennedy had many political victories, like the creation of the Peace Corps, the proposed Civil Rights Act, and the standoff with Russia over missiles placed in Cuba. But the administration's blunders ruffled the feathers of many across American business and politics. Many American presidents made mistakes, but the mistakes of the Kennedy administration stepped on the toes of some the same people who advocated for his presidency. The stakes were high; many invested large amounts of money and political capital into President Kennedy. As Valerius Torrantio said to Joe Kennedy, "Your son is our investment; we want a return."

The Mayflower Hotel was always the premier destination for movers and shakers in Washington, D.C. Many people went to the hotel to see what dignitaries were dining in town that day. On this day, the known dignitaries are at a minimum, but the importance of the meetings going on are of optimal significance. Valerius and Cecil Thomas are sitting in a secluded cove of the bar trying to stay away from pesky onlookers. The waiter pours Valerius a glass of merlot before he walks away.

"How do you drink that shit?" asks Cecil with a disgusted look on his face.

"Get some class and enjoy a drink," jokes Valerius.

"So, what do we do with Kennedy? He and his sons have really screwed us. The war, your people's prosecution, not mention just fucking lying to us. The son of a bitch needs to be dealt with!" exclaims Cecil.

Valerius continues to drink his glass of merlot.

"I am pretty sure there has really been a misunderstanding. Mr. Kennedy knows that my organization will hold him and his sons accountable. He is not stupid; he was always an arrogant asshole but not stupid," asserts a confident Valerius.

There is a growing applause in the distance. Ambassador Kennedy enters the restaurant to a seemingly hero's welcome from the restaurant's patrons. The ambassador has reveled in adoration people have given him since his son's ascension to the presidency. Both Cecil and Valerius are taken aback. They can't believe how people are reacting to the ambassador. The ambassador jaunts over to the table where Cecil and Valerius are sitting. The gentlemen shake hands.

"Mr. Kennedy, can we get you a drink?" offers Cecil.

Kennedy laughs.

"Gentlemen, my title is Ambassador," says Kennedy.

Both Cecil and Valerius squint their eyes in disbelief of Kennedy's arrogance.

"We are here because we have serious concerns about your son's presidency. We made it very clear to you that your son was supposed to be friendly to our interests. He has been anything but friendly to us. In the beginning, I thought that your sons were trying to mask the connection between us and your family's past. But now, your son Bobby is trying to bury us. His constant pursuit of Marcello has to stop. He is very important to my organization; he has been disrespected, and he helped your son get Louisiana. My people don't accept disrespect well."

An upset Cecil interrupts, "That shit in Cuba was a travesty, and this possible pull out of Asia cannot happen."

Ambassador Kennedy looks at both men with a smile. "Gentlemen, I have about 10 of these bitch sessions a week. People want to complain about what my son is not doing for them. For goodness sake, he is the president; he will get to your concerns in due time. But he can't be worried with upsetting you," states Kennedy with a smirk on his face.

Valerius leans forward on the square table.

"We put your son in office, and I told you that the promises that you made your son would be beholden to," whispers Valerius in a stern tone.

"Valerius, I understand that you are not usually told to wait, but you will have to do just that," says a flippant Kennedy.

Joe Kennedy rises up from the table.

"Good day gentlemen," announces Kennedy as he puts out his hand to Valerius. Valerius stares at his hand with contempt.

"You know you have made a grave mistake here today. I will not forget this," proclaims Valerius.

Ambassador Kennedy looks at Valerius with a look of confusion as he walks away from the table.

"*Now what?*" questions Cecil as Kennedy walks away. "That son of a bitch will not get away with this. He and his family will not get away with this," suggests Valerius as he pounds his fists on the square table.

THE CALM

The seemingly unbreakable relationship between the Americans and the Israelis has become strained over the past few months. The tensions came to a head over the last week with the resignation of Ben Gourdin, Israel's defense minister. At dispute was Israel's entrance into the nuclear community. President Kennedy has been dead set against Israel gaining nuclear capability. The Israelis think they would be able to ward off possible attacks if their enemies knew that Israel had nuclear weapons. Israel was not so secretly building a nuclear installation in Dimona. Unsuccessfully, Gourdin argued to Kennedy that tensions were growing between Israel and the Muslim countries in the region, including Syria, Iran, Iraq and most notably Egypt. The Egyptians have been moving more military resources to the border, prompting the immediate concern. The threat of a nuclear attack would keep the Israeli enemies at bay, but without a threat of nuclear holocaust, the Israeli government fears they are sitting ducks. Wesley Carter is one of the most respected intelligence officers in the world, but not even he knows the Kennedy Administration's direction of policy for Israel's nuclear development. After the failed Bay of Pigs invasion, Carter lost his affections for the Kennedy administration. Carter along with many of his 8Men cohorts were upset that the president didn't go into Cuba with guns blazing.

The mob wanted Kennedy to go in and kill Castro. He threw all the mob affiliates out of the country. The military men wanted revenge for the U.S. backed Cuban exiles that were slaughtered trying to take the island back. After Kennedy decided not to go into Cuba, all looked at him as weak and not worthy to lead. Carter was a staunch advocate for the president, but increasingly, he lessened his defense of the president his policies. A four-door black Chevrolet pulls up in front of the Lincoln Memorial, and out steps Director Wesley Carter. He looks around to see if anything is out of the ordinary and notices a thirty-something woman dressed in an all-black dress suit accented by a cream blouse standing atop the steps of the memorial. She nods to Director Carter. Carter walks toward the woman.

"Director Carter, thank you for the invite," says Danya Franck. Director Carter shakes her hand.

"Your reputation precedes you. I think both of us may have a common issue. I think former Defense Minister Gourdin was a good man. I am sorry that your country was forced to get rid of him," comments a remorseful Carter.

"I love America's monuments and memorials; maybe one day, Israel will have some type of remembrance for our fallen heroes; that is if we survive. I can't say it enough: we are on the brink of destruction. No one in the region wants a Jewish state. We are going to need you and the people in your group's help," suggests Danya.

A surprised Carter asks, "What are you talking about?"

"Director, my business is in intelligence—ours and yours," hints a smiling Danya.

Understanding that Danya is referring to the 8Men, Director Carter turns to her and looks into her eyes intensely.

"What I am about to say is off the record. If ever I hear this again, I will deny it, and I will bring the force of my position to bear on your people."

The director looks around, scanning the area to see if anyone is looking at them. He takes a deep breath before saying, "Caesar may need to go. I think that a plan should be drafted to eliminate him. Of course, no association with my government can be in on the planning," remarks a careful Carter.

Danya chuckles. "Mr. Director, I am a friend—no need for cloak and dagger with me. We understand discretion; your problem is our problem. And Caesar threatens both our nations' security. But we will need the help of some people in your government. There would be no way we could draft anything without some kind of help from the inside. But you are a resourceful man." Director Carter looks out into the distance, looking into the overcast sky to find some answers.

"I will figure something out. You start working out several plans with contingency options. I will need to call in some big dogs," says Director Carter.

VPOTUS

The Vice President of the United States of America (VPOTUS) has become viewed as the runner-up to the most powerful person in the world. Of course, the U.S. Constitution outlines the responsibilities of the position as the second in the line of succession in the event the president is incapacitated, removed or dies while in office. The position also has responsibilities as the President of the Senate—it is prescribed in the constitution as a way to break any ties with respect to voting for laws. Over the years the VPOTUS has become more of a ceremonial position than an actual player in government business. This sentiment has not been received well by Lyndon Baines Johnson; he was the Major Senate Leader before assuming the role of VPOTUS. By all accounts, Johnson was a major ass kicker in the Senate. He got legislation through the Senate that many couldn't have dreamed of getting through. He was an efficient politician, but the secret to his success was his close friendship with FBI Director J. Edgar Hoover. Hoover supplied Johnson with information on key senators' indiscretions and bad habits. It was rumored that he got a prominent Dixiecrat to change his vote upon the revelation that he had fathered a child with his Negro maid.

Sitting outside of 11005 John Paul Jones Drive in northwest Washington, Director Carter and J. Edgar Hoover sit outside the Washington home of Lyndon Baines Johnson.

The impulsive Johnson comes out of his house in an apparent huff. The VPOTUS gets into the car with an attitude.

Mr. Johnson looks into the car and notices that Director Carter and Director Hoover are in the back. It is never a good sign to see the directors of the CIA and FBI in a car together.

"What the hell do you two want?" asks Johnson.

Hoover and Johnson have been discreet friends for more than 20 years.

"Is the president sick or something?" questions Johnson.

"No sir," rebuts Director Carter.

"Well then what the hell are you rebel rousers doing here? The two of you are always in some shit," asserts Johnson in his Texas drawl.

"Mr. Vice President, we would like to speak with you in private," says J. Edgar Hoover as he motions for Johnson's driver to get out of the car.

"What the hell are you doing, throwing my driver out of the car?" utters an angry Johnson.

"Ok, just cut the shit Lyndon. We need to talk to you with the strictest of confidence. What we are about to talk about must be left in this car," declares Hoover in an unyielding tone.

Mr. Johnson is shocked by Hoover's aggressiveness and figures it may be best to just listen.

"Ok, what we say will be left in this car," says a calm Johnson.

"Mr. Vice President, we believe the president is not doing an adequate job," alleges Director Carter.

"I will agree with that; the SOB is shitting on everything. Making our military look weak, got the damn Niggers all in huff wanting that god damn civil rights legislation," says Johnson.

"Well then we agree that leadership needs to change at the top," mentions Carter.

"Sure, he has done a terrible job, but how do you change it?" Johnson has a look of confusion on his face.

"There is no way you want me run against the president in the next election cycle. That would be political suicide," proclaims Johnson.

"No, we are going to kill him," blunt says J. Edgar Hoover.

"*What!*" exclaims Johnson.

"Mr. Vice President, we need you," pleads Carter.

"What the hell are you two thinking? It's fucking treason! They would hang us all right there on the Capitol steps," responds Johnson. "Sir, understand that we would not be doing it. We will just allow it to happen. We need to know that you will support the agenda that we set forward. But we need to know that you are with us," challenges Carter.

Lyndon Johnson sits back and lets out a deep breath. He looks out the side window at his grandchildren running in the yard while weighing this monumental decision.

"Lyndon, we need an answer," demands Hoover.

"Yes, I am with you. When? Where?" requests Johnson.

"It is better that you not know sir. You will always want plausible deniability," implies Carter.

Johnson nods his head with confirmation.

"You always wanted to be president," states Hoover with a devilish grin.

CONFIRMATION

The Confirmation of young Catholics has always been a majestic event. The ceremony marks the beginning of adult life as a Catholic—no more innocence as a kid in the faith. The promises that were made at baptism must now be affirmed by the young adult. On Thursday June 5th, Valerius Torrantio is attending the confirmation ceremony for one of his 25 godchildren, Sean Cecceralli, at St. Joseph's Catholic Church in Cheverly, Maryland. Valerius and the child's father are first cousins. Much like a baptism, the Godfather stands up during the ceremony to affirm that he will support the young adult in fulfilling their religious obligations. Valerius is a devoted Catholic; he tries to go to church at least once a week as a way of cleansing his soul.

Valerius is sitting in the fifth pew. He is seated with the Cecceralli family. The family takes up the entire pew; there is a mixture of children and adults young and old. No stranger to the Catholic faith, Richard Teed enters the church from the back. Teed genuflects, then makes the sign of the cross as he dashes his forehead with holy water. Valerius notices him sitting in the back as he gets up to go to communion. After Valerius receives communion, he quietly walks to the back of the church. Valerius motions Teed to join him.

Teed gets up from his seat and walks through the large double doors leading to the vestibule of the church.

"I take it you have news?" asks an eager Valerius.

"Yes, we are a go," confirms Teed.

"Good, I want him dead," declares Valerius.

Valerius realizes that he is still within the hallowed halls of the church. He makes the sign of the cross as if to ask for God's forgiveness. He grabs Teed by the arm and whisks him outside the main door of the church.

"When? Where?" requests Valerius.

"Actually, they thought that your people would probably be better to come up with a time and place," pushes back Teed.

Valerius laughs, "They want to be able to deny everything if it goes wrong. Blame it on the mob. Whatever, they just need to play their part," utters Valerius.

"We got to do it in a mob stronghold: Chicago or New Orleans. We could never pull it off in New York; —too much press and we don't control all the officials there. He would never go to New Orleans with this mess with Carlos. Do you think he would go to Texas?" queries Valerius.

Texas is the home state of Lyndon Johnson and also lays in the territory of Carlos Marcello. The Secret Service would not be as worried about Texas; there were no known threats against the president in the state.

"I will speak with Carlos about the place to attempt this. It is time the Kennedy clan pay," says Valerius as he walks back to the church.

Any successful plan to assassinate JFK in the Gulf region of the United States was going to start in New Orleans. The only person who could make things happen was Carlos Marcello. Marcello had an ax to grind with the Kennedys. After going against his better judgment, Marcello helped the 8Men secure a Presidential win for Kennedy by stealing the Louisiana vote in November of 1960. A short six months after

JFK won the presidency, Attorney General Robert "Bobby" Kennedy had Marcello kidnapped and deported to Guatemala. Marcello felt double crossed and disrespected at the least and had an overwhelming need for revenge against Bobby Kennedy. The 8Men were going to give him the opportunity to get payback. The Black Diamond night club is one of the many legal fronts for the Marcello crime family. The Black Diamond doubles as a jazz and a gentlemen's club. Since his re-entry back into the country, Marcello has been keeping a low profile. He comes to the club pretty much every day, but normally he stays in the back office, staying away from unknown eyes.

Today, the Black Diamond has an esteemed guest, Mr. Valerius Torrantio. Valerius has had very limited interactions with Marcello, but Valerius has felt responsible for how Marcello was treated by the Kennedys. Valerius knows if Marcello had brought the Kennedys to him, he would have whacked Marcello. Valerius walks into the Black Diamond flanked by two large bodyguards. Valerius knows it would be suicide for Marcello to try something, but he also would understand why Marcello would be pissed at him. Marcello is sitting at the bar awaiting Valerius.

"Don Torrantio," says a coy Marcello.

"Carlos," responds Valerius.

Valerius puts his hand out to shake Marcello' hand. Marcello takes a long look at Valerius and his hand before shaking it, albeit begrudgingly.

"Look, I am sorry, I had no idea they would pull some shit like that," remarks Valerius as he is interrupted.

"That little fucker Bobby threw me out of the *fucking* country. That son of a bitch has to pay. I don't want to hear any of the top-level *mob* shit. This is about my respect," proclaims Marcello as he lights up a cigar.

HARLEM

The enclave of Harlem, New York, has been largely dominated by Negroes migrating from the deep South since the 1920s. Harlem has become the epicenter for Negro enlightenment and culture, but the enclave has also become ground zero for all the seedy ventures in New York City. Drugs and gambling have become the main employers of the area. The use of the drug heroin is running rampant throughout Harlem, destroying families, and those it doesn't destroy it makes fearful prisoners to the associated violence.

The secrecy of Teed's upcoming task has made him wonder who he can trust. The 8Men have said that the execution of the president is necessary to make sure that the country continues to be prosperous. It is an understatement to say Teed felt uneasy with the thought of murdering the President of the United States. Sure, the president has made some terrible decisions that may have altered global power, but he is still the leader of the free world.

At the least, Teed thinks if they are caught there will be a trial for treason, with a verdict of murder by a firing squad. He knows that he needs somebody loyal to him that is great with a gun as well. The first person Teed thinks of is Herbert "The Squirrel" Jones. The Squirrel is a great marksman; he would have been in an elite sniper unit if not for segregation. Much of the armed forces were desegregated by President Truman in 1947, but the Army's elite forces slowed their internal processes to keep Negroes out.

In an effort to reward him, The Squirrel was offered a desk job after their unit's encounter in Korea; the powers that be thought that The Squirrel would be happy to be given rank and a nice salary. Of course, they didn't know The Squirrel; he lived for the adrenaline rush. He lived for the mission; it was all about the mission. The Squirrel left the armed forces a year later. The monotony of a desk job got the best of him, and he wound up going back to New York. Unfortunately for him, he had no job prospects when he got back to Harlem; he tried to find legitimate work, but everything offered to him was menial labor. Some friends that knew his military background brought him to some local gangsters. Over the last decade, The Squirrel became the number one hit man and muscle for Harlem crime boss Bumpy Johnson.

Teed is driving on 125th Street, Harlem's main drag and most famous. He is amazed and a bit apprehensive by the sea of Negroes walking up and down the street. As he drives along the road, he notices the world-famous Apollo Theater at 253 W. 125th Street. The theater is the landmark that The Squirrel gave Teed to use when looking for Bernell's Place, located at 259 W. 125th Street. Bernell's Place is a quaint southern restaurant that is obviously popular with the neighborhood, judging by the crowded establishment. Teed enters the restaurant, and to his surprise there are some White patrons in the restaurant. The Squirrel calls out to him. "Teed!" Teed notices The Squirrel with a smile on his face and walks over to him, giving him a big hug.

"Oh, my God Squirrel, how are you doing? You look great!" exclaims Teed.

Teed looks at The Squirrel. At first glance he looks like a million dollars, dressed in a tailored olive-green suit, paisley tie, a crisp white shirt and spit-shined brown leather shoes. But as Teed looks into his eyes, he sees the soul of a man that has been hollowed by the death and carnage that he has seen.

"You too my friend. Wow, it has been a lot of years. What brings you to New York? You sounded a bit strange on the phone," comments The Squirrel.

The paranoia of Teed's of upcoming task makes him look around the restaurant to make sure there aren't any government types in the restaurant. Noticing Teed's paranoia, The Squirrel says, "You don't have to worry about anybody here. There are no G-men. They all have better things to worry about than us. Let's get something to eat." Bernell's Place is popular for its Charleston cuisine. Since many of the Negroes in Harlem were from the Deep South, the establishment was a hit.

Teed starts looking through a menu, and he sees some of his favorites from home.

He sees tasty favorites like corn beef hash, grits and scrapple just to name a few. A waiter comes over to the table to take their order. Teed looks like a kid in a candy store.

"These are some of my favorites," says a giddy Teed.

The Squirrel smiles at Teed's excitement.

"That's why I told you to meet me here. I'm pretty sure you need a reminder of home," hints The Squirrel.

Teed starts to give the waiter his order.

"I will take the grits, the corn beef hash and okra." The waiter turns to The Squirrel. "I'll take the grits and a lemonade," responds The Squirrel.

The waiter takes their order than walks away.

"So, what did you need to see me about?" asks The Squirrel.

"I need you to help with a hit," says Teed.

"Ok, who are we hitting?" asks The Squirrel nonchalantly.

"We are hitting POTUS," claims Teed.

The blood drains from The Squirrel's face. Of course, POTUS stands for the President of the United States; each and every person ever associated with the military knows the acronym. The Squirrel starts to laugh.

"What…what?" stammers a confused Squirrel.

"We are going sometime in the fall. More than likely, it will be somewhere in the south," continues a straightforward Teed.

The Squirrel continues to shake his head.

"Who are you with? I mean you just don't take out POTUS and get away with it. You do plan to get away with it?" pushes back a skeptical Squirrel.

Teed thinks to himself, '*Is this a suicide mission?' Murdering the leader of the free world doesn't allow you any room for error.* "Name your price. And whatever else you need," states Teed.

"I know if you are with serious people the money will be there; my demands will be minor, but why?" questions a puzzled Squirrel.

"The people I am with wanted POTUS to follow their agenda and he didn't. These are some powerful people. That's why I need you. I trust you; I know that you are a great gun, and you aren't connected to them," admits Teed.

"God damn, you can really fuck up a day," replies The Squirrel.

The Squirrel shakes his head in apparent doubt.

"So, are you in?" asks a hesitant Teed.

"*Fuck*…you know I am in. God damn you Teed, you are going to get me killed one of these days. Let's make sure it is not any time soon. I got your back," confirms an excited Squirrel.

The Squirrel and Teed shake hands. "*Great…great,*" says Teed. The waiter brings their food and they both begin to eat.

IDENTITY

The Lebensborn project has flourished under the guidance of Albrecht Krause. Over the past decade since Krause has taken over the project, the CIA has infiltrated different espionage and fringe organizations throughout the world. The key to success has been to acquire human assets that are credible to their organizations prior to their reprogramming. Last year, one of the program's early recruits was responsible for giving information that led to the discovery of nuclear weapons on the isle of Cuba. Without the credible discovery, it may have been months before the U.S. found out what Russia was planning. The information allowed the Kennedy administration to make a decisive decision knowing that the Russians were equipping the Cubans with nuclear weapons that could reach the continental United States.

The proven record and the secrecy of the Lebensborn program has made it the perfect cover for developing the assassination plan of the president. Director Carter, Danya Franck and Richard are observing some mental exercises given to a promising candidate from behind a two-way mirror. The candidate is sitting at a steel table with four steel chairs dressed in blue jeans and a green and white checked shirt. The candidate has been asked by a lab worker to rattle off the name of his ideological leader and what makes America bad.

"Carl Marx, he is the father of communism. Communism stresses that each citizen works for the collective of the motherland. Unlike Russia, in America capitalism hinders the progression of the collective because each citizen works for their own personal gain," espouses the stone-faced young man.

"So, what is he going to do? Is he just going to walk up to the president and shoot?" asks a puzzled Teed.

"No, he is nothing more than a human puppet. He will do what we program him to do. He will have the perfect back story for an assassin," remarks Director Carter.

"Who is he?" asks Danya.

"His name is Lee Harvey Oswald; he is a former Marine. He was an average marksman; he had a lot of discipline problems while in the service and has serious problems with authority figures. He thought the Marine Corps was an evil force bent on world domination. He became fascinated by communism and wanted to see it in practice. A few years ago, he decided to go and live in the Soviet Union. He spent a few years there," claims Director Carter.

"I guess good ole communism wasn't what he thought it would be," chuckles Teed.

"Understand, this son of a bitch is a traitor through and through; we just have been able to turn him. He believes in communism and that his murder of the president will help the collective United States," states a cold Director Carter.

Teed understands the director's feelings but thinks Oswald was once a loyal member of the United States military. At the least, he deserves a debriefing to see if he truly is a traitor. But he has been prosecuted and judged as a traitor with a sentence of impending death. *More importantly, Teed thinks, what will happen when he disagrees with the 8Men? Will they cast him aside or set him up to be branded a traitor as well?*

Teed and Danya have just left the Fort Meade military installation outside of suburban Baltimore. They are traveling back to Washington on southbound Maryland Route 301.

"America is so beautiful. The countryside is so exquisite. There are miles and miles of trees and flowers," says an astonished Danya.

The normally tough and somewhat masculine Danya shows her softer side. Riding with the car windows down, she pulls her hair out, allowing her hair to blow in the wind.

"Yeah, lots of trees," responds an annoyed Teed.

"What the hell is wrong with you?" asks a peeved Danya.

"It's this guy Oswald; I mean I know he is probably a piece of shit, but he was an American soldier and now we set him up to murder the president. If he defected, then we should charge him with treason—put him in jail—but this?" utters Teed.

Danya looks at the frustrated Teed with compassion.

"Your country is at a fork in the road. I think that Mr. Kennedy is a rather inspirational man, but he stands in the way of progress. If we don't eliminate him then the world may pay for his mistakes. There are a lot of bad people out there. They don't want to see free societies or let people have free thought. These people must be dealt with using an iron fist. Mr. Kennedy believes in negotiating with these people. They cannot be allowed unlimited negotiations. My people live in constant fear that an enemy will invade us at any moment," recites a convincing Danya.

Danya notices that Teed is still a bit uptight.

"What can I do to make you relax?" asks Danya in a sexy voice. Teed shakes his head until she starts to rub on his chest and then unbuttons Richard's pants.

"How long is the ride to Washington?" asks Danya while whispering in Richard's ear.

"At least an hour, but I will try to make it there in a half hour," hints an excited Richard.

THE PLAN

The plan to assassinate President Kennedy is beginning to take shape. Teed, on direct order from the 8Men, has begun to plot out how and where the president will be killed. Up until yesterday, Teed worried about who would be blamed for the assassination. Naturally, Teed thought that he would be used as a patsy, but that was before the introduction of Lee Harvey Oswald. Teed still feels uneasy about killing the commander in chief, but he is relieved to know this isn't a suicide mission.

The bright morning sun awakens Teed on this humid summer day in Washington, D.C. He wakes feeling tired and sweaty, but the sight of Danya's shapely nude body standing at the patio window takes away all his exhaustion.

"How long have you been up?" asks Teed.

"Since sunrise," says Danya as she looks out over the Washington, D.C., skyline.

"We need to start planning," states Danya as she lights a cigarette. There is a knock at the door. She rushes to the bed and gets her gun from underneath the pillow.

"Are you expecting anyone?" questions Danya.

A stunned Teed tells Danya, "Relax, I am expecting room service." On the other side of the door Danya hears someone say, "room service."

"It would have been nice if you would have told me," responds Danya as she picks up some clothes and goes into the bathroom.

Teed puts on his robe and goes to the door. He looks through the door peep hole. He notices a Negro waiter pushing a food cart. Teed can smell the melded aroma of bacon, hot cakes and freshly brewed coffee. Teed opens the door as the waiter wheels in the cart.

"Good morning, sir. I hope you are having a pleasant morning?" remarks as the waiter.

"How is your morning?" asks Teed as he scans the hallway to see if he notices anything out of place.

"The coast is clear," comments a relieved Teed.

"Good, these red waiter jackets are not my style," complains The Squirrel.

Teed and The Squirrel thought in order to not raise any kind of suspicion, The Squirrel would dress as a waiter. The Squirrel has a seat on the couch and begins to eat one set of the hot cakes. He notices Danya in the distance coming out of the bathroom. Danya appears to be surprised by The Squirrel; she thinks he is a waiter sitting down on a couch eating hot cakes.

"Danya Franck, this is my colleague, The Squirrel," Teed introduces the two.

"So, this is the infamous Squirrel. The savior of the Korean mission. The Squirrel, quite the moniker," says a hesitant Danya. The Squirrel laughs.

"The moniker, as you put it, is a childhood nickname. Where I am from, nobody calls you by your government name. Very few in Harlem know Herbert Jones, but everybody knows The Squirrel. Enough about me. I brought us all breakfast; please have some," utters The Squirrel.

Danya pours herself a cup of coffee.

"Danya, I asked The Squirrel to join us in the planning of our task. I thought it would be a good idea to get somebody outside the 8Men to help," discloses Teed.

Danya lets out a sigh.

"I wish you would have told me that you're inviting someone here," claims a somewhat peeved Danya.

The Squirrel starts to laugh.

"Did I interrupt something? Should I come back a little later?" jokes a sarcastic Squirrel.

"So where do we start?" asks Danya.

"Do we do it ourselves? Do we get additional help?" questions Teed. Danya answers, "We do it in tandem with another team, but we leave them out of the planning. They will be just hired guns. We will need to start looking at possible sights. We will need a copy of the president's schedule of the next three months to look at doing some dry runs."

The facial expressions of Teed and The Squirrel are in agreement with Danya.

"Wow, she is gangster. I want to take her to Harlem," says a smiling Squirrel.

DIEM

On August 29,1963, the Kennedy administration was involved in marathon discussions on the situation in South Vietnam. At the center of the discussions was the viability of the South Vietnamese President Diem. The White House was concerned that the communist backed North Vietnamese army were making large strides in taking over democratically governed South Vietnam. The Kennedy administration continued the policies of the previous administrations to hold fast against the spread of communism. Many within the administration thought that the South Vietnamese president was not taking the advances of the communists as seriously as the west. The prevailing thought was that President Diem may need to go, and he needed to be replaced by a hard-line president. The war hawks of the Pentagon thought that the U.S. should help the Vietnamese snuff out the communists, even if they didn't want the help. After days of continual meetings and conjecture on the ramifications of inaction on the part of the U.S., President Kennedy agrees to explore the option of regime change. Regime change means the murder or hopefully the escape of President Diem. The president looks around the Oval Office at the meeting's attendees: Vice President Lyndon Johnson, Director Wesley Carter and Secretary of Defense McNamara.

"Is this what we want? South Vietnam is a democratic state. They seem to be hesitant to war with their fellow Vietnamese. Are we rushing into this?" asks a pondering President Kennedy.

"Mr. President, we are exploring the possibility of regime change; that is all at this moment," explains Secretary McNamara.

Throughout the meeting, Vice President Johnson has been notably silent. The president notices.

"Lyndon, what is your opinion?" asks the president.

"Mr. President, the Soviets are marching. They can be dressed as North Vietnamese, North Koreans or even the Cubans. Their intent is to rule the world, plain and simple. We can pussy foot with them as much as we want, but they will force a line in the sand," commits a somber Johnson.

The president is a bit perturbed by Johnson's reference to the Cubans and the pussyfooting comments.

"What would you have me do? Go in and just carpet bomb the whole god damn country?" pushes back the president.

Understanding that the tension is getting thick in the room, Wesley Carter interjects. "Mr. President, you are in an unenviable position. These types of crises normally can be handled diplomatically, but the communists only understand force. If you give them an inch, they will take a mile. During the crisis last year, they understood your resolve once you drew a line in the sand. You showed great strength, and you made them understand that we would go to war if provoked," suggests Director Carter.

The president seems to be in partial agreement with Director Carter.

"I need time to process this through. If you gentlemen don't mind, I need a few moments with the secretary of defense," announces the president.

Both Vice President Johnson and Director Carter stand up and excuse themselves from the meeting. The vice president darts out of the Oval Office. Director Carter jogs briskly out of the office after the vice president.

"What the hell was that?" challenges Director Carter.

"That weak son of bitch is gonna have us fucking communists. He wants to negotiate every god damn thing. Those fuckers don't negotiate; they say, 'We want Vietnam and that is it.' Son of a bitch asks me for my god damn opinion. I give it and because I'm not hugging his nuts and agreeing with him. He gets shitty. That fucker needs to understand that we have to stand firm and say, 'We will not have it, and if you come past this point, we will destroy you,'" declares a determined Vice President Johnson.

Carter stands in front of Johnson in amazement.

"Wow, you sounded very presidential there," jokes Carter.

Johnson laughs off Carter's comments as they continue to walk.

"Where are you with your task? When are we going to get the bastard?" questions Vice President Johnson.

"Calm down, we are in a good place. You shouldn't ask about it anymore. But I do need something vital from you. After which, I don't want you to bring it up every again," states a stern Carter as he walks away.

COURTSHIP

In the summer of 1963, Richard Teed and Danya Franck toured the largest cities in the U.S. looking for possible sniper points to assassinate President Kennedy. From the outside, Richard and Danya appeared to be a loving couple going through a romantic courtship. But their intent could become the most heinous act in American history. The seemingly endless flirting and attraction exploded into a full-blown lustful affair. The couple toured NYC's Broadway, Chicago's west side, L.A.'s Rodeo Drive and a host of other cities doing recon. The couple doubles back to New York when one of Director Carter's contacts approaches Teed coming out of an ice cream shop on 34th Street in Manhattan.

"Teed!" exclaims the neatly dressed G-man.

Richard Teed accepts an envelope. He tears into it.

"What is it?" asks Danya.

Richard looks at the paper. It is the president's schedule over the next three months. There are several locations with asterisks next to them: Chicago, Tampa and Dallas.

"It's the most probable locations to get the president," states Teed as he hands the envelope and paper to Danya.

"Maybe we go to these cities to feel them out?" inquires Danya.

"I think you are right, but I promised I would show you a good time. What I was going to do over several days I will now have to do in a matter of hours," Teed commits as he reaches for Danya's hand.

The couple walk arm and arm down 34th Street, taking in the bright lights of Gotham. The couple walks into the world-famous Madison Square Garden to catch a matinee game between the New York Knickerbockers and the Baltimore Bullets. Teed and Danya stay for two quarters, the game is a blowout, with Baltimore leading by 20.

"This game is over. The Bullets are killing them. Let's get out of here. I know where you need to go," hints an excited Teed.

Teed and Danya rush down to the subway station underneath Madison Square Gardens. Danya is in awe of the subway system.

"My God, this is a like a city down here," marvels Danya.

Danya sees a number of people.

"This is how people get around in New York," says Teed.

Danya and Teed get on the train.

"This is remarkable that America has trains underground," remarks the awestruck Danya.

"Well, it isn't everywhere in America. New York is rather unique in this aspect. But I am pretty sure other cities will follow suit," concedes Teed.

Teed and Danya are standing up on the train. They have had several sexual encounters, but the intimacy of Teed opening a brand-new world up to Danya is making her feel more attracted to Teed and bringing her a closeness to him that she has never felt for anyone. She leans on Teed's chest.

"Are you on?" asks Teed.

"Yes," says Danya as she hugs Teed a little tighter.

The feeling of intimacy is mutual; Teed has had a building affection for Danya. He returns the favor to her by holding her a bit tighter to her great pleasure. The seemingly short train ride is close to an end as Teed notices the next stop.

"We are here," discloses an excited Teed.

The couple gets off the train at the Staten Island stop. Teed pulls Danya off the train with excitement.

"I want to show you the most beautiful woman in world other than you," suggests a giddy Teed.

Teed and Danya run outside; they run up the steps like school children, until she realizes she can't run so fast in her dress and high heels. Teed reaches the top of the steps first.

"Hurry," says Teed.

Danya reaches the top of the steps. She is awestruck when she steps out onto Staten Island. The ocean breeze blows Danya's hair in her face, momentarily distorting the large image in the Hudson River.

"Is that?" stammers Danya.

"Yes, that is Lady Liberty," confirms Teed.

Teed and Danya catch a ferry out to Ellis Island. The refreshing ocean air adds to the symbolic trip to view the Statue of Liberty.

Danya and Teed are hugging each other as they lean up against a gate at the back of the ferry.

"She is so beautiful. Your Washington, D.C., monuments are outstanding, but this is breathtaking," remarks Danya.

Teed nods his head in agreement.

"I hope that one day Israel will have monuments like this in Tel Aviv, Jerusalem or Haifa," says Danya.

The gravity of why Danya and Teed are in New York and traveling around the country has broken Teed out of the romantic haze of the day. Teed breaks from Danya's sweet embrace.

"What is wrong?" questions Danya.

"We are looking at the symbol of democracy. As we admire the symbol, we are planning to destroy the very principle," comments Teed.

"I hear you, and this is a powerful symbol, but there is a natural order of things. We are nothing but foot soldiers. Caesar will be taken out either way—either by us or some other unwitting foot soldiers," suggests Danya.

"As always you are right," admits Teed.

"You are correct," agrees Danya.

They share another embrace as the ferry gets closer to Ellis Island.

SCHOOL BOOK

The 8Men have been given the president's travel schedule over the next two months. The schedule is full, with trips to Texas, Florida, Chicago, California and an assortment of stops in the Northeast. By the process of elimination, the group realizes that Dallas, Texas, will be the perfect place for an ambush. All parties think Dallas is perfect. The state police are full of cronies of the vice president, and those that aren't friends of Johnson are on the mob's payroll. The New Orleans mafia runs vices in Dallas and controls much of the downtown business district, which will aid in setting up the best location.

Lee Oswald has applied for a position with the Texas School Book Depository in downtown Dallas. Lee feels good about his chances of getting the job. The schoolbook depository overlooks Daly Plaza. After his interview, Lee walks down the street toward a hot dog stand. As Lee approaches the stand, he notices a man wearing a black fedora and sunglasses.

"The interview went well. I should be packing and unpacking boxes within the week," says Lee.

"Good, make sure you are always on time and don't make any waves while you are there. In short, keep your nose clean," instructs a fedora wearing Teed.

"What is the objective of my mission?" asks Lee.

Teed gives Lee a look of non-belief before leaving Lee at the hot dog stand.

Minutes later, Teed arrives at the bed and breakfast where he and Danya have been posing as Mr. and Mrs. John Smith. Danya is lying across the bed reading the paper. The newspaper headline reads:

"The president is coming to town on November 22nd
President John Fitzgerald Kennedy will be coming to town in the
fall to begin fundraising efforts in the Lone Star State. Along with
raising money, it is thought that the president is visiting the state to
shore up Democratic support for the up-coming campaign."

"Why must your president raise money to be president?" inquires Danya. Teed does not seem to have an answer for her profound question.

"I don't really know. I guess expenses associated with traveling around," ponders Teed.

"The best leader is not always the best fundraiser, no?" asks Danya.

"I suppose. Never really gave much thought to it," answers Teed.

"America's politics are so strange," implies Danya.

"Why do you think that?" challenges Teed.

Danya jumps up from the bed to show the paper to Teed.

"Ok. Your country is involved in fights thousands of miles away. There is an article on the U.S.'s mounting involvement in Vietnam.

America has no clear reason to be in Vietnam, but they are there building up preparations for war," says a somewhat gleeful Danya.

"Why are you smiling? You enjoy this stuff?" asks Teed.

"It is fascinating. In Israel, we are united by our constant belief that others are trying to end our way of life. That is our interest. America's interest seems to be the world. It seems like your country has its hands everywhere," hints Danya.

"You are as smart as you are beautiful," comments Teed.

"So, what about Oswald, how was he?" asks Danya.

"He is an improved version from the other Lebensborn subjects. Not so much a super soldier but an everyday Marine. From what I have seen, they have worked up a really good dossier for him: a really good set-up job. Personally, he seems to really be a piece of shit, but he is a Marine," utters Teed.

"But he is a soldier. His will is not his own. He is to be used by his commanders," replies Danya.

"That fucking Lebensborn program, tricking our service men into becoming savages. I get it, there are some nasty things that go on in this world, but there are enough assholes that would gladly do the U.S.'s dirty work," alleges Teed.

"True, but most of those are mercenaries. They have no loyalty; they can be easily compromised. I don't like the Lebensborn program, but I understand the thoughts behind its genesis. Your country's politicians want to keep things in their proper order," says Danya.

THE STRAW

The planned assassination attempt of President John Fitzgerald Kennedy is getting closer. Vice President Lyndon Johnson has always dreamt of being the President of the United States. In fact, he feels that he should have been the nominee in 1960. He understands that he has to play his role until he becomes next in line. Johnson knows he is just a few short weeks from realizing his lifelong dream, but he starts to get cold feet. The vice president decides to pay J. Edgar Hoover a visit in his office. There is a knock at Director Hoover's door.

"Enter," calls out Hoover.

A large secret service agent enters the director's office.

"The vice president is here to see you, Director Hoover," barks the agent.

Moments later, Vice President Johnson rushes into Hoover's office, followed by three secret service agents.

"Edgar, we need to talk," professes a flustered Vice President Johnson.

"Mr. Vice President, exactly what is this about?" asks Hoover as he motions to Johnson about the number of agents in the room.

"Gentlemen, please excuse yourselves. Director Hoover and I need to discuss some very sensitive issues," directs Johnson as the secret service agents leave the director's office. Vice President Johnson is pacing back and forth.

"Lyndon, what the hell has got you in such a fuss?" asks Director Hoover.

"God damn Edgar. You are used to this cloak-and-dagger bullshit. But I am not. We are looking to kill the president. He is a shithead; I will give you that, but he is still the president. This is god damn treason. Are you sure we must do this?" rambles Vice President Johnson.

Director Hoover watches as the vice president paces back and forth.

"Everything is moving smoothly; everybody and everything is in place," assures Hoover as he gets up from his desk.

Hoover walks over to the vice president.

"God damn Edgar, how can you be so calm about all of this. This is not killing a drug dealer posing as a foreign dictator. *This is the god damn President of the United States,*" says an emotional Johnson.

"Sir, go home. Get as much rest as you can. In a few weeks you will be president, then you won't get any rest," jokes Hoover as both men share an uneasy giggle.

Director Hoover walks the vice president to the door.

"Go home and call your donors, make sure everyone will be voting for the president next year," suggests Hoover as he shakes Vice President Johnson's hand.

Vice President Johnson walks out the door. Hoover walks back over to his desk. He picks up the phone and starts to dial quickly.

"Come on, pick up. Hey, it's me. I am going to need that information. The vice president is getting cold feet. He is starting to get a conscience…right, have it for me before November 15th," utters Hoover as he hangs up the phone.

The election of 1964 is a little over a year away, but the sucking up for money has already begun. Texas socialite Blanche O'Leary is hosting a party for the National Democratic Party at her plush 5,000 square-foot home in the Dallas suburb of Irving. Mrs. O'Leary is the widow of former Texas Lieutenant Governor Paul O'Leary. Paul O'Leary was a descendant of old oil money. It was rumored that he was worth well over one billion dollars, but he rejected the corporate raider culture of the oil business for the hustle of politics. The National Democratic Party is starting to raise money for President Kennedy's campaign next fall. It is well known that the president will be challenged by the well-loved conservative Barry Goldwater. The National Democratic Party knows that they must raise an enormous amount of cash in order to hold back the eventual Republican challenger.

Vice President Lyndon Johnson is the guest of honor for the Texas shindig at the O'Leary estate. Lyndon Johnson has always been seen as Texas' favorite son.

Lyndon Johnson is always a big draw at these social events; he tells tall tales of conquering the big city slickers in Washington, D.C. The vice president is telling a story when he is interrupted by one of his assigned secret service agents.

"Sir, I have been asked to bring you to Mrs. O'Leary's study," states the agent.

The vice president excuses himself and walks to the study. The vice president enters the study and sees some familiar faces. Director Carter and Valerius Torrantio are sitting on a couch looking directly at the vice president as he enters the door. FBI director J. Edgar Hoover is standing at the study's window overlooking a lake in the backyard.

"What the hell is it now? I told you I hate to see you SOBs together. You fuckers are nothing but trouble," claims the vice president as he walks to the small bar to pour himself a bourbon. "So, what the hell is it Edgar? Why this clandestine meeting? This must be good. We got the leaders from the American intelligence community and the mighty godfather of the mob," comments a flustered Lyndon Johnson.

"Mr. Vice President, I am going to let you get your drink before we start to discuss," replies J. Edgar Hoover.

The vice president starts to pour his drink.

"Mr. Vice President, you are being replaced on the Democratic National Ticket," alleges Hoover.

The vice president stops drinking in mid gulp.

Edgar, that shit ain't funny," says the vice president as his face gets noticeably red.

"Mr. Vice President, it was not meant to be funny. My reliable sources have told me that the president will be dropping you from the ticket," claims a self-assured Edgar Hoover.

"The president could never pull that off. He knows that he needs Texas, and I run Texas," concedes Vice President Johnson.

"Mr. Vice President, the president has been given information that the Senate Ethics Committee will convene a special meeting to look into campaign corruption that you have alleged to have participated in," remarks Edgar.

"He couldn't. He needs me; he needs Texas," chatters a confused Vice President Johnson.

"Sir, the president does need Texas, but he doesn't necessarily need you. He has taken strides to shore up Texas," confesses Edgar.

"What?" asks a confused Vice President Johnson.

"Mr. Vice President, the president has begun to vet Governor Connelly as a possible running mate for next year," divulges Edgar.

"Does that fucking arrogant son of a bitch think I am just going to go away quietly? Does he think that he is going to be able to throw me out like yesterday's trash? He has got another thing coming," responds Vice President Johnson.

"Mr. Vice President, I have seen some of the evidence; it is quite damaging," admits Hoover.

"We can't disappear whatever it is; come on Edgar, you have disappeared evidence before. Hell, you have made up info when needed," declares Vice President Johnson.

"We cannot interfere with this investigation; it is being handled by the secret service. They have been instructed to share their findings only with the president, the minority leader and the speaker of the house," states Hoover.

"*Sons of bitches, sons of bitches.* The whole lot of them. They are going to pay. *Nobody* fucks with me. I got Jack Texas, and fucking John Connelly is going to stab me in the back. You tell me what you need to take out those fuckers. *I want them all dead,*" barks Vice President Johnson as he storms out of the study. Valerius and Wesley Carter look at each other in utter amazement.

"You played him like a fiddle. There is no vetting on Connelly. Of course, you knew that it would piss him off," says Carter.

J. Edgar Hoover smiles devilishly.

"Mr. Carter, I have learned that anger can be a great motivator. Just in case Mr. Johnson gets a moment of virtue, his anger will quell that notion. Plus, we want him to have some skin in the game for later in case he gets amnesia like the Kennedys," proclaims Hoover.

JOHN WILKES

The President of the United States has been successfully assassinated three times in the republic's history. The most recent was William McKinley; before that was the assassination of James Garfield. But the most famous and historically relevant was the assassination of Abraham Lincoln. Lincoln was as equally revered as he was despised. The Civil War, along with the Emancipation Proclamation, would change the South forever; it cannot be underestimated the financial impact of freeing the slaves. The loss of wealth was immeasurable. Family fortunes were devastated with the stroke of Lincoln's pen. Booth was a Confederate sympathizer; he was enraged by the rumor that freed slaves would soon be allowed to vote and have full rights. As a son of the confederacy, Booth's anger turned into a rage that could only be cured with the murder of Lincoln.

Much like Lincoln, Kennedy has upset the country's collective apple cart. He has shaken the establishment to its core; he has thumbed his nose at big business and given general masses a feeling of equality.

On Thursday November 21, 1963, Richard Teed is lying on the bed in the rented room that he and Danya rented as their supposed honeymoon suite. Teed is staring at the ceiling lost in his thoughts of the next day. He, Danya and The Squirrel have gone over their plans every which way. They are as ready as they are going to be; all of the teams are ready.

Richard has played over and over in his mind how the assassination will occur.

Like a quarterback before the big game, Teed plays out every possible scenario in his mind. As he thinks about the mission, he thinks about the others who came before him. He wonders if these men were patriots or just crazies that killed the commander in chief. Being from Charleston, John Wilkes Booth was an underground hero. Sure, he killed the president, but he killed a president that stood against everything that many in the South believed. Booth also was a part of a group of patriots that felt the current commander-in-chief was leading the country down the wrong path. Teed, trying to justify the assassination in his mind, thinks these men were patriots trying to right the wrong of an ill-advised president.

There is a double knock at the door. Danya and Teed worked out a double knock that both knew, letting the other know everything was ok before entering the room. Danya was returning from the bus station. She picked up Anthony Dinapoli and Daniel Mancuso; the gentlemen are Italian hit men. They came personally recommended by Don Torrantio himself. The men could have been twins, their physical characteristics are amazingly similar. Both are roughly 5'9" with short-cropped haircuts with bushy eyebrows. The twins have been trailing the president for weeks. They have followed the president and his entourage to Chicago and Tampa. They have been trying to find the secret service's tendencies to find holes in the president's protection. The assassins have taken the approach of hunting the president like big game in the wilderness. Like any hunter, the twins want to know how to hunt their prey with the greatest chance of victory. The plan is to kill the president in an area with a large building overlooking a parade route. The twins realize that the larger buildings in Dallas are not monitored by the local police and the secret service don't have enough agents to monitor all the windows. Danya pulls out a map of downtown Dallas; she points out the Texas School Book Depository.

"Here is your tall building. It sits right on the parade route," insists Danya.

"Oh shit, this will be perfect. Not only does it have a tall building, but it has several smaller buildings where a sniper's perch can be sat," concludes Daniel.

"How about any sewer systems?" asks Daniel.

Danya looks through the blueprints of the city and notices that the city has a sewer system.

"There is sewer system underneath Elm Street," claims Danya.

"We will have three snipers shooting from the Texas School Book Depository, the Dal-Tex building and we need a frontal position that is somewhat hidden," estimates Daniel.

Listening intently to the conversation, Richard Teed remembers meeting with Lee Oswald outside of the School Book Depository. Teed remembers a grassy area that sits to the right of Elm Street, about 50 yards from the street.

"There is a spot to right of Elm. There is a lot of foliage and a perfect perch on top of a fence," recollects Teed.

After his declaration, Teed finally feels his kinship with John Wilkes Booth.

THE ZERO HOUR

The plan to assassinate the president is reaching the zero hour. The team is making final preparations and tying up all loose ends. Sitting in the corner of Mr. and Mrs. Smith's bed and breakfast room are four Carcano rifles. These rifles gained prominence during World War II; they are not the greatest weapons for snipers, but the implication of the gun's usage would involve the mob. In order not to have the actual hardware traced, the twins brought the guns with them from Italy. The gun that will be left at the scene was ordered from a mail-order company in eastern Texas, which will be easily traced. The twins are feverishly cleaning their guns to a spit shine. Danya is cleaning her silver-colored handgun when she notices Teed looking out of a window. Danya walks over to him, bringing an ice-cold Coca Cola.

"Here, why don't you take a drink," says Danya. Teed thanks Danya with a kiss on the cheek.

"We are on the brink of history; either we murder the president, or we fail miserably, never to be heard from again," proclaims Teed.

"If everyone follows the plan, then we will do fine. I understand your apprehension. Your president seems to be a good man with some fidelity issues. But nobody is perfect," responds Danya.

"Exactly, nobody is perfect. So why not work to get him out of office or simply change his mind?" offers an excited Teed. Danya looks at Teed with a compassionate look.

"We are soldiers. We are given commands and we follow them out. I have questioned many commands that were given to me in the past. I have pondered what makes my higher ups positions or thoughts any better than mine. In the end, I normally see that they were correct. My higher ups normally run all the possible scenarios that I could have never fathomed. It isn't our job to come up with the mission; it is our job to implement and execute the mission," concludes Danya.

At approximately 11 am, a truck labeled "The Texas School Book Depository" backs up into the loading bay of The Texas School Book Depository. The truck is being driven by The Squirrel, and sitting passenger is Teed, both dressed in tan uniforms. Once the truck is parked, both men get out and raise the truck's back door. They both take out packages from the back of the truck. The two men walk through the lobby of the building, making their way toward the stairwell. The two men trek the stairway until they reach the sixth floor. Both men look around the normally deserted sixth floor. The sixth floor of the building has been used as a storage area for back-ordered supplies; sometimes the area is unseen for weeks. They see that the area is cleared of people.

"Let's get started," suggests Teed.

Both men rip open the packages that have the Carcano rifles inside.

At the same time, the twins are driving in a counterfeit police car dressed as policemen. They are driving on a graveled road to the north of Delay Plaza. They stop about 20 yards from a wooden fence. The twins, both wearing police uniforms, roll their somewhat hefty frames out of the car. They case the area and notice the area is secluded and bare, with the exception of some transients lying at the foot of the wooden fence. The twins walk over to the transients.

"Hey, get the hell up. This is no bedroom," roars Twin 1 as he kicks one of the transients.

"We sleep here all the time. What's the problem?" disputes the transient.

"The president is coming today. We want to leave him with a good impression of our city. So, get your asses up and don't come back until after the president leaves the city," barks Twin 2.

The transients walk away, upset that they have been interrupted from their mid-day slumber. The twins again survey the area, looking to make sure the coast is clear. With a nod of the head, they spring into action. They go into their car trunk, pulling out two gun bags. They walk the bags over to the wooden fence.

Two stories underneath Elm Street, Danya walks through a labyrinth of tunnels. Danya chose this particular mission because of her small stature; her size is ideal for the tight crawlspaces leading to the street drain under Delay Plaza. Danya is looking at her handmade map under the flicker of her small cigarette lighter. She finally finds the crawlspace directly under Delay Plaza and climbs in. She is amazed the president's security detail did not close off the drain. Danya starts to unpack her backpack. She starts to assemble a gun that is nicely packed in her bag. At approximately 12:25 pm, Lee Oswald is sitting at a lunch table on the third floor of the School Book Depository. He is eating his usual ham and mustard sandwich accompanied by his wife's homemade potato chips. He is thinking about taking his wife Maria out on a date. Lee and Maria have been in the midst of a month of terrible fights. A few of the fights are getting physical; he is very sorry for hitting Maria. Lee's temper always got the best of him. Moments later, he hears the roar of the massive crowd outside of the building. The president's entourage drives up Main Street making the turn onto Delay Plaza.

All three teams know the moment of truth is at hand. The months of preparation, the countless amounts of intelligence have led to this point of no return. Each team knows they will only get one shot. All three teams take aim at their target in the scopes of their guns. The president rides on Delay Plaza, looking like a deer in a forest, unaware of its impending demise. All three guns explode with staggered *BANGS*.

CONTRITION

It has been three days since the violent assassination of the 35th President of the United States of America, John Fitzgerald Kennedy. The murder of Kennedy sets in motion a number of events. The assassination is seen by many as an attempted coup by Cuban communists and seen by others as an all-out declaration of war by the Soviet Union. The military has been on full alert since Friday afternoon at 12:45 pm. All military bombers and nuclear submarines have been told to stay ready for an attack at a moment's notice. These events seem to pale in comparison to the pageantry of the funeral of John Fitzgerald Kennedy. The processional of family members and dignitaries from all walks of life has left on lookers awestruck. John Kennedy was not loved by all people, but he was the president. He was one of two leaders of the free world. He had a beautiful wife and very small, adorable children. As in any family, Americans don't always agree, but a tragedy normally brings everyone together.

Back in Dallas, Richard Teed has had his head in a small trash can for several hours. As he heaves chunks of green matter into the can, Teed prays the Catholic prayer, the Act of Contrition.

"My God, I am sorry for my sins with all my heart. In choosing to do wrong and failing to do well, I have sinned against you whom I should love above all things. I firmly intend, with your help, to do penance, to sin no more, and to avoid whatever leads me to sin. Our Savior Jesus Christ suffered and died for us," prays Teed.

One of the twins looks at Teed with disgust.

"What the hell is his problem?" asks the twin.

Danya walks to the bathroom to see what is going on with Teed. "What is going on, what is he saying?" questions Danya.

The twin recognizes the prayer.

"He must be Catholic, I recognize it. It is the 'Act of Contrition,' it is the prayer that Catholics pray when asking for forgiveness. I used to pray it after I did something wrong as a kid. He has been praying it for the last three days. He has got me worried. We don't need a stool pigeon getting a conscience," utters the twin as he walks away.

Danya silently agrees with the twin but knows that she must snap Teed out of this emotional funk. If he is to be a good operative, he is going to have to be able to kill without hesitation. Danya looks at Teed with compassion.

The twins' mission is now complete. It is now time for them to go back to Italy, understanding that the American military will pretty much shut down travel for several days in and out of Dallas and its nearby metropolitan areas. The twins are going to make the trek to New Orleans, then take a cruise ship to Cape Town, South Africa. Once in Cape Town, they will hop a plane to Palermo. The twins are carrying their two small luggage bags to the car. Danya escorts them to the car.

"You know you are a hell of a shot. Maybe we should hook up again, plus you are very easy on the eyes," comments Twin 2 as he flirts with Danya.

Danya scoffs at the twin's assumption.

"I guess that is a compliment, but I only involve myself in missions for the betterment of Israel," admits Danya.

The twins shrug their shoulders.

"Oh well, we need to settle our payment," declares the twin.

"Of course, please open your trunk," demands Danya.

The twin opens the trunk to find three duffle bags of money. "Wow, you got to love America," he says as he closes the trunk.

"Thank you both," says Danya as both twins get into their car.

Danya waves to the twins as they pull off. She walks back into the hotel room. She notices that Richard is sitting on the couch watching the president's funeral. An unfazed Danya walks over to Teed and sits next to him on the couch. The physically drained Teed lies across Danya's lap. She looks down at Teed like a sick child. Danya starts to sing a bedtime limerick.

"Blessed are you our God, who casts sleep upon my eyes and slumber upon my eyelids. May you lay me down to sleep in peace and raise me up in peace. Blessed are you who illuminates the entire world with your glory. Sh'ma Yisrael Adonai Eloheinu Adonai Echad. God of Israel may Michael be at my right, Gabriel at my left, Uriel before me and Raphael behind me, and above my head the Presence of God," sings Danya as she strokes Teed's hair while they continue to watch the president's funeral.

MOMMA

Richard Teed has not seen his mother in over 13 years. He hasn't seen her since he left for the conflict on the Korean Peninsula. The drama of the Kennedy assassination made Teed think that it was time to go home. He needed a different perspective; he needed to get out of the intelligence bubble. Unfortunately, his mother will not be at 400 Ashely Avenue to greet him for his homecoming. She has become a patient at the North Charleston State Mental Hospital. The mental stress of Teed and Cap's disappearance drove his mom out of her mind. Teed received a letter from Jen, his high school sweetheart, a few weeks ago about his mother's condition. From the letter, Ms. Teed has been in the North Charleston Mental Hospital since 1955. The moment Richard saw the year 1955, an anxiety came over him. He thought to himself that he was the second man to have left his mother. Of course, Richard's dad died in the second world war, and he was pretty sure that it was assumed that he expired somewhere on the Korean Peninsula. Teed thought that maybe he could give his mother some kind of comfort by letting her know that he was still alive. But Director Carter made it apparent to him that no one was to know he was still alive.

It was not just to protect him but to potentially protect anyone that he may love. Teed decides against the two-hour flight to Charleston, instead deciding to take the 17-hour drive to the Palmetto State.

The drive gives Teed some time to process the things going through his mind. He cannot get the explosion of the commander in chief's brain all over Delay Plaza out of his mind. As he replays the terrifying scene over and over in his head, Teed can feel the recoil of the Carcano rifle against his shoulder. The constant question that goes through Teed's mind is, *Am I a patriot or a traitor?* He remembers a conversation with his father about one man's traitor was one man's liberator. He taught Teed that nearly 200 years ago the people in England called the colonists of the New World traitors. A Virginia sheriff's police car is visible in Teed's rear view mirror. His heart starts to beat faster and faster as the car approaches. He wonders, *Is the jig up? Have I been sold out?* In his mind, he thinks, *Did the 8Men sell me out like they did Oswald? Is it predetermined that I will be killed on some backwater road?* He thinks, *Hell, I'm already dead as far as anybody already knows.* The Virginia sheriff's car passes Teed's car, providing a moment of relief.

Hours later, Teed arrives at the mental hospital. He pulls into a parking space in the emptied parking lot. Teed gets out of the car as a fog begins to surround the grounds of the hospital. He gets an eerie feeling; it is a feeling more reserved for a graveyard. Teed's first impression is that this place is where dead souls are stored. He walks up the cracked steps and into the building. Teed sits in the office of the hospital's administrator. He thinks to himself, *"who will I say I am? Can I say I am a nephew, a cousin or even a concerned former neighbor?"* He realizes he can't say he is her son back from the dead, her son that has been dead for more than 12 years. The administrator walks into the office. Teed decides to say he is her nephew. There is no paperwork needed, and he feels he would rather say he is a family member.

"Hello, my name is Dr. Williams. I am the head doctor and facilities administrator here at the North Charleston State Mental Hospital. How can I help you?" asks the raspy voiced gentleman.

Teed answers, "I would like to see Mrs. Teed. I am her nephew." The administrator seems to be a bit surprised.

"I am sorry son; we just have not seen any visitors for Mrs. Teed. She has been here for a number of years without any visitors. She has gotten progressively worse over the years. She has not responded to much of anything," reveals Dr. Williams.

With each word, out of Dr. Williams's mouth, an additional pound of guilt is placed on top of Teed's heavily weighted shoulders.

Teed is led down a long corridor by an orderly. As Teed walks down the hallway, he notices a patient lying on a mobile bed as drool spews from their mouth. The orderly tells Teed, "The patient is very distant. She may not respond to you. In my three years here, I have never seen anyone visit her."

The words from the orderly cut Teed to his heart. The orderly opens the door to the padded room. He is hesitant when he sees his mother draped in a straitjacket. All the feelings of guilt rush back to Teed. He wishes he could turn around and run away. Mrs. Teed is sitting on the cold tile floor, looking down, not even acknowledging her son's entrance. Teed slowly walks over to his mother. He is thinking, *what will I say? What will she say back to me if she recognizes me?* Teed stands in front of his mother, and she looks at him as if looking into the sun. Mrs. Teed blinks several times before being able to focus on her son's face.

"You have a handsome face. You look like somebody I used to know…um um…somebody I used to know," rambles Mrs. Teed.

Mrs. Teed looks down at the tiled floor and continues to say, "Somebody, I used to know." One long tear rolls down Teed's face. His mother does not recognize him. The emotion strikes Teed straight at his heart. The woman who birthed him does not recognize him. He thinks to himself, *how much have I changed? Is it the hair color? Is it the mustache? Is it the number of years that I have been gone?* Teed is looking for some type of excuse to rationalize why his mother does not recognize him. A visibly shaken Teed excuses himself and runs out of his mother's room. As Teed runs out of the room, he thinks to himself, *where do I go. Who can I turn to?*

Richard Teed is sitting in his car outside of the North Charleston Mental Hospital, sobbing. The emotion of seeing his mother in an unnerving mental state has caused him to question everything he has done over the past 13 years. Teed questions if his mother's mental state is worth the time he spent away from her. Teed thinks his mother is a shell of herself. Where is the woman that would give him a hug every time she saw him? What happened to the beautiful woman who was his mother just 13 years prior? Teed hoped that he would come to Charleston to visit his mother and in some kind of way she would make him feel better, with hopes of forgetting the horror that he had inflicted. The thought of assassinating President Kennedy is now a distant memory.

The condition of his mother becomes front and center. He wonders what he can do. Should he come back to Charleston to take care of his mother? Teed begins to sob again. He drops his head into his hands.

Through the grief he is feeling, Teed hears the clack of shoes approaching him.

Teed takes his right hand off his face and reaches under his seat and pulls out his silver .45 magnum and points it out of the driver's side window at the person approaching.

"Wow, are you going to shoot me with the gun I gave you?" recites Danya.

Teed lowers the gun as he sees Danya's friendly face. She walks around to the passenger side door. She opens the door and sits in the passenger seat.

"Danya, what do you want?" questions a distraught Teed as he puts his head back into his hands.

"I want to help," insists Danya.

"What can you do? Can you make my mother get better? Can you take away this feeling of guilt I have?" challenges Teed.

The usually stoic Danya begins to cry as a single tear rolls down her rosy cheek.

"I want to take you away from here," asserts Danya.

Teed lifts his head.

"Take me to where? Do I leave my mother? Do I just forget what has happened over the past week?" he asks.

"Of course not. But what is done is done now. We can make sure your mother gets the best care possible. There is nothing you can do for her now. The other thing…there is nothing you can do about that…let us be clear; you must snap yourself out of this," states Danya forcefully.

Danya has been told by the powers that be that if Teed's mental state does not clear up fairly soon, he will have to be dealt with. She knows that means that if Teed doesn't get it together he will be killed, if not by her then by someone else.

"I have been given a mission by my government. I don't know all the details of the mission, but I know it is a covert mission as husband and wife. I want you to come with me. Come with me, get your head together and put this strife behind you…. I know you are apprehensive to leave your mother, but we will get her out of this god-forsaken place and get her better care," promises Danya. Teed wipes his face; he tries to snap himself out of his funk.

"You are going to have to trust me. We are going to leave the country soon, and we won't be coming back anytime soon. Ok?" says Danya.

The gravity in Danya's voice sobers Teed to the situation. He nods his head in agreement. She leans over and kisses Teed on his forehead. She kisses him as a sign of comfort to let him know that everything will be alright.

THE PREACHER

In the summer of 1967, the Vietnam War is in full swing. There are over 300,000 American troops in the war. The war has cost the U.S. approximately 20,000 troops' lives and approximately $30 billion dollars, without any end in sight. The U.S. began its efforts in Vietnam back during the Eisenhower administration, so the dollar amount related to this conflict is well north of $70 billion dollars.

War has always been a motivating virtue for all imperialistic societies: the Roman Empire, the Greeks, the Babylonians and yes, the United States of America have all shared these principles. The use of war allowed all these powers to take natural resources and strategic lands in the name of a cultured society. Unlike the prior three imperialistic societies, the current U.S. war machine is being presented to the American public through the medium of television as a war the country can't win. The war has gone from many strategic covert missions under the Kennedy administration to a full-blown military engagement under the Johnson administration. Those that wanted war got exactly what they wanted, the American infantry is fully engaged with the Viet Cong. Cecil Thomas' company, Steadman Technologies, has profited well from the war. The company has made a staggering $15 billion dollars during the hostilities.

Steadman's lucrative contracts with the U.S. government have the company providing aircraft, tanks, retrofitted vehicles, clothing, guns, etc. Steadman Technologies has offered themselves as a one stop shop for the American military during the conflict. The U.S. government has in effect written the organization a blank check. Cecil's relationship with the 8Men has provided him with a financial windfall that his father-in-law could not have imaged for his company two decades ago.

The 8Men are sitting at their round war table laughing about good times and smoking cigars. The mood in the room is very jovial. The group has gathered in order for Cecil Thomas to disperse funds to the members. Today is the first of many paydays to come. Steadman has been making a killing off the suffering of American soldiers and their families, but today it is time for Steadman to pay tribute to a few of the power brokers that made their newfound bonanza possible. Cecil hands out individual checks in the amount $500,000. The amount is staggering, but it is a pittance to the amount Steadman has raked in.

Senator Hampton Capers looks hard at the check and exclaims, "Whoo wee! Thomas I think I love you. And I think my family and friends are going to love you too." The entire group starts to laugh.

"This is a wonderful token, and I hope there is more to come." Senator Capers gives Cecil Thomas a short glare. Thomas gives an affirming nod back.

"Good. Gentleman, I think we may have an obstacle that may derail our gravy train," claims Senator Capers.

The group looks puzzled.

"The Nigger preacher Martin Luther King has turned his attention from the colored people's issues to telling the coloreds and the poor White trash not to go to Vietnam. He is questioning why we are over there and why those that are disenfranchised here in the United States should go fight over there," remarks Senator Capers.

Murray Smith takes a long toke off his Bacardi-dipped Cuban cigar before he speaks.

"Gentleman, we have tried to quell the spread of King's message, but the Negro press and other underground publications have caught on to his message."

Smith passes out copies of the Afro-American newspaper. The headline reads, "Whose War are we Fighting?"

"I have seen polls where 70 to 80% of Negroes are against the Vietnam War. There have also been accompanying polls that are showing declining support from low-income Whites. If we lose both of those groups, who will fight the war? More well-to-do Americans of soldiering age are getting deferments or all-out leaving the country," confirms Murray Smith.

The once jovial atmosphere has changed. There is an indiscriminate shout of "we can't allow this."

Director Carter speaks up. "I will look into this. Maybe Director Hoover is already on it."

COINTELPRO

J. Edgar Hoover led a very secretive program to disrupt and destroy Black organizations and individuals he deemed subversive or communists. This initiative was called the Counterintelligence Program but became known as "Cointelpro." In Hoover's view, any person or group disagreeing with the U.S. government fell into this category. All the civil rights advocates and those speaking out about the mistreatment of Black and brown folks were in the FBI's crosshairs. At the top of Hoover's Cointelpro list was Martin Luther King Jr. Hoover has loathed Martin Luther King Jr. since he was nominated for the 1964 Noble Peace Prize. Hoover saw King's nomination, then him winning the Noble Peace Prize, as a slap in his face. In the beginning, Hoover wanted to stop all the Black liberation efforts because he saw them as kin to the communists. The thought was that King needed to be neutralized because many believed he was the Black messiah. Hoover hated that Martin Luther King was trying to achieve equal rights for Negroes. Hoover felt that Negroes were beneath him and that their achievement would cause the second Civil War. Hoover is not crazy about the Ku Klux Klan, but he didn't want that element to rise in the face of so-called equal rights.

Director Carter reaches out to Director Hoover in an effort to find a joint solution to the so-called Martin Luther King problem.

Director Carter is sitting in Hoover's office reading a file labeled "Cointelpro MLK." Carter looks up from the file.

"You sent him letters telling him to commit suicide?" asks a baffled Carter.

"Sure, that way we wouldn't have to waste bullets on him," mocks a laughing Hoover.

Director Carter always had a respectful opinion of Director Hoover. Carter thought Hoover did a lot of good work during his fight with the gangsters of the 1930s, but since then he thinks the director has been an errand boy for the mob and a chief looking for headlines instead of criminals. Even though they never had a conversation about it, Carter knows that the powers that be in the mob have been blackmailing Hoover since the late 1940s. Carter saw the pics of Hoover caught in a compromising position with a man. Carter always thought it was ironic that Hoover persecuted many Americans because of their suspected homosexuality.

"So, you think he should kill himself because he may or may not have had sexual relations with anyone but his wife?" questions a doubtful Carter.

Hoover rises out of his seat angrily.

"Of course. He is supposed to be a man of the cloth, a clergyman, the so-called Black Messiah. He is nothing more than a sexual beast. People need to know; he needs to be exposed as the fraud he is. King is leading many Black people into an unwinnable war with the U.S. government. If we can destroy him, the so-called Messiah, the rest won't dare challenge us," concludes a passionate Hoover.

Hoover's office phone rings. He answers. "Yes, excuse me Miss De Lour, I forgot they were coming in today. I will be right out. Director Hoover hangs up the phone,

"I need to take care of a few things. I will be right back," states Hoover as he leaves the room. Director Carter is in awe of Director Hoover's thinking. He notices that Hoover has several poster boards on several easels throughout the room. One of the poster boards illustrates, "Nation of Islam." The poster has pictures of Elijah Muhammad, Muhammad Ali, and Malcolm X, with deceased written over his face. Poster two has the heading "The Black Panthers." The pictures that Carter recognizes are Bobby Seale, H. Rap Brown, Stokely Carmichael, and Geronimo Pratt.

The third poster is the obvious prize. It is a large picture of Martin Luther King during his "I have dream" speech.

The picture has a crosshair over the top of it.

Carter realizes that he must be careful involving Hoover in any plans that he might have. Hoover's apparent hatred may cause unforeseen problems.

"This fucker is out of his damn mind. I think I had better take a trip to Israel," proclaims Carter to himself.

DIMONA

It has been a little over three years since Danya and Teed left the states. They settled in the Israeli city of Dimona. The city sits in the Negev desert. The couple has settled in the town as a part of a covert mission to monitor terrorist activities against the Negev Nuclear Research Center. The facility was kept a secret for a little over a decade until recently, when French officials who assisted in its construction believed the facility should be regulated. After the murder of President Kennedy, the Israeli government began to build its secret nuclear installation in Dimona. The installation was going to allow the state of Israel to build nuclear weapons and keep all its nearby enemies at arm's length. With no opposition to their nuclear ambitions, the Israelis were free to build an arsenal that could level all its known enemies. The Arabic Liberation League (A.L.L.) has vowed to destroy the facility as well as the state of Israel. Publicly, Dimona has come under much scrutiny by the international community, but many in countries outside the Middle East are secretly in full agreement with Israel's actions. Since the discovery of the atrocities found during the Jewish Holocaust, many countries have looked the other way on many decisions the Israelis have made in the name of self- preservation. Many of the countries including the US, looked the other way while the Nazis began their reign of terror.

Danya and Teed are posing as shopkeepers; they have owned the shop for a little over three years. They have been gathering valuable intel since coming to the area. Many in the community relay information unwittingly to the couple. The pair received a tip a little over six months ago. An A.L.L. operative was planning an attack of the nuclear facility. Danya and Teed foiled the plot and gained valuable intel on the group's operations and plans. After a brief shootout injured an A.L.L. operative, Danya and Teed took him to a warehouse to be interrogated. The A.L.L. operative was a solider of the movement. From the tattoos he had, the operative was an Egyptian prisoner from the infamous Liman Tora prison. It was rumored that the A.L.L. brotherhood grew out of the frustration of many of Muslims felt with the growing domination of the region by the Jews.

As two children run out of the shop, a whistling Director Wesley Carter walks into the shop. He takes the couple by complete surprise; then they realize that if Carter is in Israel, then he wants something; he surely wouldn't be here on vacation. Carter looks around the shop to make sure no one else is in earshot. He picks up an apple and takes a bite without paying for it.

"My favorite assassins, how's Israel? Both Teed and Danya roll their eyes at Director Carter. I am going to need to bring you both back into service. Your vacations are effectively over," states Director Carter.

Teed has been keeping up on U.S. politics by reading the *New York Sun*. He has read that Bobby Kennedy may be vying for the democratic nomination for president in 1968.

Teed asks Carter, "Another Kennedy is getting to close?"

Carter scoffs at Teed's comments.

Carter responds, "We will get to Bobby in due time, but we have more pressing issues with the Negro preacher Martin Luther King." Teed is perplexed by the 8Men's concern for Martin Luther King.

"He is just a preacher. He has no real power," comments Teed. Carter starts to laugh.

"I love this kid. You are so naïve. C'mon Teed, Jesus Christ was a preacher. The Jewish establishment said he had no power; how did that whole thing turn out? No disrespect to your religion Ms. Franck," apologizes Carter.

"None taken," rebuts Danya.

"What did he do?" questions Teed.

"He meddled in some business that was not his to venture into. The whole business with the colored rights was quite admirable, but now he is affecting people's business. And we can't have that. So that's where you two fine people come into play. I know you've been playing house for the last couple of years, but now you need to be called back into service," asserts Carter.

"Director Carter, we are on a mission," rebuts Teed.

Director Carter seems to be losing his patience debating the issue of Teed and Danya coming back to the states.

Danya interjects, "Richard you go back to take care of the director's request, and if we resolve the issues here, I will join you there. Get your things; I will be alright," she says.

Teed slowly walks toward the back of the store, eyeballing Director Carter, obviously showing his displeasure. Once he walks in the back of the store, Director Carter leans over the counter to speak to Danya,

"I wish you were going to be there to help him, but I know your loyalties lie here. But when you are ready to come back to the states, I have a solo mission for you. I am sure you will relish this mission," hints Director Carter as he grabs a Coca-Cola before the exiting door. "Don't be a stranger now," remarks Director Carter as he walks out the door.

24 HR FLIGHT

Richard Teed has been on Director Carter's plane for a little over 12 hours. The first two hours, he watched as Director Carter snored rather loudly as they passed over Iran and Iraq. After Richard settled in, he began to reflect over the last three years in Israel. Teed and Danya went to the biblical holy land to protect the Dimona nuclear facility from possible sabotage from terrorists. Fortunately for everyone, no such attack occurred, but during this period, Teed and Danya fell in love. The two have flirted and even had sexual relations, but time in Israel gave the two time to explore each other's dreams and inner demons. Danya told Teed about her experiences during the Holocaust. She told him about her extended family being herded into a gas chamber and listening to their cries as the gas fumes began to choke them. She expressed her gratitude for still being alive but is still deeply scared by her own trauma. Over the past several months, Danya has alluded to being raped by a number of her Nazi captors. She has maintained that she is not a victim. Danya makes it clear that she has already passed judgement on her wrongdoers. The guilt of surviving the Holocaust has stuck with Danya over the years, even though she encountered her own horrors.

During their time together, Teed discovered how vulnerable Danya truly was. Before her rape, Danya was a very naïve 16-year-old that really did not know despair, but since her encounter with the Nazis, that is all she has felt.

Teed feels his own guilt for leaving Danya. He feels the Israelis fight is an admirable fight, but he sometimes questions their methods. Some of the major gripes with the Nazis were their merciless tactics to inflict pain but Teed has seen the Israelis perform similar tactics.

Director Carter awakes from his two-hour slumber and notices Teed looking out of the plane window onto a dark sky.

"This part of the world doesn't really have great scenery at night," comments Director Carter.

Teed turns toward the director.

"I didn't notice," mentions a somber Teed.

The director chuckles. "Missing your love?"

Teed starts to blush with embarrassment. He starts to stammer as he tries to respond.

"Son, it is ok. Danya Franck is a beautiful woman. I completely understand your interest. But she is a broken woman; she has a past you can't imagine," asserts Director Carter.

"Sir, she has had unspeakable things happen to her," remarks Teed.

"Have you ever seen any of the classified pics of what the Nazis did to the Jews? Downright grotesque…some of the shit makes you just want to throw up. They killed the Jews like they were sport. All I saw were pictures, she lived it, and I can't imagine the burden she carries," admits Director Carter.

"Me neither," responds Teed.

"Either way, your focus must be on the task at hand," declares Carter.

A doubtful Teed questions, "Sir, has anyone tried to talk to Reverend King or even try to scare him?"

Director Carter opens a manila folder with Martin Luther King's name on it.

"Hoover is so consumed with hate when it comes to these Black groups. I personally couldn't care less about the civil rights thing. Hoover can't see straight when it comes to King. A number of different efforts have been attempted. Hoover was initially tasked with this, but his band of bumbling idiots alerted King he was being monitored. We had tapes of him and his inner circle having wild sex parties. But the god damn FBI sent him a letter telling him to kill himself." Carter leaps out his seat in a huff and goes to the window.

"For the life of me I don't know why those idiots thought he would just kill himself. So, we are all out of ideas; to get him to stop now we must eliminate him. Come up with a plan and tell me what you need. That is the mission," states Director Carter.

BEN'S CHILI BOWL

A staple of the District of Columbia's Negro community is the great Ben's Chili Bowl restaurant. The eatery has become a swanky diner that sits in the District's U Street corridor. Ben's Chili Bowl has been popular with many Negro artists and entertainers for years since it sits just a block away from the Negro landmark, the Howard Theatre. The establishment brings people from miles around to eat the great chili and the assortments of hot dogs and sausages.

Teed has been plotting a possible location for the assassination of Martin Luther King Jr., but he knows that he has to cultivate a team as efficient as the one that worked with him before on the Kennedy assassination. Teed knows that he needs to call his most reliable ally outside of his pretend wife. Teed calls the always dependable Squirrel; he knows he can count on his help and his veiled silence.

Teed walks into Ben's Chili Bowl. The smell of fried sausage and chili are overwhelming. Teed takes a look at the menu, knowing that he will be coming back to the counter to order something in response to his instant hunger. He notices The Squirrel eating in the back of the establishment. Teed walks through the sea of Negroes to get to The Squirrel.

"My God, it looks like you have never eaten before," says a laughing Teed.

The Squirrel continues to eat as he momentarily chuckles at Teed's comments.

"Teed, New York needs one of these places. These are the best god damn hot dogs I've ever had. The damn chili…oh my God. I know I'm going to have the shits tonight, if I make it that long," jokes The Squirrel.

Both of the men start to laugh.

"Where you been? That cute little fox got your nose opened? She is a fine little thing," utters The Squirrel.

"So how do you like D.C.?" asks Teed.

"D.C. is fucking great. I love it. There is an ass load of beautiful Black women here. Between the women and this here place, I might just relocate," remarks a laughing Squirrel.

"So, what's up, man? I appreciate that you invited me to D.C., but I know there's got to be something you need," claims The Squirrel.

"I do need you…I have another job to do. This will be a smaller team, probably just you and me," hints Teed as he reaches for one of The Squirrel's hot dogs.

"Good, I really didn't like those Italians. Y'all good with this prez?" questions The Squirrel apprehensively.

"We are good with this one. The folks I am with are ok with him," comments Teed.

"Well then who?" asks The Squirrel.

Teed leans in to speak to The Squirrel.

"If we do this, you will be a very rich man," discloses Teed.

"Sounds good to me, I am all ears," anticipates The Squirrel.

"I have orders to neutralize Martin Luther King Jr. He is to be neutralized within the next calendar year. My orders are to make sure he is gone by the end of the summer of 1968 so that it will not have a major impact on the presidential election," whispers Teed.

The Squirrel drops most of his eaten hot dog bun in utter amazement. Then starts laughing.

"I have never known you to be a jokey guy, but this has to be some sick joke," asks The Squirrel.

Teed solemnly shakes his head.

"You are like my brother…you saved my life from that god damn Viet Cong. I would do just about anything for you—anything…but this; is there some other way?" demands The Squirrel.

Again, Teed shakes his head.

"This is just wrong. He doesn't have any power. He is like the Black messiah…. I can't be a part of this one," states The Squirrel.

Teed realizes The Squirrel is not going to do the job.

"Money is no object; tell me what you want," asks Teed.

The Squirrel is somewhat insulted as he touches his heart.

"You know it was tough to do President Kennedy, but you are my man so I went along with you…but being a Negro I just can't. I can't be responsible for King's death," reveals The Squirrel with a finality in his voice.

Teed is very disappointed by The Squirrel's answer, but he understands. Teed reflects on his feelings about the murder of President Kennedy. The Squirrel takes a long breath.

"I know you are going to fulfill your orders. If you are going to do this, you will need a good patsy this time. I never really agreed with that Oswald guy. He was too connected. You need a cracker racist from the South or Midwest who is a prison escapee or something. Make sure he is a known racist. After he is caught, the racist connection will make it an open and shut case. For your sake, people won't look further into it…. Ricky, when does this stop? We ain't no better than all those fucked up countries we were sent into to liberate. Here we just kill the liberators," challenges The Squirrel.

Teed looks out the window with a look of confusion.

PATSY

The assassination of John Fitzgerald Kennedy has awakened a conspiratorial view of America's government. Many Americans believe that forces within the U.S. government participated in JFK's murder. It has not been lost on "Joe Public" that Lee Harvey Oswald seemed to be an Army operative. Oswald also seemed to be well connected to current and former government officials. After meeting with The Squirrel, Richard Teed meets with Director Carter about trying to find the right person to take the fall for Martin Luther King's murder. Unlike the Kennedy situation, the 8Men's thought is to find someone to be a lone-wolf murderer. Following The Squirrel's suggestion, Teed wants to find someone that most Americans both Black and White could look at and agree was the killer. Director Carter has requested information on all White men who have escaped prisons within the last six months in the Midwest. Director Carter is looking at the *Washington Sun*. The *Sun* is reporting that Martin Luther King is leading a poor people's march. The *Sun* is tying together that poor young people are dying in Vietnam while their more well-to-do counterparts are not making the ultimate sacrifice of dying in war. Many rich White kids are receiving deferments to escape the possible draft. Most poor people are enlisting in the military optimistically hoping for a quick resolution.

In a separate article, it shows polls that Americans' opinions on the war are declining. Director Carter throws down the paper down and looks out his large bay window. "We got to do something about this fucker," says Carter to an empty room.

There is a knock at the door.

"Enter," barks Director Carter.

Three delivery men come in with boxes labeled "confidential." The delivery men place the nine boxes in front of Director Carter's desk. The director starts to look through the boxes. Teed walks into the director's office, and the director notices him.

"Your information has come in; why again do you need this information?" asks Carter.

Teed starts to look in the boxes.

"We are looking for a young to middle-aged White male with a reason to kill Martin Luther King. We need someone who looks like a criminal. We don't want any governmental ties this time. We will not have to get rid of this patsy. In fact, we want to make sure this patsy will rot in jail. We need him to be someone that will convince Joe Public that this guy hated Martin Luther King so much that he had to kill him," conspires Teed.

Director Carter smiles at Teed. Teed notices the director smiling at him.

"What?" asks Teed.

"You have changed. You have become an insightful operative. I knew you had it in you. Others were worried about you, but I'm glad you have come into your own," rebuts Director Carter.

Teed smiles at the director. His smile becomes a frown as he realizes maybe he has lost his soul. Teed thinks to himself, *"Am I now a soulless person?"* He wonders, *"Have I lost the boy from 400 Ashley Avenue?"* As

Teed contemplates if his soul will burn in hell, he notices a file picture of a scraggly gentleman named James Earl Ray.

The Underground Railroad is a little-known secret about a resource used by escaped prisoners in the Midwest. The escapees go to different predetermined locations throughout the Midwest to receive help and avoid capture. Several years ago, the CIA found out about the Underground Railroad. The Agency was tipped off by Chicago crime boss Sam Giancana's people during the run up to the JFK assassination. The thought was that if they needed anybody to purchase guns and/or to be used for a likely cover story, it would have been very hard to convince the American public that a lone escapee was responsible for the death of the president. Instead of the CIA letting the appropriate law enforcement know about the Underground Railroad, they opted to exploit the resource. The Agency has employed many of these escapees in covert missions in the U.S. and abroad. The CIA has looked at these folks as expendables. The Underground Railroad usually provides money and identity changes for the escapees, and no organization disappears people like the CIA.

Butchie's is a local low-brow bar in Cahaste, Missouri. Teed walks into the bar, and he is immediately repulsed by the heavy stench of stale cigarette smoke. He walks over to a secluded booth. A waitress follows him to his table as he sits in the booth.

"What may I get you?" asks the gravelly voiced 40-something waitress.

"I will take a scotch on the rocks," replies Teed.

A skinny, scraggly, middle-aged man walks into the bar. Teed immediately recognizes James Earl Ray from the picture he saw in Director's Carter's file. Teed tips his fedora in James Earl Ray's direction, signaling him to come over to the table. Ray walks in the direction of Teed's table. Ray does not look like the typical crook. He is scrawny and unsure of himself. Teed feels somewhat sorry for Ray; he wonders how a guy like this could survive in jail. He looks terrified to be in such an establishment.

"Hi, I am Ray," stammers James Earl Ray.

Teed pauses for a minute. He looks at the wall and notices a picture of singer Raoul Mendez. Teed realizes that he cannot give Ray his real name. He says to himself, "This patsy is going live. He can't know my real name. I need to give him a name I can abruptly walk away from. Teed extends his hand to Ray.

"Hello, my name is Raoul," announces Teed.

They both sit in the booth. "I understand you are trying to disappear?" asks Teed.

"I am, but I don't know how, and I don't have any money," replies Ray.

"I understand your dilemma, but I will need you to do me some favors to work off the debt," discloses Teed.

Ray nods his head in the affirmative.

"It could be anything, delivering money, drugs, or even guns. Will any of that bother you?" inquires Teed.

Ray shakes his head.

"Let me ask you another question. How do you feel about Niggers?" asks Raoul.

Ray looks around the bar, looking very confused by Raoul's question. He shrugs his shoulders.

"I really don't care either way. I stay out of their way, and I hope they stay out of mine," utters a nonchalant Ray.

"Great, here is some paperwork. This is your new identity." Teed hands Ray an address. "I will meet you in Toronto," says Teed.

TORONTO

The brisk Canadian air is foreign to Richard Teed. The native Charlestonian stays away from the north. He had been to New York City, but very rarely in the wintertime. Even New York City is no match for Toronto's fall air. Teed thinks it is a good idea to meet James Earl Ray in Toronto, away from the prying eyes of any potential American agents. He thinks that since he is in Toronto, it would be a great idea to meet Ray at the McLaughlin Planetarium. Teed is very interested in the planets and stars. He always wondered what was going on outside of the realm of the planet Earth. So, Teed will be killing two birds with one stone once his meeting with Ray has finished.

The nervous James Earl Ray walks toward Teed, known to him as Raoul, sitting on the park bench outside the McLaughlin Planetarium.

"This is an interesting place to meet," says Ray.

"Not really, I am going to look at the planets and stars once we finish. I believe there is life outside the planet Earth. Good to see what is going on in the galaxy," responds Raoul.

Ray sees the brown duffle bag to the right of Raoul.

"Is that bag for me?" asks Ray.

"You are very perceptive. This bag has ten thousand dollars in it. I want you to go to Los Angeles to purchase some guns from a contact of mine. You look at the guns and see if you can't get a lower price. If you are able to talk him down, the money is yours. Whatever you do, don't make my contact feel like you are taking advantage of them. If they feel insulted, they just might kill you. And that would be bad for both of us. I would lose credibility and you, frankly, would lose your life," responds Raoul.

Ray is visibility shaken by Raoul's frank discussion.

"I don't know about this. If I say the wrong thing, they could kill me. What the hell are you getting me into?" questions a somewhat emotional Ray.

"Calm down, nobody is going to kill you. I was messing with you. My contact knows who I am. They may want to put the fear of God in you, but they won't touch you. Ten thousand should cover the merchandise," says a calming Raoul.

Ray seems to be a little more at ease but still has questions. "After I get the guns, what should I do with them? Do I come back here?" he rambles.

Teed laughs at Ray.

"Are you kidding? We are in Canada. As bad as Canada's border security is, there is absolutely no way you could bring a trunk full of guns back here. No, I want you to drop off the car in Chicago. I will pick up the car there," clarifies Raoul as he hands Ray an envelope of 20 crisp $100 bills.

"What is this for? You already gave me the bag with ten thousand," asks Ray in amazement.

"It is for your expenses getting to and back from L.A. Don't stay out there long and don't make too much noise. Remember, you are a prison escapee," reminds Raoul as he stands up to button his coat. "If you will excuse me, I am going to look at the planets and the stars.

Richard Teed's strategy of making James Earl Ray a patsy is going according to plan. James Earl Ray's back story is starting to fill in. With Ray escaping from prison, he is the perfect patsy. He has been conditioned to run and avoid any contact with so-called normal folk.

Teed walks into the planetarium. He slowly walks through the halls of the planetarium, taking in all the sights and looking at the vast reaches of the galaxy. Teed walks over to an exhibit called "The World Was Flat." The exhibit highlights the period in which people believed that if they sailed far enough, they could fall off the earth. Teed is looking at the exhibit when he is approached by a man wearing a baseball cap and very dark sunglasses.

"Are you Raoul?" inquires the gravelly voiced man.

"I am," responds Teed as he steps back to make sure no one else is with the man.

"You came alone?" asks Teed.

The man smiles devilishly at Teed.

"I never go anywhere alone. I have people with me; don't worry, they are here in the shadows. You are Raoul, I presume?" questions the man.

"I am, and you are?" asks Teed.

The gentleman laughs. "I have many names, but all you need to know is that my name is Sam," reveals the gentleman.

Teed is amused by the man's overblown arrogance. Another man comes out of the darkness with a briefcase. He hands the briefcase to Sam. Sam begins to open the briefcase. Teed motions to the man to not open the case.

"No need for you to open the case. I know that you want Dr. King dead; I know you won't shortchange your mission," suggests Teed. "You are quite smart, young man. So, when can we expect that trash to be taken care of? We are getting tired of seeing him. He is getting all our Southern Niggers all uppity. Got them thinking that they can vote and sit with good self-respecting White folks. We can't have it. We will not have our way of life changed because some Niggers are feeling they want change," proclaims a frustrated Sam.

Teed listens to Sam's frustration, but he doesn't really give a damn about his problems with Negroes. Teed's mission is to neutralize Martin Luther King so that he will not awaken the poor Americans that are needed to fight the war in Vietnam.

POW WOW

P ope Paul VI declared January 1, 1968, a day of peace. Thousands of lives have perished in the Vietnam War, both Vietnamese and American. The hope was that the day of peace would help both sides realize that they should end the conflict. The number of causalities are piling up without either side looking to find a creditable solution. The war doesn't seem to be breaking for either side; both seem to be digging in their heels on their respective sides. The continued conflict is exactly what the 8Men want.

The 8Men have decided to meet at the Annapolis Yacht Club in Annapolis, Maryland. The club sits on the beautiful Spa Creek, with the angelic St. Mary's Catholic Church serving as a backdrop. The club is also home to Murray Smith's massive yacht, The Smitty Bear. The men have assembled in the club's meeting hall. They are joined by some beautiful 20-something young ladies wearing very skimpy dresses. The festive atmosphere is a little too much for Teed. He walks out of the glass doors that lead to the marina pier.

"Ladies, could you all please excuse us?" asks Murray Smith.

The young ladies gather their belongings and begin to exit the room.

The gentlemen start to make their way to a brown, oval-shaped table.

"I love how you boys put a party together," utters Maximillian Love.

Everybody chuckles at Love's comment.

"Gentlemen, thank you all for convening here in Annapolis. We have had the pleasure of some beautiful young ladies…but now it is necessary that we all get down to business," conveys Murray Smith.

Hampton Capers and Lance Bowen light up cigars.

"Gentleman, we continue to prosper as a unit. Steadman's profits continue to climb, so of course your profits have climbed as well," claims Cecil Thomas.

Cecil passes around envelopes to everyone at the table. The gentlemen open their envelopes. The envelopes contain checks for $1 million dollars for each of the 8Men. There are also checks for Teed and Danya that Thomas puts to the side.

Hampton Capers takes a toke on his cigar and begins to laugh. "Yee haw!" yells out an excited Capers.

"I hope you all are pleased with these proceeds," says Cecil Thomas.

"God damn Cecil Thomas, I think I love you. Boy, make sure you keep the money faucet on," jokes an amused Capers. Cecil Thomas takes enjoyment in his response. "Gentleman, I am glad that you are pleased with your gains, but we must speak about some possible barriers. Number one is this notion of possible peace. As we all know, today is supposed to be a day of peace. The Pope's attempt won't last long, but King's continued efforts are making inroads with Negroes and even some poor Whites. We need to have all these people fighting continually. We need them using planes, we need them shooting bullets, and we need them using resources so that we can replace them. This is how we can continue to make money. We must do something about King. The longer he is out there preaching to the masses, the more people will heed his message," replies a concerned Cecil Thomas.

"I thought we discussed killing the Nigger? What are we doing? I thought we agreed that he would be neutralized?" remarks Capers.

"We have agreed, but we wanted to make sure everybody was still on board. We have been planning; we should be ready in the next month or so," hints a stern Wesley Carter.

"Is everybody in agreement?" probes Cecil Thomas.

All the 8Men raise their hands in agreement.

"Fine, we are in agreement," confirms Cecil Thomas.

"What is next?" questions Maximillian Love.

"The next issue is a possible presidential run by Bobby Kennedy," announces Director Carter.

The 8Men are very surprised. There is an immediate concern.

"Are you sure? I have not heard any of this before," asks Valerius.

"I have a couple of sources that assert that Kennedy will make a run. The president is looking very weak right now," reveals Director Carter.

"What in the hell? That would be political suicide for Bobby. A presidential run from somebody in the same party as the sitting president?" suggests Hampton Capers.

"Senator, I would ordinarily agree with you, but this is not ordinary. The person possibly running for president holds the sitting president responsible for killing his brother—a brother that his world revolved around. In this instance, all the normal rules should be thrown out the window. So, I would be derelict if I didn't ask you all what you would like to do," asks Carter.

"We can't allow Kennedy to run. His brother was eliminated because of him. He would be impossible to deal with as president. We cannot allow this," declares Valerius.

"So, what do we do?" asks Carter.

"I suggest that if he formally runs, we must take him out before we get to the general election," replies Hampton Capers.

"If he decides to run, then we will take care of him. We will work up preliminary plans for Kennedy," proclaims Director Carter.

"Are you going to have the same team on Kennedy that will be doing King?" asks Cecil Thomas.

"No, I will get another team to work on that," says Carter.

Teed is sitting on the Smitty Bear dressed in his Sunday best. He is wearing a powder blue suit accented by a red and blue-striped tie and white bucks. He is loving the unusually warm winter day in Maryland. The setting of the day has not been lost on Teed; his mind is on the task that he must tackle in the next few months. He is joined on the boat by Director Carter.

"You didn't want to stay in the meeting?" asks Carter.

Teed looks off into the distance.

"No, I am not a part of the 8Men. I am a solider, not a thinker like you Director," replies Teed sarcastically.

Carter laughs at Teed's assertion.

"I think and I know the others value your opinion," rebuts Carter.

"Ok, answer me this. Why are we killing a preacher? It is really hard for me to wrap my mind around this. All he is doing is inspiring people. Where is the patriotism? That is why we were doing this, right?" says a bothered Teed.

"Look, I understand that sometimes it is hard to see that patriotism isn't black and white. There are many levels of gray. The men that broke from the British were branded traitors. They were to be hung on sight. So, depending on who you were talking to on that day, they were traitors. Today, what do you call them?" challenges Carter.

Carter's words have left Teed with some ideas to think about.

Teed is not going to let a perfectly warm January day go to waste. He is riding through downtown Annapolis checking out the post New Year's festivities going on in the capitol city. People are out with their young children enjoying family time and the many outdoor restaurants. The United States Naval Academy is a short one-mile ride from the Eastport

Yacht Club. Teed drives over to the Naval Academy's west gate on his way to Hospital Point. Hospital Point is a large green space that was used for Plebe training during the week and used for youth sports on holidays and weekends.

Teed pulls up to one of the many fields filled with young football players, then walks across the field. Off in the distance is a woman sitting on a picnic blanket with a picnic basket. The woman is wearing a royal blue dress with a white head scarf and dark sunglasses.

"You fixed a picnic basket. How thoughtful of you," says Teed. "Thank you, sweetheart," says Danya as she takes her extremely large sunglasses off her face.

"I love the scenery. Is this a meeting or a date?" asks a smitten Danya.

Teed smiles. "It is a bit of both," he flirts as he bends down to kiss Danya on the cheek.

Teed reaches into his sports coat's inner pocket. He pulls out the envelope the 8Men wanted Danya to have. Danya opens the envelope and sees the one-million-dollar check made out to Danya Franck.

"America pays well. When we leave the country, I will deposit this in my bank in Geneva. So, what is the purpose for our date?" asks Danya.

"I really need your help. I thought I could do the King Job by myself."

Danya pulls out a bottle of wine.

"But I realized I can't, and you are the best in planning jobs," reveals Teed.

Danya starts to gleefully giggle. "You say the sweetest things. And yes, I will help you."

Danya pulls out wine glasses and starts to pour the wine.

"You will need to get the target's schedule over the next four months. The target will be easy once we get his pattern. The two of us will do the job. Ask Carter to get the information, then we go underground. No more contact with anyone after that," discloses Danya. Teed nods his head yes.

INSIDE MAN

As a part of the Cointelpro program, J. Edgar Hoover assigned a Black CIA agent to keep tabs on Martin Luther King and his group of advisors. The planted agent has been able to gain the trust of King's group; this has allowed him to place bugs in hotel rooms and meeting places ahead of King's arrival in different cities. Director Carter has set up a meeting between Teed and the agent, Anthony Montgomery. Montgomery was snatched from the District of Columbia Police Academy. He tested off the charts while at the academy. Without giving him too much credit, the academy officers had never seen a Negro cadet score perfect scores on the aptitude and physical test so consistently. Montgomery's achievements did not go without notice, knowing that feds were looking for a Black agent. The academy commandant, Eugene Rudder, the former marine lieutenant, reached out to his former boss, Wesley Carter. Rudder knew that Carter was looking for a Negro federal agent and he thought that Montgomery could fit the bill. Montgomery was being brought in to be a sort of Trojan horse. Up to now, the federal government had not been able to infiltrate any of the so-called black organizations because they didn't admit white members, or with the case of Dr. King's group, they just didn't trust non-Black participants. Wesley Carter knew that Montgomery wanted to be in law enforcement but would probably have reservations about taking part in an operation that would eventually lead to King's death. So, Carter has decided to compartmentalize the information he gives to Montgomery. The cover story for Montgomery is that he is to protect King and make sure there are no communists sympathizers within the group. One of the points of contention that Hoover had with Dr. King was that his group was a front to further the communist message in America. Carter made it apparent to Montgomery that he was to protect King. Many different factions within and outside of the government want to destroy Dr. King. Director Carter assured Montgomery that the CIA didn't want anything to happen to Dr. King or his message. Montgomery was to act as King's bodyguard and to keep tabs so that there could an assessment of potential threats.

The North Carolina A&T State University graduate should have been able to apply to the FBI academy at the least, but with the bureau's unfavorable outlook on minority candidates, Montgomery, like many others of the day, had to settle for coming into law enforcement through other means. Montgomery decided to become a peace officer while in college. While at North Carolina A&T, Montgomery witnessed many of the injustices related to the Greensboro sit-ins. Montgomery thought that if he became a peace officer that maybe some kind of way, he could level the playing field. Montgomery is on a break from protecting King's group. King and his advisors all planned time to be with their families ahead of the coming Poor People's marches.

Teed wants to ensure that Montgomery's cover is not blown. He decides to meet Montgomery on rural Route 17 in Stanton, Virginia, just one mile south of Bowen's gas station. Teed is sitting on the shoulder of the road in a mustard-colored Chevrolet Camaro. About three minutes later, Montgomery pulls up in a White Ford Fairlane. Montgomery immediately gets out of his car and walks up to Teed's Camaro.

"Are you Teed?" asks a hesitant Montgomery.

Teed shakes his head yes. He throws the loose papers sitting on the front seat into the back.

"How was your trip?" asks Teed.

"Ok. I understand you need information about King?" questions Montgomery.

"I do. How far out is King's schedule?" requests Teed.

"Hard to say. He has events scheduled six months from now, but he always fills things in," reveals Montgomery.

"How is the security for King and his inner circle?" inquires Teed.

"Not good. As political a figure as King is, I would think he would have more security. Many police departments have a good faith presence when he is in public, but after that he is a sitting duck," discloses Montgomery.

"That is very interesting," replies Teed.

"Also, tell Director Carter that Stanley Levinson has been in contact with Dr. King," utters Montgomery.

"Levinson?" pushes back a puzzled Teed.

Stanley Levinson was an advisor of Martin Luther King Jr.'s until 1963. President Kennedy asked King to end his relationship with Levinson because of his connections with communist group within the United States. After consulting with others in his organization he asked Levinson to leave. But over the years he has continued to write letters to privately counsel King.

"Here are some letters he has written," remarks Montgomery.

Teed takes the letters unsure of their importance to the mission.

"Are you guys going to get him some better security? He really needs it," interjects Montgomery.

Teed is shocked that Montgomery does not know the reason for his Intel. Montgomery passes Teed a piece of paper with some scribbled dates and addresses. Montgomery gets out of the car. Teed folds up the paper and places it in the glove compartment.

SANITATION

Teed and Danya decided to do some recon on Reverend Dr. Martin Luther King. Unlike President Kennedy, the pair figured getting close to King would not be as daunting a mission. King was normally followed by local police and under-cover FBI agents, but he did not have a protection detail. Many found it strange that a Black man that received so many death threats and traveled so regularly through the racist south wouldn't have a visible show of force around him. Teed and Danya heard that King would be in Memphis giving a speech, so they decided to observe him there.

The deaths of Memphis sanitation workers Echol Cole and Robert Walker touched off a strike of the city of Memphis' sanitation workers. At the center was the issue of malfunctioning equipment that caused Cole and Walker's death. The frustration of no response from the city brought the lack of wages into the spotlight. It was being reported that full-time sanitation workers were on welfare and received food stamps to keep their families afloat. Some of the sanitation workers reached out to the Memphis clergy with hopes they could make some inroads with the local government. The local clergy, led by Reverend James Lawson, went to Memphis Mayor Henry Loeb to address their concerns. Mayor Loeb asked the small group of clergymen for time to fully address their concerns. The clergymen, already frustrated by the lack of movement of local civil rights issues, thought it may be best to reach out to Reverend Dr. Martin Luther King Jr.

On March 18, 1968, Dr. King addressed a crowd of roughly 25,000 people in Memphis.

"I am so proud of you all. You have stuck together as powerful forces have tried to pull you apart. The cause of the Memphis sanitation workers is the same cause as the Poor People's movement. We are fighting for equality and a sense of respect. We are asking only for what any successful business should want… Look out for its employees, pay them a fair wage and treat them with respect. The city of Memphis' mayor has never even acknowledged the deaths of Echol Cole or Robert Walker. If the authorities in Memphis do not show respect toward it workers…how do the people have the confidence they will hold the private businesses responsible?" recites a passionate Dr. King.

There is a thunderous applause for Dr. King. Richard Teed and Danya Franck sit 10 rows back from the stage. They rise to their feet as the rest of the crowd rises; they want to make sure they don't seem out of place.

"He is quite electrifying," marvels Danya.

"He is," replies Teed.

"Gentlemen, I encourage you to all strike. The strike must stay non-violent. You must show the powers that be that you are committed. I will not tell you it will be easy, because it won't be. There will be brothers that will cross the strike line. You will be impacted by loss of income, but you must keep the faith," orates a smiling King.

An hour later, Teed and Danya are ordering dinner at a local diner.

"I will have a BLT with chips, and the young lady will have a salad," states Teed.

The waitress completes their orders.

"King is a good speaker," admits Teed.

"He is, but you know we must complete the mission," asserts a stern Danya.

Teed nods his head in agreement.

"I never listened to his speeches before, but he does make some striking arguments," proclaims Danya.

Teed is intrigued by Danya's interest.

"Like what?" inquires Teed.

"Negroes here are like the Jews were in Nazi Germany. Well not exactly, but we were second-class citizens to the Nazis. Negroes have been destroyed as a people. I dare say they aren't even second-class citizens here," expresses a sadden Danya.

Teed is shocked by Danya's assertion. Americans have regarded the atrocities by Germans during World War II as some of the most heinous acts against mankind in all of history. Teed thinks to himself that America hardly mentions the devastation of the slavery era. Teed wears a look of disbelief.

CABAL

The 8Men learned many valuable lessons before and after the assassination of President Kennedy. The most valuable lesson was the thought that the American public would not swallow any story they were given by its government. The group underestimated all the glaring connections. The convenient murder of Lee Oswald heightened the calls for a conspiracy investigation. The cabal to kill Martin Luther King had to be kept close to the vest by the 8Men. Director Carter knew he was going to need to bring in Director Hoover to pull off the King job. Director Carter had a cordial relationship with J. Edgar Hoover. He had always admired Hoover from a far. Carter respected the fact that he was a major power broker through some of America's most trying times. Hoover earned much respect for killing the communist scare of the 20's, rounding up many of the key gangsters of the 30's and taking on the Nazi spies in the 40's shortly before the US' entry into World War II. But as Carter rose through the ranks, he heard stories of Hoover bending the rules for his purposes. Either way, Carter knew Hoover could be helpful.

Director Hoover called on some of his old contacts to help pull of this caper. Knowing that King had decided to help the sanitation workers in Memphis, Hoover thought it would a good idea to reach out to his former branch Chief, Robert Powell. Powell was one of the powerful men in the state of Tennessee, surely the most powerful in Memphis. Powell has been in retirement for a little over ten years. From time to time, Hoover reaches out to Powell to get his opinion on Dixie issues. Powell is a son of the South; he is not necessarily a fan of the Klan, but he doesn't want Negroes to live equally in Memphis either.

Powell decides to invite Director Hoover to his friend Bessie Brewer's restaurant.

The director has decided to bring Teed and Danya along to the meeting. The trio enters the sparsely populated restaurant. They are greeted by the bubbly Bessie Brewer.

"Hi y'all doing? Welcome to Bessie Brewer's," greets Bessie.

"We are meeting Mr. Powell," claims a stoic Director Hoover. Understanding that the stranger means business, Ms. Brewer directs Director Hoover to the back.

"Mr. Powell is in the back," directs an expressionless Bessie Brewer.

Director Hoover walks through the restaurant with Teed and Danya in tow. The portly Powell sits in the back of the restaurant eating a slab of barbeque ribs.

"Director, can I offer you some ribs?" asks Powell.

Director Hoover, Teed and Danya sit at the table across from Powell.

"What in the hell have you done to yourself," remarks a somewhat disgusted Hoover.

Powell laughs. "Director, I thought just the two of us had business to discuss."

"You can discuss anything in front of these folks. They are with the group I was telling you about," mentions Director Hoover.

Mr. Powell motions for everybody to sit down.

"So, the Nigger preacher is really screwing up things for the bigwigs?" asks Powell.

"He is making things very inconvenient. We need to be rid of him," responds Hoover.

"I think you need a two-man team. Or maybe a one man and one-woman team." Powell laughs as he looks at Teed and Danya. Neither is amused by his assertion. "The shooter and the spotter," estimates Powell.

"I think we have that covered," replies Hoover.

"So, will there be a cover story. You plan to escape, right?" questions Powell.

"We got a cracker patsy. His cover story is in the works," discloses Hoover.

Powell takes a long gulp from his large beer mug.

"Looks like you have all your bases covered," states a smiling Powell.

"This is your city. You know the ins and outs and you have your finger on the pulse of this city. We need your contacts and need you to reach out to the people to make this go smoothly and without incident," suggests Hoover.

"Director you are so kind," laughs Powell.

"Are you going to assist us?" interjects Danya.

Danya has grown tired of the continuous banter between Powell and Director Hoover.

"You are surely one spicy Philly. Relax, this is what the director and I do," utters Powell.

Director Hoover motions to Danya that everything is ok.

"Powell, are you still friendly with the higher ups in the Memphis Police Department?" asks Hoover.

"Sure, I play poker with the chief every Friday night. He owes me a couple of big favors he needs to pay back," hints Powell.

Powell is confident the Memphis City Police Chief Bradley Wayne will help him. He helped get rid of a young woman that claimed Wayne got her pregnant 20 years ago. The young woman was 16 years old. The scandal of an underage young woman and the adultery would have sunk Wayne's career. Powell is a second cousin to Bradley's father, but they were more like brothers. Knowing also that Bradley isn't the greatest fan of Martin Luther King, he knew he could get him to go along.

THE PLAN

Over the week of March 27th, Powell plans how they would neutralize Martin Luther King. Dr. King has planned several events over the next week. All the events are going to be public. Powell has maps of the entire area and blueprints of every building of all planned events. Powell seems to be stumped.

"God dammit," utters a frustrated Powell.

"What?" asks Teed.

Powell takes out a pack of cigarettes.

"Killing him is not the problem. Getting somebody close enough and still getting away will be a problem. The churches he will be speaking at…we can't get someone in there when he is marching…no one would believe your patsy would have been the killer. We gotta get him to a place that your patsy could possibly take the shot," ponders a frustrated Powell.

Powell gets up and takes a walk while Teed gets up to look at the maps hanging on the wall. Powell walks through the back of the restaurant where the cook is making Bessie's signature barbeque sauce. He intrusively gets a piece of rib and dips it into the sauce.

"Tastes great," says Powell.

The cook looks at Powell with disgust. Powell continues through the kitchen out the back door. He digs deep into his pockets to pull out a pack of Camel cigarettes, then walks around in the alley between the restaurant and the Lorraine Motel. Even though Powell is retired, he yearns for the approval of Director Hoover. He relishes the idea of Hoover coming to him to plan for black op missions. He knows that he has come up with a creative way of killing King without any links to the bureau and largely the government. The Lorraine Motel is upscale lodging for well-to-do Blacks visiting Memphis, and many of the city's visiting Black musicians stay at the motel. He briskly walks across the court that joins the back alley of the restaurant and the parking lot of the Lorraine Motel. Powell starts to get an idea of King staying at the motel. He walks to the sidewalk that is underneath the balcony and notices that several rooms of the boarding house could be perfect perches for a sniper. Powell needs to keep in mind that the shooting needs to be plausible. He needs people to believe that an average crack pot could make the shot. Powell mentally lines up the shot. He steps back onto the parking lot and looks up.

"The second floor would be a perfect shot from the rooming house. It could be one of any of those rooms," claims a smiling Powell.

He walks through the back of the restaurant singing the Southern favorite "Nigger Go Home" by Johnny Dixie.

"Nigger Go Home, we don't want you down here no more, shut up cook my food and clean my floor. Take your half breeds and darkies and never come back to Dixie," Powell softly sings.

Teed is looking at a blank notepad.

"I know how we are going to do it!" exclaims Powell.

Robert Powell was one of the most valued tacticians at Director Hoover's disposal. Maybe it was fate that Martin Luther King was on Powell's home turf. It had been rumored that Powell was responsible for several coups in Latin American countries in the late 50s and 60s and even more chatter that he was responsible for many of the clean-up murders associated with the Kennedy assassination. Powell had a talent for completing a covert task while diverting attention away from the actual perpetrators, which always protected those ordering the act.

He brings Danya and Teed up to room 5B of Bessie Brewer's rooming house. Powell walks both into the bathroom.

"I want both of you to look at this location," says Powell.

Teed and Danya walk over to the window. They look out the window and see the Lorraine Motel in the short distance.

"What are we supposed to be looking at?" queries Teed.

"Exactly," expresses Powell.

Teed and Danya are confused about what Powell may be implying.

"Could you get a good clear shot at room 306 at the motel across the street?" asks Powell.

Danya gets a good look at the room and shrugs her shoulders.

"Either of us should be able to hit that mark with no problem," assures Danya.

"Good," says Powell.

"Now what?" asks Teed.

"Now we plan," states Powell.

The location for King's ambush has been found, but now King and his inner circle need to be convinced to stay at the motel.

"You still have a way of getting in touch with Montgomery?" asks Powell.

"Yes," answers Teed.

"Get in touch with him and your scapegoat. We need to start to pull this thing together," directs Powell.

Teed walks down the street from Bessie's Brewer's rooming house to a pay phone. He takes out a crumbled piece of notebook paper. The paper has the numbers of Ray and Montgomery. Teed walks into the phone booth. He takes out a pocket full of dimes and places them on the phone booth shelf. He dials Montgomery's number first.

"Hello, is Montgomery there? This is Teed…I am ok. I need you to move where Dr. King will be staying. We just don't think he is safe in his current location…where? We want him to go to the Lorraine Motel. It's a Negro-owned motel. We think he would be safer at a Negro-owned motel. Can you make that happen? Good, we want you to request rooms 305 and 306 for him and his associates. Great, thanks for your help," says Teed.

Teed hangs up the phone from Montgomery. He takes a deep breath, steps out of the booth and vomits in a drain outside of the booth. Teed wipes his mouth and pulls himself together. He goes back into the phone booth and begins to place a call to James Earl Ray.

"Ray…yeah this is Raoul. I need you in Memphis. I want you to come straight here. I want you here tomorrow. No excuses. Did you pick up the package in Birmingham? Bring it with you. Make sure it is fully wrapped… Alright, make sure you are here tomorrow. Ray, no *goddam excuses*," commands Teed.

STRESS

The Vietnam War is officially entering its fourth year. It has been a short four years since the controversial incident in the Gulf of Tonkin that catapulted the United States and its citizens into the conflict in the small Asian country. The massive death tolls and ballooning military presence make many question the country's values and question its government's moral compass. The Vietnam War led many young Americans to boycott and to protest the war at every turn. The once beloved and trusted presidency of the United States is being questioned. The buck stops with the president, and Lyndon Johnson is hearing it. Johnson is literally hearing from Americans; droves of citizens are camped outside of the White House screaming a barrage of insults aimed at him. The one that seems to bother him the most is the constant slander of "LBJ the baby killer." President Johnson had been called some of the worst names in his day, but normally that was from politicians who were made to bend to his will. Not the American public, these were the people who had loved him, they were the ones that swept him back into office after the assassination of President Kennedy.

Against the counsel of his inner circle, President Lyndon Johnson calls for a press conference on March 31, 1968. The president outlines his plan to limit bombing and proposes that there be peace talks.

"We will continue the bombing in areas just north of the established demilitarized zone. We will be doing this in order to protect Allied positions. I will also be asking for an additional two billion dollars in fiscal expenditures and an additional 14,000 troops to Vietnam," says a somber President Johnson.

Director Wesley Carter and Senator Hampton Capers are watching the president's speech. It has been a pleasure to their ears thus far. The men are watching the president's speech in Director Carter's office. Excited by what they have heard, Director Carter jumps up to fix a drink.

"I love that Texas fuck. Do you want a drink?" asks an excited Carter.

"Don't mind if I do. Never really liked anything from Texas before Johnson," jokes Senator Capers.

Both men laugh. They know they are about to make some serious money with the president committing an additional two billion dollars over the next year with additional troops going to the region. They both know that if troops and additional resources are committed to Vietnam, that more is to come over the next couple of years. That means the 8Men will continue to line their pockets with cash. The Director and Senator Capers are watching the television when President Johnson reveals, "I will not be seeking the Democratic nomination for President this fall."

Director Carter drops his glass in shock.

"What?" recites a confused Director Carter.

"Som bitch…Son of a bitch," yells an upset Senator Capers in a very deep South Carolinian drawl.

"*Fuck*…who will be president now?" asks Carter rhetorically.

"With Johnson dropping out, Humphrey becomes the heir apparent," answers Capers.

"It will be Bobby," rebuts Carter.

"Kennedy," utters a stunned Capers.

"Bobby will not be able to pass this up. And there is no way people will be able to resist voting for him. The back story is overwhelming. The little brother is running for president so that he can avenge his brother's murder and fulfill his dreams. He will obviously reverse everything that has to do with Vietnam. Bobby was the reason Jack wanted to pull out. Jack didn't really give a shit, he would have pushed for Vietnam if Bobby wasn't in his ear," suggests Carter.

"Will he come for us?" questions Capers.

"He would almost have to. Bobby will open up a true investigation into his brother's death… If they weren't up to their necks in that whole Cuba covert shit, he would have come sooner. The death of Jack has sat on Bobby's heart for a while. He will come after us, the mob, surely he breaks up the CIA without a doubt," rambles Director Carter.

"So, you know what we must do. Shit, Bobby has always been the problem. Jack was not the problem. He would go along to get along but Bobby…that fucker would push him. If that little fucker becomes president, we all will be strung up," hints concerned a Capers.

"He will have to go, too," states a resolute Carter.

MOSES

Martin Luther King has led the effort of the Negro people to gain full equal rights. King has championed civil rights since he stepped on the scene in 1955. No one could compare in their efforts to help the Negro gain full American citizenship. King headed the efforts to boycott the bus system in Montgomery, Alabama, which led to abolishment of segregation and the Civil Rights Act of 1964. Recently, King has been leading efforts to level the playing field for the nation's poor, regardless of race. Many in the country quietly admire King for leading the effort to integrate the country. After the protester beatings by the ravenous southern police departments, many think it is time to face the original sin of the United States.

But as King starts to delve into equal housing and the Vietnam War, he begins to run away many of his previous supporters. President Johnson was once of one of King's greatest advocates in his civil rights fight. Johnson helped King and his movement with federal assistance after the Alabama State Police beating of Selma marchers on March 7, 1965, an event also known as Bloody Sunday. Without Johnson's cooperation, the movement probably would not have received any help from the government. But King did not feel obligated to support Johnson's efforts to bring war to Vietnam. In fact, Vietnam was at the center of King's attack on America's policy to entice poor young Americans to enlist in the war.

Dr. King is relaxing in his room at the Lorraine Motel. He is feeling a bit under the weather; he has a bit of fever. Dr. King is lying across his bed looking at the TV. Anthony Montgomery is sitting in a chair talking with him. He is sitting with Dr. King while the rest of his entourage attends a gathering at the Masonic Temple.

"How are you feeling?" asks Montgomery.

"I will be ok with some rest. I must continue to forge on," says King.

"Maybe you need a vacation. Just go somewhere and sit down," jokes Montgomery.

"I do need one. I need to take my family away. I signed up for this; they didn't," remorsefully comments King.

"How much longer do you think you will be in Memphis? Maybe you can take the family on vacation after you leave here," responds Montgomery.

"I may leave in the next couple of days, but I will have to come back. The sanitation workers strike is not going how I had hoped. The city government is sticking to its guns. They really don't want to give anything," claims an insightful King.

"If you come back, what will you change?" queries Montgomery.

"I don't know, but I have to try," replies King.

"Those troublemakers from today's march didn't make things any better," mentions Montgomery.

"Young Mr. Montgomery, those are what you call government plants. We have been getting more of those here recently. For too long, too many of our peaceful marches have been too peaceful. The government has realized that they must show America that our movement has some thugs so when they beat them down, the police are looked at with a sympathetic view. Defenseless Negroes are not good for the evening news. It is good ol' intimidation from Big Brother. We know the government has been watching us for some time," admits King as he gazes at Montgomery.

Montgomery feels a bit nervous. He is not sure if King has figured out that he is an FBI agent. Montgomery tries to change the subject.

"Why does it seem like things have changed over the last couple of years?" pushes back Montgomery.

"What do you mean?" asks King.

"It just seemed like there was a feeling of marching for our rights as Negro people. But now it seems like it's not just about Negroes," asserts Montgomery.

"That's because it is not just about the Negro people. The Negro is a victim, as is the poor White person. We have won some rights for the Negro people, but what good are those rights if you can't live where you want or get the same wage as any other person? The war is the greatest tragedy. This country is sending young people to die for an unnecessary war. As an agent of God, I must speak about this injustice," declares King.

"Doesn't it seem like some people have turned against you?" asks Montgomery.

"Maybe they have. My heart and soul tell me it is the right fight, so I will follow that," concedes King.

There is a startling knock at the door. Montgomery goes to the door with his hand inside his suit jacket, tugging at his service revolver.

"Who is it?" barks Montgomery.

"It's Andy," answers Andy Young.

Andrew "Andy" Young is one of Martin Luther King Jr.'s most trusted advisors. He has argued many of the crucial legal briefs that have helped the movement.

"Marty, we need you at the temple. We know that you want to rest and frankly you need it. The crowd found out you weren't going to speak tonight, and they started getting restless. Nobody wants the other preachers; they want to hear from you," implies Andy Young.

Dr. King takes a deep breath and rises to his feet.

"Let me take a quick shower and then I will give them a speech they won't forget," replies a smiling King.

There is a knock at the door of room 1015 of the prestigious Peabody Hotel. Teed and Danya are sleeping as they are awakened by the loud knock. The clock reads 8:25 am. Teed yawns as he rises from the bed. He stumbles as he walks toward the door. Teed looks through the peep hole; it is a hotel waiter. The hotel staff wheels in a breakfast cart. The cart has freshly cut fruit, two glasses of orange juice, eggs and bacon, and a steaming pot of coffee. The aroma of the coffee instantly shakes the sleep cobwebs from Teed. Teed wheels the cart into the bedroom where Danya is still sleeping. The smell of the coffee also wakes her up. They both go and sit at a small coffee table in the room. Danya looks inside the trays.

"Bacon, yuk," utters a disgusted Danya.

"What's wrong with bacon?" asks a confused Teed.

"You spent three years in Israel. Jews don't eat bacon," says Danya.

"My mistake," smiles Teed. Teed and Danya share a slight chuckle. Danya begins to read the newspaper. The front-page article centers on Martin Luther King's speech at the Masonic Temple that has been dubbed "The Mountain Top" speech. The article speaks to King's vision for Negro America. The reporter's opinion sees Kings' speech as defeatist; he thinks King has given up. The article goes on and says it sounds like King might be leaving the Civil Rights Movement. The report thinks maybe the years of scrutiny finally caught up with him. For years, rumors have run rampant of King's extramarital activities and his own inner demons.

It is inferred that as a teenager King tried to commit suicide. All that aside, the article speaks to the speech as one of the most inspiring speeches to the Negroes of Memphis. King told the crowd to press on and not let the minor setbacks stop progress. He was referring to the recent riots after the marches in downtown Memphis. Danya and Teed continue to eat their breakfast. They pass each other eggs and fruit. Teed stands and pours two cups of coffee. Minutes later, the couple finish their breakfast. They both get up and walk to the bathroom. Like most couples, Danya and Teed start their day in the bathroom together. They both brush their teeth, then take a few moments to make love in the shower. The passion between the two could not be more evident. Teed and Danya get out of the shower and dry each other off. They share one last passionate kiss. As if a switch has gone off, both Danya and Teed's faces become all business. They step out of the bathroom and go to their adjoining suite. The suite resembles a military command center. On one wall, maps of the center city are blown up to show the best places for snipers and the best possible escape routes. Danya and Teed do not think they will need an escape route, but they want to cover all their bases. Dressed in her favorite black cat suit, Danya sits at one of the coffee tables and begins to check the rifles in the green duffle bag. Danya checks the scope on the gun to make sure the scope will pick up the correct distance.

"The rifles are ready," assures Danya

"Are you ready?" asks Teed.

Danya nods her head yes. Teed goes into the suite's coat closet and pulls out a baby carriage. Danya places the rifles back into the duffle bag. Teed picks up the bag and places it in the carriage and throws a blanket over the entire carriage.

"Well mama, it is your turn to get ready," suggests Teed.

Danya pulls back her damp curly hair into a ponytail. Teed walks over behind Danya, holding a girdle stuffed with foam. The purpose of the girdle is to give Danya the appearance of a mother who has recently given birth. If it takes a while to leave the boarding house, no one will suspect a new mother.

4/4/68

The city of Memphis is all abuzz from Dr. King's speech the night before. The feelings of the residents fall along racial lines. The city's Negroes feel his speech gave them all a reinforced resolve toward their fight for human rights. The city's White population feels that Dr. King and his Yankee cronies riled up the city's Negroes. There is an uneasy feeling that has gripped the city—Negroes and Whites have kept their distance from one another.

A puke-green Chevrolet pick-up truck pulls up to 422 South Main St., in front of Bessie Brewer's Boarding house. Teed steps out of the driver's side and proceeds to the passenger side to help the pregnancy-impersonating Danya out of the truck. Even though she is not actually pregnant, the girdle she is wearing is very uncomfortable and restrictive. As Danya is getting out of the truck, her purse drops to the ground. A Negro man bends down to pick up the purse.

"Ma'am, you dropped your purse," says the deep-voiced Negro man.

Danya turns toward the man.

"Thank you," says a thankful Danya.

Danya gazes at the man for a second before she realizes the man who picked up her purse was no other than Martin Luther King. Baffled that they could have run into him, both Teed and Danya appear to be momentarily star struck.

"Dr. King, my gosh, I can't believe we ran into you. We are both big admirers," proclaim Teed as he enthusiastically shakes his hand.

Dr. King smiles at the couple.

"I thank you both. I was just out getting a Coca-Cola. If you will excuse me. God bless both of you and your child," remarks Dr. King as he continues down South Main St. For Teed and Danya, the awestruck feeling of meeting one of the most transformational figures in history is replaced by the feeling that they need to complete their task. Teed and Danya walk into the rooming house. The couple walks past the front desk, as they already have keys to room 317. Teed and Danya climb the three flights of steps to the third floor. They are greeted by Robert Powell. The couple scoffs as they walk into the room.

"Mr. Powell, nothing better to do today?" asks Teed.

"Just thought I had better keep an eye on you two," jokes Powell.

Danya rolls her eyes at the sarcastic Powell. She picks up a bag and takes it into the bathroom.

"I noticed that the two of you ran into the Nigger preacher. Y'all had a lot of small talk. Just a yucking it up," mentions Powell.

Danya hears Powell, and she rushes out of the bathroom.

"So, you were watching us. If you think we can't handle this, why don't you pick up a gun and do the job yourself," states a pissed-off Danya.

"I was right, you two don't want to do the job. You got some kind of feelings for the Nigger," asserts Powell.

Teed tries to calm the situation. In his heart, he thinks that Powell may be correct. Both Teed and Danya have grown to admire Dr. King.

"Hold on Powell, we are here to do a job and we plan to complete it. Danya, let's just get ready. No more arguments are needed," directs a decisive Teed.

Danya walks back into the bathroom while giving Powell a death glare. Powell shakes his head as Danya walks away.

"You got a fiery one there," Powell whispers to Teed.

"Do you have your people in position?" asks Teed.

"We are simply waiting on a time. Have you talked to your contact?" responds Powell.

"He said that Dr. King will be leaving to go to dinner at Reverend Joseph Lowery's house around six pm," affirms Teed.

"Sounds good. The police will get scarce around five thirty then," claims Powell.

"You have an escape plan?" asks Powell.

Teed takes a long hard look at Powell and thinks to himself, *"this guy is a master manipulator and king of the assassination plot."* Teed knows the 8Men wouldn't betray him, but Powell is a different type of character.

"We are just going to slip out," implies Teed very nonchalantly.

Powell scoffs at Teed's half-ass answer.

"Good enough, what will your patsy be driving?" asks Powell.

"Why?" questions a confused Teed.

"So that the police have a description of the car. We want the police to catch the killer of the good Dr. King," says a devilishly smiling Powell.

MUSTANG

James Earl Ray spent a busy April 3rd purchasing a rifle and ammunition in the name of his alias, Eric Gault. He purchased a rifle and enough firepower to take down a herd of elephants. Ray was following orders given to him by Raoul. Raoul said that after their upcoming deal, Ray would have fulfilled his debt for springing him from prison. Raoul also promised Ray that he would have a plane ticket for him to travel from Canada to South Africa. Ray knew that once he got to South Africa, he would be free. He was excited to be on his way to starting a new life, after he dropped off the newly purchased shotgun.

Ray pulls up to Bessie Brewer's rooming house at 3:15 pm. He recalls several of his conversations with Raoul. Raoul has made it clear he wants Ray to be discrete when they have interactions. Ray decides to drive into the alley directly behind the rooming house, which seems to be clear. He surveys the area before pulling out a duffle bag and long brown paper wrapped package. Ray walks back to Main Street and into the rooming house.

The door to Room 315 squeaks as Mrs. Brewer opens it to let James Earl Ray in the room.

"My God, my husband is going to have to fix this damn door. I will get him up here first thing tomorrow," complains Mrs. Brewer.

Ray carries his large army green duffle bag to the room's twin-sized bed. He drops the bag and takes a deep breath before unpacking. Ray unzips the duffle bag and takes out several pairs of dusty dungarees and an assortment of wrinkled plaid long-sleeve shirts. He brought enough clothes to stay in Memphis a few days; he didn't know what Raoul had in mind for him. As Ray begins to fold up his emptied duffle bag, Raoul steps out of the bathroom.

"All unpacked?" asks Raoul.

"Jesus H. Christ!" exclaims a startled Ray.

Raoul starts to laugh uncontrollably.

"What the fuck? Why wouldn't you just say something?" asks Ray.

"Oh boy, that was funny," jokes Raoul.

Ray begins to pick his things that fell on the floor. Raoul sees the wrapped-up rifle next to the door.

"Good, you got the rifle wrapped," comments Raoul.

"Yeah, it's nicely packaged for you," replies Ray.

Raoul walks over to the package. He picks up the rifle to verify in his mind the gun is in the package.

"So, what time does the buyer get here?" demands Ray.

"About that, it may be best for you not to be here. People get a bit nervous when they don't know everybody in the room. I don't want to spook the guy out of the deal. You understand?" pushes back Raoul.

"Sure, I guess, but what am I supposed to do while you're meeting the guy? I don't know anything about Memphis," questions Ray.

Raoul shrugs his shoulders.

"This is a pretty popular area. Go catch a movie," suggests Raoul as he begins to dig into his pocket.

"Here is $20, go catch a movie... Oh, this is Memphis. Get something to eat. They have some of the best barbeque in world here," claims Raoul.

"I am a bit hungry," utters Ray as he grabs Raoul's $20-dollar bill.

"What time should I come back?" asks Ray.

Raoul looks down at his watch. He knows that King is supposed to leave around six pm, so a half hour should give him and Danya time to get out without being noticed.

"It is about three thirty now; come back after six thirty. We should be done by then. And we both will have our big pay day," says Raoul as he gently pushes Ray out of the door.

Minutes later, Teed goes back to room 317, where Danya is making preparations for Dr. King. Danya is oiling the rifle, looking very intently at the gun. She wants to make sure there are no unforeseen issues with the gun. Danya was taught by her Mossad trainers that she needed to be prepared and then prepare for the unthinkable—to eliminate the most probable obstacles.

"How are things coming?" asks Teed.

"Making sure the rifle is in good working order," says Danya as she continues to oil the gun.

Danya jumps up and goes into the bathroom. She looks out onto the alley across from the Lorraine Motel.

"What time is he supposed to leave?" asks Danya.

"My understanding is that he will be leaving around six o'clock. To be sure, let's prepare for five thirty. They may decide to leave early," suggests Teed.

Danya nods her head in agreement. She leaves out of the bathroom, then walks into the bedroom and sits down on the bed, staring off into space. She then begins to take a drink of water. Teed notices that Danya has been quiet, and he is concerned about her state of mind. Teed sits down on the bed next to Danya. He tries to console her, and he places his hand on the small of her back.

"What is wrong? You seem to be deep in thought," says Teed.

"What are we doing? I have always questioned some of the motivations of my superiors. I always carried out my end, but normally things played themselves out in a way that I could understand…this one has me truly baffled. This man of God is not a political figure; he didn't cause mass death and he has no real power," searches a flustered Danya.

"Talking to some of the 8Men, it is not that King is any of those things you just said. His ideals are counter to many of the power brokers. King is changing minds. The 8Men don't want the people to wake up," proclaims Teed.

Both Teed and Danya do not like the idea of assassinating a man of God. But they do understand their place. They questioned many of the prior decisions made by their benefactors, and much like the prior times, the couple prepares to carry out their mission. Around 5:20 pm, Danya starts to set up her sniper's perch in the bathroom tub. The perch is a converted 35 mm film camera stand. She has been rehearsing the shooting in her mind over the last two weeks. Danya starts to daydream about her Mossad training. She remembers having to find an area in the Negev desert where she could set up a sniper's perch and wait on her prey. Most of her prey were small indigenous animals that were quick but posed no physical threat. The small animals allowed Danya to practice without reprisal. As Danya became more proficient with eliminating the smaller animals, her trainers decided to introduce larger and deadlier prey. The trainers decided to have Danya track a striped hyena. Danya knew the hyena was a formidable adversary; she knew that if she missed the hyena that it would not take the animal long to turn the tables on her. Unfortunately for the hyena, Danya rarely misses her target. She knows that she is much more precise and self-assured than the young girl who left the Negev desert so long ago. Danya snaps herself from the daydream.

"I'm ready," affirms a determined Danya.

Time ticks by slowly. Teed continues to look out of the window as Danya stands outside the tub trying to keep herself stretched out. There is no activity in the Lorraine Motel parking lot between 5:30 and 5:50, then a flurry of activity begins. Several large black cars drive into the parking lot. The cars are filled with Black men who empty out onto the parking lot. They all walk up to room 306. Several of the men go into Martin Luther King's room while the others stay outside talking and smoking cigarettes. Danya and Teed find it hard to believe that King doesn't have an extensive protection detail. Many in his entourage are lawyers, preachers and other community activists. None of these men could protect themselves let alone King. All at once, King's motel door opens, with several men exiting. King is not a part of the initial group leaving the motel room. Those that exit motion to those standing outside the room to go to the cars. They must be getting ready to leave.

"I think this is it," says Teed.

Danya sets the rifle and gets herself into position. She begins to adjust the rifle scope. As Danya starts to focus her scope, which is set on Dr. King's room, Anthony Montgomery walks out of the room. Teed looks down at his watch: 5:58 pm.

"He should be following him very soon. That is only the bodyguard," whispers Teed.

Danya takes a deep breath. Her heartbeat speeds up and her palms become a bit sweaty. Dr. King steps out on the mezzanine in front of his motel room. He acknowledges several people in the parking lot. Teed looks back down at his watch, it now reads 6:00 pm. He looks at Danya; she seems to be a bit unsure.

"Danya, do it. He is out there. You have to do it," says an anxious Teed.

She takes another deep breath while adjusting her scope. Dr. King's face is in Danya's crosshairs.

"Danya," shouts Teed.

Danya pulls the trigger. A large blast billows from the rifle. Moments later the face of the Dr. Martin Luther King explodes, tearing away most of his jaw. Danya and Teed take a moment to look at the carnage. Dr. King is lying on his back with much of his blood sprayed on the room doors and the members of his entourage that were close by when the bullet hit. As Danya and Teed begin to leave, the last thing they see is Anthony Montgomery trying to perform CPR on the mortally wounded civil rights icon.

AFTERMATH

The genius of Dr. Martin Luther King and his non-violent protest movement was the thought that most Americans were good people that abhorred violence. Even though many Americans weren't necessarily comfortable with the racial and social changes Dr. King was advocating for, the brutal beating of non-violent men, women and children protesters were even harder to stomach. Many in the Black community thought Dr. King was a fool to allow the barbaric beatings that those in his movement received. But once he was killed, those who thought his methods were foolhardy became incensed. Many Negroes wondered, with the murder of Dr. King, what did he do? King tried to be non-violent. Many Negroes thought King was willing to take the crumbs that White people were willing to give, and he still was killed. The anger of the Negro community spills onto the urban streets of America. Cites all over the United States are on fire. Spontaneous fires have been popping up throughout the country. The largest cities are on fire include New York, Chicago, Baltimore, Newark, Los Angeles and the nation's capital. The presence of the federal government does not quell the frustration of the Negroes in Washington, D.C. Several businesses have been set ablaze along the 14th Street corridor. There have been reports of White people being pulled from their cars, beaten and then having their vehicles set on fire. News reporters have been warning Whites to avoid the Negro areas of the city. The National Guard has been mobilized to protect the Capitol and the White House.

Senator Hampton Capers is oblivious to the burning of the District of Columbia, never mind the rest of the cities in America. Capers leaves the Capitol around 8 pm. He is trying to tie up some last-minute legislation ahead of next week's Easter break. As Senator Capers' driver pulls out onto Constitution Avenue from the Senate garage, Senator Capers notices an armada of army tanks lining both Constitution and Independence Avenues. It appears the tanks are a visible line in the sand for the rioters who may have thought to burn anything in the National Mall. Capers' car travels up to North Capitol Street, and he notices that the city is a virtual ghost town. Off in the distance, Capers sees many little fires.

"What the hell? Is all this about King? asks an annoyed Capers.

"I am not sure, sir," responds the driver.

As Capers' car rides up to P St., there is a red light in front of them.

"What are you doing? Go through the damn light," commands Capers.

As Senator Capers moves up in his seat to give his driver a piece of his mind, a Molotov cocktail hits his window, igniting the entire passenger side of the car. Before a frightened Capers can look at his car door, the door opens violently. He is pulled out of the car and thrown to the ground. Senator Capers looks up, and six young Black men are standing over him wielding large pieces of wood and pipes.

"Y'all motherfuckers killed him," yells one of the Black men.

"Killed…I didn't kill anyone," responds a shaken Capers.

Senator Capers has realized the gravity of the 8Men's latest mission. Senator Capers thought of Martin Luther King as that "Nigger preacher."

He never thought of Dr. King as a moral and spiritual leader. He just thought of the Rev. King as an impediment to him making money. But the young men standing in front of him lost a leader, even if they don't believe in his non-violent stance.

"What do you want from me?" questions a frightened Capers.

"We want you to die for killing King," barks the leader of the young men as he moves toward Capers.

Suddenly Capers is overcome with an extreme tightness in his chest. He grabs at his chest. There is a loud gun blast. The sudden blast stops the young men in their tracks.

"Go!" screams Senator Capers' driver as he points a gun at the group of young men.

The young men run off. The driver runs over to the senator. He picks up Senator Capers off the ground.

"Why?" asks a rambling Senator Capers.

The driver gets Senator Capers off the ground and gets him back into the car. The driver sees the Senator is in obvious pain. Capers is grasping his chest as he pants heavily.

"I'm getting you to the hospital, now," says the driver.

The driver makes a left on the emptied New York Avenue.

"Stay with me Senator Capers," hollers the driver.

Capers takes several quick breaths as he slumps over in the back seat.

ROUTE 301

The death of Martin Luther King has rocked the entire nation. Unlike the Kennedy assassination, the King mission had a personal tie for Teed and Danya. They met King; he was nice to them. He seemed to be a genuinely sincere man. He was nothing like the man that the 8Men presented him to be. The explosion of the bullet hitting Dr. King continues to replay in the minds of Teed and Danya. The memory bothers both of them, but the incident brings back the memory of Danya's family being executed by the Nazis. Up to this point, she had always rationalized why she killed for the greater good. She had always thrown the persona of the Nazis on the person she was ordered to kill. But reflecting on the death of King, Danya can no longer simply make that comparison. Danya now thinks she isn't any better than the barbaric Nazi murderers who killed her family and six million other Jews. Danya wonders if some of those same Nazis would say she did it because she thought it was for the greater good.

Teed and Danya are driving on Route 301 in rural North Carolina. They have sat in virtual silence since completing their mission in Memphis. Teed pulls off the road. He is trying to find a slightly hidden road.

"Where are we?" questions Danya.

"We are in Roxboro, North Carolina," answers Teed.

"What are you looking for?" asks Danya.

"I am looking for a road. It is around here somewhere," claims Teed.

Teed finds the road.

"Here we go," he says.

Teed makes a right onto the road. The dirt road is very choppy and dark; it appears to be going further into darkness. After riding for about three minutes, a barn appears in the distance. The pair pulls up to the barn. They go to the barn door, and Teed opens it. Sitting in front of them is a shiny black Chevrolet Camaro. In the back seat of the Camaro are two backpacks of supplies and clothing. Teed and Danya change their clothes. Teed goes through the backpack to find two canisters of water, a care package of assorted dried fruit, and some blankets.

"Fucking fruit and water," utters Teed.

Teed continues to rummage through the bag. He notices a pack of cigarettes and a mason jar.

"Aww some smokes and..."

Teed smells the jar.

"Good ole Hooch," exclaims a happy Teed.

Danya goes and sits on a bale of hay. She is still distracted by the events in Memphis. Teed goes and sits next to her. He hands her a canister of water and a bag of fruit.

"How can you eat?" inquires Danya as she walks away.

"I am starving," replies Teed.

He walks over to Danya. He tries to console her.

"The mission is over. We have to leave it back in Memphis," declares Teed.

"I want to. I really do. I just keep seeing his blood splatter everywhere. It is what my parents' execution looked like; the difference is I pulled the trigger this time," reflects Danya.

Danya walks out of the barn. It is obvious that she wants to be left alone.

Senator Hampton Capers was pronounced dead on arrival at George Washington University hospital at 9:17 pm. He apparently died from a massive stroke. The stress of being pulled from his car and his not so healthy lifestyle of overdrinking scotch and vast daily assortments of fatty meats may have finally caught up with him. The funeral of Hampton Capers is a who's who of Washington, D.C. politics. Capers had been involved in D.C. politics for over four decades. The most impressive part of the senator's resume was his military service. Before he was a senator, Capers was a colonel in the United States Army. He received 15 medals and awards, including the Bronze Star with valor, the Purple Heart and France's Croix de Guerra, a result of his involvement in the Battle of Saint Michel. Capers used his much-celebrated patriotism to catapult him into public office. When Capers came back from Europe after World War I, he wanted to make a difference. He ran for city council of Charleston, South Carolina, in 1920. Two short years later, Capers ran and won as a Dixiecrat for the U.S. Congress. Capers presented himself as a good ol' boy that fought for the common South Carolinian. He was for a strong military, and he was a strong anti-equal rights voice, putting him in line with the values of most voting South Carolinians.

The politically high-profile funeral is beginning at the famed Arlington National Cemetery in Arlington, Va. The cemetery sits on a hill in the shadow of Washington, D.C. From the cemetery, one can see the picturesque landmarks of the capitol city. Those who have served in the military can only wish for the distinct honor of being buried at Arlington National. The last high-profile funeral at Arlington National was for President Kennedy. The funeral proceeds without a hitch. Pastor Irving Harris from Senator Capers' church in Charleston officiates a solemn service. At the end of service, as a bugler played Taps, Senator Capers' widow is presented with a neatly folded American flag by two four-star generals. All the dignitaries begin to pass Mrs. Capers, offering their condolences. Director Hoover approaches Mrs. Capers to offer his condolences.

"Mrs. Capers, I offer my sincere sympathy," remarks Director Hoover as he shakes her hand.

"Thank you very much," she responds.

As Director Hoover begins to walk away from Mrs. Capers, Hoover notices Wesley Carter and several of the 8Men huddled 20 yards away. Director Hoover briskly trots over to the huddle.

Wesley Carter is telling some stories about the late Senator Capers to the 8Men.

"He was one of kind. One tough son of a bitch, he was," says a reflective Carter.

"He was tough. He surely would play hard ball when needed. You didn't want to be his enemy. Hopefully you were his friend," says Hoover as he interrupts the 8Men's private conversation.

All of the 8Men look at Hoover with contempt. The 8Men have partnered with Hoover on certain issues, but none really like him and even less trusted him.

"Senator Capers was a very influential figure; he knew how to get things done," comments Hoover.

"He was our rock...the country's rock," responds Carter.

"I was thinking, you guys need...may need a new member. The 8Men are down to seven. I am pretty powerful in my own right," says Hoover.

"Goddam Edgar, the body is not even cold yet," says Wesley Carter.

"My apologies to the dead. But I've been known to pull off some pretty impressive things. I think you all know my resume. No pressure of course," says Hoover as he devilishly laughs as he walks away from the 8Men.

The gathered men collectively shake their heads at Hoover's apparent self-invitation into their stealth organization.

"Did that arrogant fuck just invite himself into our group?" asks Valerius Torrantio.

"Yup, he sure did. He is going to be a problem," replies Carter.

THE BIG PAY BACK

Operation Paperclip allowed the United States government to bring former Nazi scientists and intelligence agents into the United States intelligence apparatus. The move did not sit well with governments around the world and even some American politicians. The underlying reason for Operation Paperclip was the build-up of military might by the Soviet Union. The United States did not want to be caught without intelligence on the Soviets. During World War II, the Nazis made many inroads with regards to intelligence on the Soviets. It was believed that many of the Nazis had contacts and found ways to gain access to Soviet-controlled areas. The conversion of many of the Nazi agents was quite fruitful for the U.S. efforts. The Nazis integrated themselves successfully into American life.

Most Americans are unaware that the Nazis are working in aeronautics, finance and banking, ammunitions, and most notably the sciences. The Nazi scientists are known for their vicious war machine, but it is their advances in the sciences that made their people so coveted after the war. Nazi scientists are working on a host of avant-garde inventions, including the booster rocket, an early computer program, and countless medical discoveries. Many of the medical discoveries come as a result of the varied grizzly experiments the inhumane Nazi scientists performed on the defenseless Jews at the concentration camps around Europe.

The Israelis do not like the United States' arrangements with the former Nazis. The U.S. feels that its quiet agreement to allow the construction of the Dimona Nuclear Plant will ease tensions with the Israelis. The Israelis have been begrudgingly muted for several years, but with rise of radical Islam, the Jews are a bit nervous. The Israelis don't want the radicals to get any inspiration from unpursued Nazis, not to mention that they want plain ol' revenge for the Holocaust. Director Wesley Carter has always been able to walk a fine line with the Israelis. He knows that the United States must continue to cajole its only Middle East ally. To keep the Israelis in the American's good graces, it is time the U.S. offers some sacrificial lambs.

Danya Franck has visited Langley several times over the years, but this time she is going straight to the director's office. She is not going through the basement or the over one thousand inconspicuous entrances that lead into the CIA stronghold. Danya is walking through the long vestibule on her way to the director's office. She walks up to the director's secretary.

"Hello, I have an appointment with Director Carter," says Danya. Danya walks into the director's office. As she walks into the director's office, the director is looking out of the large bay window in his office.

"Good afternoon Director Carter, I hope my time away has been fruitful," says Danya.

Danya walks over to the director's desk. She takes off her right-handed glove and extends her hand to the director; he kisses her hand.

"Yes, your time and your efforts were very fruitful. We want to thank you for everything that you have done, and I thank you in advance for everything you will do," conveys the director.

Danya rolls her eyes as she feels that she is being conned.

"My superiors asked me to come and meet with you. So, I am here; what would you like to discuss?" asks Danya.

Director Carter takes two files out of his top drawer. The director pushes the two files over to Danya. The first file is labelled Gerhard Mehrhoff. Mehrhoff was a head prison guard at the Dachau concentration camp located outside of Munich, Germany.

He was known as the "Butcher of Bavaria." The files describe a few of the acts perpetrated by Mehrhoff. He was a lover of the German Shephard dog breed. To amuse himself and his guards, Mehrhoff would starve some of the dogs for weeks, then put them in a cage with several concentration camp children, then watch as the famished dogs literally ripped the flesh from the defenseless children's bones. The second file was labelled Wolfgang Geschwind. Geschwind was dubbed "Doctor Evil." He was an experimental doctor, some would say barbarous. He performed experiments like detaching the eyeball from one twin and attaching it to their twin's eye. If that was not heinous enough, Geschwind experimented with the creation of viruses. He would inject viruses into an array of prisoners. No group was off limits to Doctor Evil's diabolical exploits. He gave toddlers hepatitis to see how long it would take to destroy the child's liver. As Danya reads the horrible acts that these Nazis performed against the Jews, a single tear rolls down her face. Director Carter reaches into the desk and pulls out a file labelled Albrecht Krause. He slides the file over to Danya. He reaches into his desk and pulls out to two glasses and a large bottle of Scotch.

Danya looks at the file label and notices the name. She looks up in the direction of Director Carter. The director gives Danya a wink. She flashes back to having a knife to Krause's throat and wishing she had killed him.

"Why now? What is your angle, Director?" challenges Danya.

The director takes a very long gulp of scotch.

"We owe the good people of Israel some retribution for the horrors of the Holocaust," replies the director.

Danya smiles. "What are you afraid of Director? Do you think you have fallen out of favor with Israel?"

"Maybe, I am figuring this could be a down payment for favors to come in the future. These bastards should be taken out and shot down like the dogs they are," responds Director Carter.

"We want them killed and we want everyone to know that these Nazi bastards were hunted down," concedes an impassioned Danya. The director nods his head.

"What if it were in a few national newspapers with their stories, speaking to the fact that they are escaped Nazis that must be hunted down?" says Director Carter.

Danya nods her head in agreement.

"Will you handle all three?" asks the director. Danya looks at Krause's file.

"I don't know about all three, but I will certainly take my time with this one," affirms a cryptic Danya.

Director Carter is in full clean-up mode. He knows with Hoover's possible power move against the 8Men, he is going to need to purge most of the possible connections to the group. Carter knows that at some point his most trusted assets, Teed and Danya, will move on to greener pastures. Director Carter knows that the couple's missions have been some of the most sensitive covert missions ever performed in U.S. history. He knows that there are loose ends out there that needed to be taken care of. Director Carter also knows that it is in Danya and Teed's self-interest to get rid of those loose ends. Danya has already gotten her marching orders. He knows convincing Teed of his upcoming mission may be a little more difficult.

Moments after his meeting with Danya Franck, Director Carter walks down the hall from his office to meet with Richard Teed in a secluded office. Teed is sitting at a large square table.

"Mr. Teed, can I get you anything?" asks Carter.

"An explanation to why I am here," responds Teed.

"Can't a friend ask their friend to come to visit them at the Central Intelligence Agency without wanting something?" suggests a sarcastic Carter.

Teed is looking at Carter with a look of anger.

"Look, in all seriousness, we have to eliminate some loose ends," hints Carter.

"No, Danya and I need to clean up the mess," replies Teed.

"That is an accurate statement. You and Danya need to eliminate the loose ends," says Carter.

"So, what are we supposed to do?" challenges a suspicious Teed.

"Well, you are going to take out the undercover officer that was tasked with protecting King," directs Carter.

"What?" exclaims Teed.

"I figured you would be a bit upset, but either we get him, or somebody will sooner or later come get you and Danya," claims a deadly serious Carter.

Teed realizes as much as the 8Men have valued him, once he has outlived his usefulness, he too could be eliminated.

"Look, I understand you may have some affection for Montgomery. I know he unwittingly helped with the assassination of King. And he may never speak a word about knowing and meeting you. But it is a chance that we cannot take. He is distraught and out of sorts. A person like that will sooner or later have a moment of clarity and may tell all they know. We simply cannot have that," explains Carter.

Teed rises out of his chair.

"Is that all?" asks Teed.

"No, I have one more thing I will need you to do," says a cryptic Carter.

CLEAN UP

The Monday October 28, 1968, edition of the *Washington Sun* has the headline "Two Suspected Nazis War Criminals are Murdered in Two Separate Grizzly Acts." The article describes the horrors that both perpetrators inflicted on the Jews in the concentration camps during World War II. The article purposely makes sure to include the Gerhard Mehrhoff and Wolfgang Geschwind's new names and their American addresses. Both Mehrhoff and Geschwind had assimilated into a normal American life. Mehrhoff became a police officer with the Anne Arundel County Police Department in suburban Baltimore. Mehrhoff served as the department's point person on training the department's corps of German Shepherds. He was discovered shot several times laying in his bed next to the decapitated head of his beloved German Shephard Luka. The article also noted that Geschwind was working as a lead laboratory technician with the University of Maryland's biology department on its Baltimore County campus. Geschwind was working in conjunction with the National Institutes of Health on new research as it relates to the human immune system. Geschwind's body was found in the basement of his Catonsville, Maryland home brutally murdered. It appeared that he had been tortured for a lengthy period. Geschwind had been beaten with a pole, had both legs and arms broken, stabbed under both armpits and lastly had the tips of three fingers cut off. The murderer for good measure injected Mr. Geschwind with a syringe of cyanide which they left in his limp body. Geschwind and Mehrhoff's bodies were draped with Swastika flags to leave no doubt who and what they are. The publication of the murders would surely put all former Nazis residing in America on notice, that there is a vigilante out there trying to get retribution for the Nazis crimes.

Danya Franck arrives at the National Institutes of Health in an unassuming Yellow cab. Albrecht Krause is working in his lab. He is looking at several slides under his numerous microscopes lined up next to each other. Krause looks up from a microscope to log some information into a notebook. He changes the slide under the microscope he is currently working on. He talks to himself as he thinks through his theories.

"So, this virus will replicate within months. Any possible antibiotics will be rendered useless," says a somewhat joyful Krause. He recognizes a familiar scent in the distance.

"Is that you, Ms. Franck?" asks a hesitant Krause.

Danya Franck steps out of the shadows.

"I cannot forget your fragrance. Your essence has been seared into my brain. I can still smell your body fluids all over me," remarks an aroused Krause.

"You are a sick man. Time has not cured your vulgar ways. I would have thought that you would have atoned for your wrongdoing," says Danya as she holds a .22-caliber handgun pointed directly at Krause's heart.

"It is so hard to believe that you are the same young girl who played with dolls," reflects Krause.

"That young girl was killed by you and your guards," says an increasingly angered Danya.

"I never touched you. You can't blame me for what those savages did to you," utters a defensive Krause.

"You were there; you were in charge. You let them take advantage of me. I saw you. You walked in and then walked right out, like you didn't see anything," proclaims Danya.

Krause realizes that Danya's hatred for him is because she was raped by four of the guards at the Dachau camp that he oversaw as the head doctor. For two decades, Krause believed that Danya didn't like him simply because he was a Nazi.

"Danya, I am sorry. I am really sorry. I wish that I was brave. I may have been the official in charge, but I had no power. Can you forgive me? I am eternally sorry for what they did to you," says a remorseful Krause.

Danya has a tear roll down her cheek.

"The sad thing is I almost believe you," says a stoic Danya. Krause begins to snicker. "What did you not believe? Did I spread it on too thick? I practiced that monologue several times. I knew that you would come for me one day," admits Krause.

Danya now feels vindicated for wanting to kill Krause. Many in Mossad and in the American government feel that Krause is just a scientist that got caught on the wrong side of history.

"You thought that time would soften my heart toward the Zionists. Well, it hasn't. Your people are an abomination. The Jews destroy any civilization it becomes a part of. In due time, they will destroy America too," rambles a breathless Krause.

The anger builds on Danya's face as her eyes lock with Krause's. Danya pulls the trigger of her gun three times, hitting Krause in the chest. He stumbles from the force of the gun shot, knocking over his desk before falling on the floor. Danya walks over to his profusely bleeding body. She takes a moment to reflect on the horrors cause by Krause. Danya places a Swastika over Krause's face. She turns around and walks out of the lab.

ANACOSTIA

Anthony Montgomery went on the run after the assassination of Martin Luther King. Anthony knew he was being used by the FBI to keep tabs on Dr. King, but he thought that he could use his position to help and protect the civil rights icon. After Dr. King was put into the ambulance after the shooting in Memphis, Montgomery had a moment of clarity. He realized that he was probably giving Dr. King's location to the would-be killers. Montgomery knew that not many people outside of King's circle would have known that Dr. King had changed motels. He also knew that he was a loose end who would surely need to be tied up sooner rather than later.

Montgomery was originally from Danville, Virginia. But he, like many Negroes, moved to Washington, D.C., after graduating from North Carolina A&T in hopes of finding a good job. Montgomery was a promising police academy recruit when he was asked to join the FBI.

In the mid-sixties, the FBI did not have any Negro agents. Not having any Negro agents made the agency's surveillance efforts of the Black radical groups and the civil rights organizations close to impossible. It was also useful to the FBI that Montgomery was a son of the South.

Montgomery had a slight country twang when he spoke; this would endear him to many of the civil rights workers that were also country boys.

Over the last few weeks, Montgomery has been laying low in the mostly Negro enclave of Anacostia in the southeastern portion of Washington, D.C. Montgomery's time in the FBI helped him learn that if you want to disappear, you need to get completely off the grid. Montgomery is staying in an abandoned apartment building off the busy Alabama Avenue. He has taken on a rougher appearance. He is no longer clean shaven and wears a new style of dress, with baggy jeans and oversized sweatshirts replacing his manicured appearance and tailored suits.

Montgomery walks to Jake's liquor store, one of the many liquor stores along the route. He walks into the store and purchases a six-pack of Miller High Life beer. Montgomery pays the cashier in exact cash. He walks back to the apartment building, and he is careful to take stock of his surroundings. He knows that someone will be looking for him. Montgomery walks back into the building; he surveys the building and makes sure nothing is out of place. As Montgomery walks into the building, he is hit in the head from behind. A couple of hours later, Montgomery wakes up from his unwanted slumber. He is bound to a chair. Teed is sitting in a chair across from Montgomery.

"I knew it would be you," states Montgomery.

"You should be lucky that it is me," responds Teed.

"You set me up. You killed me," suggests Montgomery.

"It is complex," hints Teed.

"No shit," responds Montgomery.

"All of this got out of hand," claims Teed.

"Man, just do me. I don't want to hear your excuses. You used me to kill Dr. King. I helped kill Dr. King. I am going to hell. You have damned me to hell," utters Montgomery.

"It wasn't supposed to happen like this," says a remorseful Teed.

"C'mon man. How was it supposed to happen? You killed the Black Messiah. You made me Judas. I didn't want to be Judas. I wanted to help him; I wanted to protect him—all of them—but I led the killers right to him," sobs Montgomery.

Teed sees the pain that Montgomery is in. He notices the tears rolling down his face.

"Man, just kill me. Put me out of my misery," pleads Montgomery.

Teed walks out of the room. Moments later, he walks back with a large black bag across his shoulders. He throws the bag on the floor in front of Montgomery. Teed sits back in the chair across from him.

"Look, I was supposed to come here and kill you," reveals Teed.

Montgomery looks nervously at the black bag.

"Get on with it then," challenges Montgomery.

"You were as much a victim of this whole mess as Dr. King. You never asked for any of this. You thought you were doing a service for your country. You thought you were doing something good," admits Teed.

He walks over to Montgomery. Teed pulls Montgomery's wallet out of his pants. Teed pulls the cash out of Montgomery's wallet and places it back in his pocket. Teed bends down to the bag and unzips it. There is a corpse in the bag. The man in the bag could be a twin of Montgomery.

"Striking image I would say," says Teed.

"What the hell?" asks a baffled Montgomery.

"It is simple. Today, Anthony Montgomery will die in an apartment building fire in Anacostia. You, my friend, will need to find a new identity," recites Teed.

Teed places Montgomery's identification in the corpse's pants.

"So, you are going to just let me walk out of here?" asks an apprehensive Montgomery.

Teed walks out of the room again. Moments later he walks back into the room with a large black duffle bag.

"There is ten million dollars in this bag. I want you to get lost. There is a Brown four-door Lincoln across the street. The keys are in the sun visor. Get out of D.C. You are too easy to find here. Also, if you ever need to get in touch with me, call my friend, "The Squirrel." mentions Teed as he places a piece of paper in Montgomery's pants pocket.

Teed walks over and unties Montgomery. Montgomery immediately jumps out of the chair.

"You stay lost so that we both can stay alive," begs Teed.

Teed picks up a can of gas that is in the room.

"Am I supposed to say thank you?" questions Montgomery.

"No, you are supposed to say goodbye," proclaims Teed.

Montgomery quickly runs out of the apartment. Teed throws the gas can in a corner of the room. He pulls out a book of matches and strikes a match and throws it on the floor. A small fire starts. Teed looks around to make sure that he hasn't left any evidence behind. He rushes from the apartment. Teed walks out onto Alabama Avenue. He looks back to see fire erupting from the building. There are shouts from people on the streets.

"Fire! Fire! Somebody get help!" shouts a voice from the crowd.

Teed walks back to a black Ford Thunderbird. He gets into the car and continues to look at the fire burning.

"You did a good thing. He can start his life over and you can have some type of peace of mind. Now, it is time for us to leave," declares Danya.

Teed nods his head, agreeing with Danya as they pull out of the parking space. Teed looks at his rear-view mirror and sees a smoky Alabama Avenue in the backdrop.

DEVIL'S DEAL

The death of Robert Kennedy by an assassins' bullet all but assured the fall presidential election to Richard Nixon. No other Democrat could possibly win the election; the Democratic Party was looked at as a political party in disarray. Nixon was viewed as a strong executive that would get America back on track. Thoughts of Nixon becoming president made many in America harken back to the days of the Eisenhower administration. The Eisenhower administration had kept the communists at arm's length and gave Americans a sense of security. None of the 8Men had a relationship with Nixon, making all of them a bit nervous with him probably becoming president. Wesley Carter knew that J. Edgar Hoover had a relationship with Nixon. From what Carter had heard, they actually had a good relationship. Hoover tended to stay on the good side of those with realistic chances of becoming the president. Hoover had hoped Nixon would have won in 1960; the two men shared a paranoid view of the world. In Hoover's mind, Nixon would have allowed many of the covert activities Hoover wanted to push.

Wesley Carter has been mulling over the possibility of inviting Hoover to join the 8Men. Carter had relationships with President Johnson and many within the Kennedy administration, but he had not really crossed paths with Richard Nixon. Director Carter knows he needs to make a decision about inviting Director Hoover into the 8Men. He meets up with his 8Men colleagues Valerius Torrantio and Murray Smith at Charlie's Bar and Grille in southwest Washington, D.C. The gentlemen are sitting in a secluded back room. A waitress brings the gentlemen a couple of bottles of Jack Daniels before exiting the room.

"In honor of our esteemed colleague and friend," comments Carter as he raises his drink glass.

Torrantio and Smith raise their glasses out of respect for Senator Capers.

"Ok, gentlemen, the reason for our meeting of course is to pick a new member of our group," mentions Carter.

"Who are you thinking?" asks Murray Smith.

"The obvious choice is Hoover," replies Carter.

"But?" asks Valerius.

"I don't trust him. I don't trust many people. Most of the time it is a healthy distrust of people. But this time, I got a bad feeling about him. Hoover makes me think he is up to something," suggests Carter.

"So, what do you want to do?" asks Valerius.

"I am thinking we will go with Hoover," says an unsure Carter.

"He won't get too far out of hand. We still have leverage on him. He doesn't want those pictures to see the light of day," claims Valerius.

"This is not Hoover's first rodeo. There have been many that thought they could control him, and he turned things around on them. We just have to keep a close eye on him," asserts Carter.

"So, have you replaced your two assassins? You pulled a masterful job with Bobby," congratulates Murray.

"Yeah, we couldn't have it look like his brother or King's murder. The solider program worked out well," explains Carter.

"So, what about your assassins? Are they out now?" asks Valerius.

"It is probably time for them to take a break. The King job took a toll on them. The JFK murder was tough for them, but I think killing King made them question what they were doing this for. I think they need to take a sabbatical," suggests Carter.

"Whatever happened with that undercover FBI officer that was assigned to King? What have you done about that?" asks Torrantino.

"You don't watch your local news. Mr. Anthony Montgomery met with a very unfortunate demise in an apartment fire in Anacostia. Director Carter your people are good. I could have never found him let alone in the Blackest area of the city," says Murray Smith.

"Your people did that? Are they holding classes? I got wise guys who could use their expertise," remarks Torrantino as he laughs.

"It was quite a masterful job. Now that we are rid of all the nonsense, we should be able to move on to more important business," says Carter.

"What do you think is going to happen with Vietnam?" asks Murray Smith.

Director Carter gets up and refreshes Smith and Torrantino's glasses.

"Well, Johnson has given us a gift by committing resources for the next couple of years but what hoops we may have to jump through will be another story. Cecil has not had to explain much and the Defense Department pretty much has written Steadman Industries blank checks. We need to continue to get that money so that we can continue to invest. The Middle East will be the next frontier," forecasts Carter.

THE TAKEOVER

Wesley Carter has gone back and forth for weeks about inviting J. Edgar Hoover to join the 8Men. Carter has had several long intense conversations with each one of the other six remaining members. The conversations focused on the pros and cons of Hoover. The group knows that Hoover could bring some added resources, but they worry about the possible negative attention he could also bring. One of the collective attributes that all the 8Men share is discretion. Hoover does not share this quality with his potential colleagues. In the end, Carter decides to bring Hoover in because of the resources he can provide, along with his access to President Nixon. With the absence of Senator Capers, Carter envisions getting Hoover's FBI to spy on many of the top Congressional Committee chairmen. Carter also wants to get access to the hordes of private files Hoover keeps on many Americans, including congressmen and captains of industry.

The 8Men are meeting at their original headquarters in northwest Washington. The remaining six members are drinking and smoking when Hoover walks in.

"Maybe I arrived a little too early," says Hoover as he coughs from the heavy cigar smoke.

The group starts to laugh. Hoover walks over to the seat that was vacated by Senator Capers.

"Gentlemen, thank you for coming today. The reason we are here is to formally bring Edgar into our organization. Edgar, we want to thank you for accepting our invitation to join our group," declares Carter.

All the 8Men stand and applaud Hoover. Hoover tries to stay humble as the group applauds him.

"I thank you gentlemen for inviting me in. There are so many things that we all can do as group," suggests Hoover.

"Thank you, Edgar. We truly appreciate you joining us. We—" says Carter as he is interrupted.

"I know that I am just joining the group, but I was hoping we could get moving on certain things," interjects Hoover.

The group seems somewhat baffled by Hoover 's assertion.

"What's on your mind, Edgar?" asks Carter.

"I appreciate you indulging me," says Hoover.

Hoover motions to his people to bring in some materials. Several FBI agents are scrambling to get the director's materials.

The agents bring in three easels with posters of Black nationalists, the Vietnam War and energy independence.

"What the hell is this?" exclaims Carter.

"Since I am the director of the Federal Bureau of Investigation, there are so many issues that I am privy to. We are going into a new decade with a new presidential administration. Mr. Nixon will be a different type of president. He will be a bit more hands on, and from my conversations with him…very willing to put down any adverse actions from anybody or any organization not in lock step with his ideas of a new America," says Hoover.

"What do you suggest?" asks Cecil Thomas.

"First, we should look to infiltrate all the Black nationalist groups. These groups will spawn much upheaval in the years to come. Second, we should increase programs to get young men into the military. This group makes a hefty amount of money from the country's involvement in the Vietnam War. We should really try to increase those numbers to increase our profit margins. Lastly, energy independence, most notably gas, will be a major issue in the years to come," utters Edgar.

"What are you proposing we do as a group?" asks Carter.

"Much of the energy exploration prior to now was done in the southwestern part of the United States, but recently the Middle East has become a major player in the world's oil market. We will need to keep our eyes on this region and the players in the market. Ignoring this market could lead to financial ruin as well as putting this country's national security in peril. I know my entry into this organization was partly because of my relative connection to the president. I have had discussions already with the incoming President about much of what I have outlined here. And he is completely on board," discloses Hoover.

The group chats quietly as Wesley Carter realizes the control of the 8Men is slipping away from him.

THE JOURNEY

The year 1968 is a very turbulent one. It is momentous for the United States, but the turmoil is not confined to America. The Jewish state of Israel finds itself under attack by Arab terrorists. It is believed the terrorist attacks are the result of Israel capturing the Sinai Peninsula, the Gaza Strip and the West Bank in the Six-Day war in June of the prior year. Israel won the lopsided war by launching preemptive attacks on the Egyptian and Syrian air forces, rendering the countries' ground forces useless as the Israelis were able to end the war by attacking from the ground and air. The war was originally seen as a way for the Arab nations to come together to defeat and drive the Zionists from the region.

The overwhelming defeat leaves many Arabs demoralized and angry. Many young Arabs feel that their governments did not have the will or the fortitude to properly challenge their oppressors. The young Arabs decide to take on the Zionists directly by staging attacks in Israeli public centers.

The recent uprising of terrorist attacks has caused the Mossad to bring Danya out of her mini retirement. She has enjoyed the flexibility of coming and going as she pleases, but the director of the Mossad has found it necessary that Danya find and track down the genesis of these attacks.

She is meeting with the Mossad Director's second in command, Alon Levy.

"Agent Franck, you look as lovely as always," remarks Alon Levy as he kisses Danya on both sides of her face.

"Thank you, Assistant Director Levy. What can I do for you?" asks Danya.

"We would like to bring you back into service for the Mossad," says Levy.

Assistant Director Levy slides pictures of several different attacks in front of Danya. The pictures show destroyed buildings and bloodied bodies covered by white sheets.

"There is no need for you to show me these pictures. I am in America right now, but I follow what is going on Israel," comments Danya.

"Well then, it is clear we need you to come back into service," replies Levy.

"I am not sure if it is the right time," pushes back Danya.

Director Levy pulls out a small bag of money. The bag consists of all $100 bills. It looks to be several hundred thousand.

"This is just travel money. The director has told me to tell you that you will get your regular payment as well as expenses," claims Levy.

"I am not worrying about the money. I need to make sure my companion will be coming with me as well," asserts Danya.

"I don't see why not," rebuts Director Levy.

"Is there any intel about who could be financing the attacks?" questions Danya.

Director Levy goes into this briefcase and pulls out a file with the name "Wafai" on it. He slides the file to Danya.

"There is a group named the Arab Liberation League. Their leader is…" Director Levy interrupted.

"Wafai," says Danya as she nods her head. She remembers that Teed and the 8Men tried to sell weapons to the group prior to Danya blowing up the plane.

"Friend of yours?" asks Director Levy.

"No, just unfinished business," hints Danya.

Moments later Danya walks into her hotel room. Teed is looking out of the patio window. He is contemplating his future. Teed knows that his soul can no longer take being an assassin and an errand boy for the 8Men. He feels that somehow, he must atone for his sins. Teed knows that he must go underground. Maybe he should go back to Charleston to oversee the care of his mother.

"A penny for your thoughts?" asks Danya.

"Thinking about what to do now," replies Teed.

"So, what did you come up with?" inquires Danya.

"Nothing," utters Teed.

"Well, if that is the case, I may have a solution," states Danya.

"What is it?" asks Teed suspiciously.

"The Mossad wants me to come back, and I want you to come with me," offers Danya.

"What will we be going into?" asks Teed.

"There has been a rash of terrorist incidents in Israel. They believe it came from the ALL organization. They have been gathering strength and the new-found wealth from some of the Middle East barons is helping to fund the attacks. They want me to find the leaders of ALL and eliminate them," shares Danya.

"Sounds a bit dangerous. You go after these targets, you better get them…they shoot back," proclaims Teed.

"I shouldn't have asked…it is too dangerous," declares Danya.

Teed moves toward her. He throws his arms around her.

"No, I want to go with you. I can't think of a place I'd rather be than with you," confesses Teed.

Teed and Danya share an embrace and a passionate kiss.

FRIENDLY SKIES

The 8Men have accomplished many of the goals they set for themselves. The group has been very successful in shaping geopolitics around the world after the devastation of World War II. The faction has been influential in slowing the spread of communism and equally successful in destabilizing the Middle- and Far-East regions of Asia. The assembly of 8Men have sold heavy artillery to both sides of the Zionists and Arabic battles in the Middle East. They have eliminated three of the most powerful voices in opposition to their goals. The organization's misplaced patriotism was rewarded with unlimited profits. The society of heavyweights has reached its goal with no deterrent in sight.

The 8Men are no longer in need of the services of Teed and Danya. The duo served the 8Men admirably; they questioned many of the group's directives but followed them in the end. The election of Richard M. Nixon is a good departure point for Teed and Danya. The couple helped to shape the 20th Century, but they know it was time to aspire to greener pastures.

Teed and Danya are riding in a Yellow cab going to Washington's National Airport. Teed has taken many cab rides through the streets of Washington, but during this ride he seems to absorb the symbology of the monuments. Teed looks at the Washington Monument and thinks about the men fighting with then-General Washington. He compares himself to those gentlemen because they thought they were patriots as well but remained fearful that they could be deemed traitors.

"Washington, D.C. is truly a beautiful city," remarks Danya.

Teed nods his head in agreement.

"Not as beautiful as you," flirts Teed.

Danya hugs Teed as the cab drives over Washington's 14th Street Bridge heading into Arlington, Va. A few minutes later Teed's cab arrives at Washington National Airport. He and Danya walk into the airport looking like a couple who has their entire lives in front of them. As the couple walks toward the gate, a figure they both recognize stands in the distance. They soon can make out the face of Wesley Carter. Carter is smoking a cigarette as the couple approaches.

"I wanted to personally thank you both. You have done a great deal," comments Carter.

"Thank you, Director Carter. You came all this way to say thank you?" asks a suspicious Danya.

"Not exactly," replies Carter

"Figured as much," jokes Teed.

"Danya would you please excuse us? I would like a word with Teed."

Danya gives Teed a kiss on the check as she eyes Carter suspiciously.

"She is very protective of you," says Carter.

"She is great," declares Teed affectionately.

After Danya is out of earshot, Teed turns his attention back to Carter.

"So, what do you need?" challenges Teed.

"I needed to talk to someone. I know we have battled about principle and why we created the 8Men," rambles Carter.

"Where is this coming from?" asks Teed.

"I thought if we could put together a group of powerful men that influence global policy and could keep the Russians out of our backyard…" reflects Carter.

"But haven't you done that?" questions Teed.

"We have, but at what costs?" questions Carter.

"Do you regret anything that has been done?" asks Teed.

"Of course. I wanted Kennedy to work out. I wish King would have left Vietnam alone. But I really wish Capers was still here. He would know how to navigate through all this shit," claims Carter.

"How is his replacement working out?" asks Teed.

"He is a bully. Always has been. He is going to fucking ruin us," forecasts Carter.

"So now what? No enemies?" alleges Teed.

"There are always enemies. Even if you have to invent them," suggests Carter.

Carter sticks out his hand to shake Teed's hand.

"Teed, you and Franck be safe," states Carter.

"Thank you, sir."

Teed walks off toward Danya. The couple begins to make their way to an awaiting plane.

FIN

APPRECIATION

To those that have helped and inspired me. 8MEN would not have been possible without you. Your words, your kindness and your tough love made a difference. I am eternally thankful to you.

John & Bernell Smith, Pamela Love, Sean Smith, Sierra Smith, Terry Watkins, Bryant & Rachel Watkins, Kevin and Kelsey Allen, Addie B. Johnson, Florence Smith, Romaine Parker, Tonya Love, Christal Gaston, Nana Afrieye, Dr. Nana Kokoroko, William & Patricia Love, John & Blanche Harris, Melvin & Nancy Parker, Scott & Craig Carrington , Richard & Meka Parker, Aaron Harris, John I. Harris III., Shelly Davis, Bryanna Carter, Dian & Kevin Carter, Jason Carter, Elaine Carter, Andre & Kristie Harvey, Chauka Reid, Brenda Leake, Steve & Erica Bates, Andre' & Anthony Savoy, Al & Paul Green, Reggie "Reckless" Coleman, Kenneth "Black" Riley, Camille Thomas, Cecily Bush, Michael Grisby, Shannon Day, Terrae Brown, LaChelle Hyman, Germaine Smith, Patricia Taylor, Rae Swann, Ricardo Fox, Larry Beavers, Flo Ann Taylor, Tina Moreland, Meico Green, Ramona Simms, Jeanette Davis, Trisha Quarles, Marcy Allsup, Ayanna Green-Harris, Zanette Burrell, Stacey King, Tracy McKinney, Ramsay Johnson, Teresa Bradshaw, Raymond & Margaret Steadman, Raymond Steadman, Jr. Carol Fox, Diane & Mary Gadsden, Monica Brown, Luis Grillo, Micha Harris, Norman Parker,

Tim Massey, Tracy Miles, Theodore Hicks, Randy Banks, Robert Monk
, Monique Richardson, Eugene Rudder, Andel Owens, Johnny Garnett,
Jeff Flournoy, Keenon James, Mike Williams, Lonnie Stancil, George
Parson, Otis Adkins, Charles Twitty, Daryl and Lisa Watson, The
Brothers of the "U", Trevor Morris, Hania Al Saket, Malika Carey,
Anthony Johnson, Jr. Brown Family (Charleston SC), Kevin Thompson,
Angela Johnson, Chris White, Grace Morris, Guy Coates, Dana Lyons,
Denise Wilkerson, Harold and Michelle Scott, Marjorie & Walter
Winston, Malcolm & Lauren Augustine, Kara Penn, Carol Vance,
Glenard Moulden, Rhonda Stenson, Paula Sparrow, Evelyn & Curtis
Bennett, Tara Shea-Newsome, Paul Leonard, St. Mary's family
(Annapolis) , SAS family, Bay Boyz, 4th Ward family, Sheik Njie, Michael
Crutchfield.

Thank you all